The GCP The First Resurrection

The GCP The First Resurrection

Frantz Charles

Godly Visionz

CONTENTS

ISBN: 978-0-578-76974-5 (ebook)
ISBN: 978-0-578-76973-8 (Print)

For more information about special discounts for bulk purchases, live events, and booking please contact the author at frantzcharles.com

Printed in the United States of America

Frantz Charles, 2020

To God, my humble gift to you. Thank you for keeping me and making me a better man. To every GCP member out there fighting the fight that isn't seen, you're the true heroes.

1

I Need Help - Cade

The sirens broke my meditation. I shot open my eyes as my heart began to beat fast. Sensing hundreds of gods miles from here, my hands started to shake in fear. The sirens were always taught to recruits that if you heard this sound, that the highest level of danger was at hand and to report to your leader with your holy item for further instructions, but it was highly unlikely the siren would ever ring. A motley crew of GCP members barged inside my all-white room.

Moses came up front, sweat dripping from his pale face. "We've been looking for you."

I nodded. "What's happening?"

"Something's gone bad with the mission to aid England. The gods are overtaking the headquarters in Scotland, Northern Ireland, and Wales." Moses shook his head. "The Republic of Ireland is reported to fall any minute; they're under attack by the gods that were held prisoners underground in London. Hurry now." Without waiting for my reply, he turned and ran out.

I got up and rushed with the others to the front of our US headquarters, crowded with members viewing the screens on the walls showing the events taking place at various locations worldwide. I stopped to watch a screen that showed hundreds of gods flying past cities in New York, knowing they were making their way here. Switching my focus to the primary concern, I got as close as I could to view the screens projecting images from Heaven's Eye, an enormous computer that allowed us to see anyone or anything on Earth.

Before studying the screens, I stood by Moses and whispered, "Their mission was to aid England in wiping out those gods. Now you're telling me that the gods who were turned to stone have been revived? How is that possible? They would need—"

"The Golden Water." Moses gave a sharp nod. "The gods have twelve containers of it. They killed George Proctor, who was protecting it before getting into a teleportation pod to this location. They were statues like usual, monitored twenty-four hours a day by Guardians and members alike. Then, the next minute they were awakened and simultaneously attacked in a coordinated way almost like this was planned."

"Vera ... Please tell me she wasn't resurrected." I stared into his eyes, wanting an answer. "Did they tell you anything about her?"

"No, we've heard nothing so far but Vera is the only answer for this, don't you think?" He turned to face me. "She's the only one able to lead the gods to a successful revolt."

I pursed my lips, thinking about Vera, the daughter of Ominous—one of the three royal god figures—since Moses was right about her being the only one capable of successfully leading such an army.

Moses put his hands in his pockets. "After all, Vera controlled the strongest army in her universe and never lost a war."

"My father and Marie Proctor both fought Vera and took her down." I stared down at the floor. "My father has never been touched in battle, and I remember him telling me that when he faced her, it was the only time he didn't refuse help from others. She's not someone to take lightly. Legend says her kind respected her as their queen despite being under her father's rule."

"Nonsense. Your father would have taken her or any other god out without breaking a sweat. We have footage to prove that."

"He didn't fear her fighting abilities. He feared her mind—her ability to lead an army and take out this universe. If she's been resurrected, we're goners."

Moses closed his eyes. "Colvin knows what's at stake. He would've told us." He slowly opened his eyes. "And he wouldn't allow someone so powerful to be resurrected. He wouldn't let things go that bad."

"You speak of my brother as if he's some—"

I stopped talking when a large group of our members walked up to the crowd around us to witness the overthrow of the UK Headquarters. The gods who were held captive under the British Isles exploded out of the ground. Many of the screens in front of us showed different views of members from the UK fighting alongside their Guardians—supernatural beings from our universe who came to Earth to use their amazing powers to help us fight the gods.

At this point, their help didn't make any difference.

Seeing the carnage happening live, I turned and asked, "How many gods were revived?"

"Millions, in England alone. We're outnumbered and losing by the second. And now the gods are here at our doorstep. What do we do? All of the US Protectors are in England, so we're shorthanded here."

I shook my head, accepting the reality of things. This is what we were chosen for—our destiny. As GCP members—God's Chosen People—we were created to protect the most powerful items in all four universes from the gods, who sought full control and destruction of humanity and the Afterworld, a planet where all souls ended up. We fought for the protection of the living and the dead.

For the first time, the end seemed to be close at hand, maybe in minutes.

"Also, there's no response from Washington or New York," Moses said as he made his way closer to the gigantic center screen. "And we did receive a report that the gods are planning on using the Golden Water to revive a supreme deity—a god who can't be awakened by anything other than the Golden Water."

Names like "Washington" and "New York" weren't states or cities in a geographical sense, but code names used for the GCP members in those locations. A member with a city, town, or village code name protected that specific area, along with the unique item given to them by the GCP—so these were called Protectors, one of the job classifications within the GCP. If an individual had a state code name, then he or she served as a captain over all those in that region.

"Understood," I said to Moses, knowing that he meant both the Washington and New York captains were likely dead.

I pushed forward and made my way through the throng of members to stand by Moses in front of the central screen. Beneath that screen sat a long workstation with a single keyboard that required multiple people to work Heaven's Eye properly.

"Millions got revived, but it looks like there's a couple thousand on that island. Show me the exact locations of every god who's been revived and who we're dealing with," I said.

"Sir!" said a communicator as he got up from his seat and faced me, even as the other communicators continued to work. "England just sent word that Vera was the first to be resurrected."

Moses and I shared a glance, then I nodded, and the communicator sat back down to begin typing on the shared keyboard again.

"There," I said, pointing at a smaller screen to my right, where a live video stream showed several gods descending into Florida. A still image of a teenage girl appeared on the side of the screen.

"Sir," another communicator said, "gods are entering the state of Florida."

"Yes, just seeing that, thank you," I said. "The gods must know that the rest of the Golden Water is somewhere in that state. Who's the girl?"

"Heaven's Eye is showing us Angela Proctor, Marie Proctor's daughter. To the outside world, she goes by Angela Lopez. She lost contact with the social world after her mother's death."

I frowned, then reached into my pocket and took out my holy item—the Karui, a soul necklace from the Kokoro collection. A necklace made of a rare celestial stone holding what looked like a cross except there were three lines horizontally across instead of one. Each end of the cross had an arrowhead and three diamonds down the middle. It was only two soul necklaces, the Karui and the Kurai. The Karui Kokoro was from my home planet, Planet Avia and only the purest could wield its power.

The Kurai Kokoro was taken from the gods by my father and later given to Colvin by the GCP. Only the darkest being who was able to control the evil within the necklace could wield the power it contained. For years, no one on Earth could control such power until it reached my older brother's hands at eight years old. Both necklaces were connected somehow and notified each user whenever each was close to death. The Karui enabled its user to project pure astral power from the universe—but I didn't put it on just yet.

Looking back at the communicator, I asked, "How long do I have before they get to Angela?"

Another communicator turned around in his chair to face me. "A few hours, maybe less."

I continued to stare at the live footage. "This state won't last long now that they're here. If any hostiles get near our location, go to Code Red. Right now, power up this building to collect all the energy possible from every base in America and center it to this city alone. If the gods get here, it'll be the end of this world. I have to get the Golden Water, as well as Angela Proctor."

Moses came up and pulled me aside. "You're talking about leaving every base in every city in this country defenseless. What if a god happens to land at one of our bases and realizes it's not protected? Each base has intel that can put us at risk."

"I know, but as long as we have all the holy items here, nothing else matters. There are twenty-four containers of the Golden Water, and you know as well as I do that the gods can use the tiniest drop to resurrect anyone. They already have twelve. You know Marie stashed the other twelve before she died. I'm guessing that Angela knows something about their location even if she doesn't realize it, but if the gods get to her, it's over."

"I know, but—"

"Then why are you trying to stop me? Humanity is at the risk of extinction. We have no leader, so it's up to me. Notify every country about what's going on. When you hear from my brother, send him to my location asap."

Another alarm went off, and Heaven's Eye showed a large group of gods flying toward our location in Closias, New York.

"Code Red! And why isn't that force field up yet?" I said as I hurried back toward the workstation.

"Doing our best, sir," one of the communicators said. "Almost done pooling all the energy from other US bases." Typing as fast as he could, he stared at the screen. "Alright ... there! Engaging force field, sir."

What looked like an antenna atop of our building shot a beam of light upward, slowly creating a domed force field that would cover all of Closias. I switched my gaze back and forth between two screens: one showed the blue force field's progress, and the other showed hundreds of gods approaching the city.

A member near me shot an impatient look at the communicators, then yelled, "Speed up the process! They're coming!"

Moses ran forward and shoved one of the communicators aside. "Move it! I know a few tricks from the old days."

I looked back up at the screens and saw an individual in black armor flying out in front of the gods, who seemed to be only seconds from entering the city.

I shot a glance at Moses. "Hurry up!"

"Almost there!" Moses barked back.

The force field abruptly finished covering the entire city, appearing as a sparkling blue dome.

One communicator stood up and pointed to a small screen showing a single god. "There! That god levitating above the others has the Golden Water."

"Galoriah," I said.

"I say we evacuate this city now," Moses said.

I nodded as we all focused in on the video that showed a figure covered in black armor—Galoriah, a seven-foot-tall god notorious for killing GCP Protectors and innocent bystanders for centuries. His armor looked similar to a bulletproof vest, and he carried a war-hammer.

Galoriah looked down at our city of Closias, then slowly descended to land on the ground, shouting, "I know you can hear me ... even see me! We've killed your superiors, your fellow Protectors, and those Guardians in the UK. They're all dead. They've failed to stop us, and the rest of my kind will soon find their way here."

I could hear several gasps and cries around me as I studied this blood-thirsty monster. After a moment, I said, "Put all civilians to sleep ASAP. They could be exposed to the truth."

I looked at Moses, who glanced at the other communicators to confirm they were carrying out my order. Seconds later, the dome unleashed a white spark of light that put every non-GCP person in the city to "sleep"—meaning they would continue doing their usual activities, yet remain unaware of what was happening present time.

"We're clear," Moses said. "Everyone is asleep. I'll also command them to stay indoors to prevent any casualties."

I nodded and Moses walked over to a part of the keyboard that held a mic to control anyone who was sleeping. As Moses spoke into the mic, I watched Galoriah raise his war-hammer, aiming it at the force field.

"You are to hand over the rest of the Golden Water and every holy item confined in that building you're all hiding in," Galoriah said as his long black hair raised from the heavy wind outside. "You do this without the slightest resistance, and I will show mercy when killing you all."

Moses backed away from the workstation to stand next to me. "What now?"

The army of gods descended to join Galoriah on the ground, and then one of them walked to the edge of the force field, where Galoriah stood. This god wore no shirt but a long black jacket, black pants, and black boots. His shoulder-length blond hair shone in the bright sunlight. Lucius: a foe not to be toyed with.

I folded my hands, waiting for their next move. "We've collected all the energy in America, so this is an incredibly strong force field. No way can they break through it."

Heaven's Eye now zoomed in on a portal that had appeared beside Galoriah and Lucius. Out of the portal stepped a goddess with blazing red eyes and short black hair that stopped midway down her neck. As the portal disappeared, every god and goddess bowed at her presence. She wore a red thin plated armor and a black cape with red reflective scale patterns.

I pursed my lips and looked at Moses, who only shook his head.

"Wait!" a female communicator said. "Whoa whoa whoa! That's her." She got up and backed away from the screen. "That's ... that's Vera!" She turned to look at me and Moses. "We were instructed to leave immediately if we ever encountered her."

I kept quiet, thinking of the options left to me, and Moses just pointed the communicator back to her workstation.

On the main screen, Vera opened up her hand revealing three small black orbs that floated forward to touch our force field. The orbs shone red and I watched as the orbs began to drain the power of the force field.

We looked on as she turned toward the other gods, then said, "Soon this barrier will be diminished. Get what I've requested and I will liberate you all from this planet and restore balance back home." She looked to her right, opening up a portal, then left just as quickly as she'd come.

A GCP weapon-smith made his way through the crowd around me to say, "I've studied those orbs. They're attracted to life and energy. Once they suck the energy out of our force field, they'll kill us next." He looked at me. "We can fight another time. We have to hand over the location of the Golden Water."

With every second that passed, our force field became more transparent. I could sense the others waiting for me to make a decision. I shook my head and said, "I'm not handing over any info on the rest of the Golden Water. Marie Proctor died protecting it from the likes of Vera. What we do today determines if the lives of those who died for the GCP were meaningless or not. If we die, let it be because we fought for the future generation and those in the Afterworld who have already paid the price. They won't taste death a second time." I clenched my jaw, remembering how many had died fighting the gods. "But I also just can't leave now." Thinking of my options, I said to myself: "Angela is just going to have to wait."

"Then what do you expect us to do?" Moses said as he looked at the horrified people around us, then back to me. "We aren't Protectors like your brother. We weren't born for this. There are orphans here who are still learning to be Protectors. You only have weapon-smiths, doctors, nurses, communicators, and technicians here. What exactly is your plan?"

I looked at Moses. "We hand over information on the Golden Water, and this universe will be gone. You understand what's at stake?" I looked around at everyone. "If we let them kill us and they find out about Alice and what's inside her, they will kill her and resurrect Genesis. We have to fight." I looked back at the main screen, studying Galoriah's face. "Even if we do what Galoriah says, he'll kill us once he finds out we don't have what he needs."

I nodded toward the entrance of the HQ and began walking that way. Moses got the hint and followed along.

"Marie Proctor died without telling us where she hid the Golden Water, other than it's somewhere in Everglades City," I said to him. "Seven years later and we still can't locate it. But Gabriel said the one who is destined to be the Protector of Florida would find the Golden Water—and I think that's Angela. That's why we can't give in to this fiend. Brighter days are ahead." I put on the Karui necklace, summoning my armor. "I'm going to keep fighting and protecting for the sake of humanity. That's my purpose; it's my destiny."

A hand from behind grabbed my wrist, and then a familiar female voice said, "You're heading out there, aren't you?"

I turned. "Alice ..."

Her green eyes caught and held my attention, but she said nothing else.

"I have to do this," I said. "You go to the vault and put on the ring. Once you do, raise your hand, and the ring will shine, collecting all the holy items we have stored. To release one of the holy items, or all of them, simply call out the name of the item or items you need." I leaned in closer to Alice. "I need you to carry the ring."

Avoiding Alice's stare, I stepped over to Moses. "Power up the building and put this entire city underground."

Alice grabbed hold of my hands. "Don't go alone! Wait for Colvin."

I hated it when she brought his name up—like he was the answer to all our problems. "We're in this situation because he couldn't kill them off," I said.

"I had a dream of you dying last night." Alice squeezed my hands, then got closer. "If you go, you won't return."

I squeezed her hands much tighter. "I'm not letting one innocent life die out there. Today won't be the day I die either. I made a promise."

"I know, Cade, I know!" She pulled her hands from mine. "You're not listening to me. You're going to die if you go out there! My dreams are accurate most of the time."

Alice's red hair matched her inner fire that exploded whenever she was upset. I always believed my scruffy brown hair and personality represented the rock that became a foundation to her happiness—and the rock that extinguished the fire whenever she was hotheaded.

"I'm going to fight," I said.

She shook her head. "You don't even like fighting. You're only doing it because of your father and how the GCP will look at you if you don't fight. We can just leave and finally be together."

"I'm not leaving!" I glared at her. "My brother is somewhere in the UK fighting for his life and you want me to leave?" I started to breathe heavily through my nostrils. "If any god kills ..." The thought of him dying only made me angry as I clenched my fist. "If any god kills my brother, I will end them all."

Alice looked up into my eyes and got closer. "You know better than anyone that Colvin can't be beaten. The gods fear him. He's built for this and you're not."

"Then why don't you just go be with him?" I stepped back. "Every time you say his name, it's always a praise."

"Don't say that!" Alice spat back. "I've known him my whole life. He's just like his dad: he can't lose. I'm just telling you the reality of it. You're hiding from the fact."

"My father entrusted me to take care of Earth ... You really don't believe in me?"

She looked down. "Just scared that's all ... Listen, there's a small chance that good could still come out of this. That can only happen if you save Angela. If you go out there now, only stay long enough to buy us some time, then leave and save her. Don't put your life at risk trying to save anyone but her. The GCP needs you both."

I looked at her for several moments, then nodded. "Agreed."

Alice offered a small smile. "Cade ... I know how it feels to lose a father. My mom is just this miserable and depressed person. I don't want to be like that. Please don't die. I can't imagine living without you."

"I know. I still love you."

I glanced over at the door. Moses nodded. Turning back, I could see tears in Alice's eyes. I gave a small nod to her, then I headed toward the exit. I knew she couldn't say anything. I was now a GCP Protector. I had just taken on the mantle of New York, and so I was obligated to protect the entire state. But more importantly, it was my duty to protect the GCP holy items from the gods who sought to destroy this universe.

"Just wait ..." Alice looked at the floor. "I don't want to be like my mother. I - I'm ... pregnant, Cade." She looked into my eyes. "Please don't die."

I froze, staring at her face as fear crept up inside me. "Wait, what?" I said, walking toward her.

I halted when a loud bang came from afar.

"This isn't the time!" Moses said. "They're trying to break inside." He looked to the door. "Go save the world, Cade."

I glanced at Moses, then at Alice as my head began to spin. "Right ..." I closed my eyes, trying to concentrate. Her news was something I wish I hadn't heard right before doing this.

Opening my eyes, I looked into Alice's green eyes and then teleported to the far side of the city where Galoriah stood with his army. Being surrounded by acres of open grasslands and farm fields—nowhere near the city of Closias—I focused on what was now inches from my face: Galoriah. The only thing that stopped us from starting to fight was the force field that separated us at the moment but was rapidly disappearing by the second.

Galoriah lifted his face with a smirk. "Cade Walker ... son of Gage

Walker. So you chose mercy rather than fighting as a Protector. Coward, but then again, a smart one. And yet, here you are."

"Eh." I shrugged. "I don't like dying without putting up a fight. The rest of the Golden Water won't be yours, not ever. I'll make sure of that."

Even while keeping eye contact with Galoriah, my thoughts were elsewhere—focused on the news Alice had told me. My mind was spinning with what I should do now ... What does all this mean for our baby's future? More importantly, how would I be able to protect a pregnant girl?

Galoriah's face remained calm. "I was expecting nothing less actually. Fighting, you should be a nice warm-up."

Making their way to the front of the group, Aerozayle, a goddess with green eyes, long black curly hair, and rosy lips, flew to Galoriah's side with Lucius following behind her. They didn't say a word; they only stared at me waiting on their leader's next move.

I flew back as I saw that the force field had nearly disappeared now. "Moses, are you underground yet?" I said in a quiet voice, knowing he would hear me via the subdermal communicator implanted behind my right ear.

Moses's voice replied: "This is the first time going to Code Red in the city your father built. It's going slow; we'll still be descending once the force field is gone."

I flew into the air, keeping my eyes on Galoriah, Aerozayle, and Lucius as I replied to Moses, "I intend to fight 'til you are all safe."

Closing my eyes, I transcended past reality to one of the celestial realms in the West Universe. I got into my meditation posture and closed my eyes, moving into the Avex Realm. I saw an army of Avexes standing in front of me, in complete darkness, and waiting for my command. Avexes had previously been Avians like myself, from Planet Avia. Once an Avian died, he or she turned into a white astral entity called Avex.

"I need an army." I announced.

In this dark realm, an Avex flew to me. "An army you shall have, my lord."

I opened my eyes back on Earth—with an army of Avexes by my side, awaiting my command.

Flying downward, I landed on the ground. "Let's go!" I shouted just as the force field disappeared, along with Vera's orbs.

As the Avexes came forward, the army of gods charged at us.

I pulled out my bow and drew the string, causing an arrow of white energy to appear. I released the string and the arrow shot forth, with multiple arrows following from behind me from the army of Avexes. Many of our arrows struck the gods, piercing their armor and then exploding, turning them into stone.

My army of Avexes now flew straight into the remaining gods. I followed behind, transforming my bow into a sword. Teleporting to the first god, I drove my blade into his chest. Seeing two more coming my way, I extended my right hand to send forth a bright light, blinding them. I moved in, summoning another blade. I sliced the two blades into bodies on my right and left, and both gods turned to stone.

"Cade!" came Moses's voice in my ear. "At your nine o'clock—that's Amentous. You have to fall back!"

I looked over and saw another one of the royal gods—Amentous—striding toward me, wearing his infamous gold armor, supposedly impenetrable against any power or weapon in the four universes.

"I fall back; he gets to the city," I replied. "Moses, I have no choice."

As I finished saying this, I saw that many Avexes had already begun to surround me, shielding me from Amentous.

Continuing to walk forward, Amentous kept his attention on the Avexes protecting me. "You're all beneath me," he said.

Then Amentous opened his hand and shot a red wave of energy—wide enough to destroy the city. I watched the Avexes ahead of me quickly disappear as the wave hit them.

Moses's voice returned. "If that wave hits us, we're all dead ... and we're almost underground!"

"It won't," I said, lifting off the ground and flying back toward the city even as the wave followed behind.

I saw that the city of Closias was almost underground, with just the tops of a few buildings showing. The ground around the city began to close.

"This is it!" I called out, closing my eyes to summon more Avexes from their realm.

As soon as they appeared, I shouted, "Make a shield strong enough to block that wave!"

In unison, the Avexes created multiple force fields. I looked down to see that the ground was seconds away from closing up and sealing the city safely below. But the energy wave still posed a threat if it reached the gap before it disappeared.

"Moses, I'm going to give it everything I got," I said.

Then I touched my wrists together and closed my eyes to transcend to Planet Avia. "Phase one," I whispered.

At that moment, multiple Avexes flew into my physical body on Earth. Feeling a surge of energy racing within me, I opened my eyes as my heart started to race. I extended my hands toward the red wave, feeling the power of my home—Planet Avia—coursing through me.

My skin shone as I shot out a large mass of energy, destroying the red wave.

"Over here," came a familiar voice from behind as Amentous touched my left shoulder.

I turned around to no one.

"Over here." The voice came from my right this time.

I switched my attention and looked up to Galoriah. My body completely froze as Galoriah descended in front of me and extended his hand toward me. Then, using his telekinesis, he turned my body around to face Amentous.

Aerozayle flew over and hovered by Amentous's side. Lifting my chin, she stared into my eyes. "Tell me, where's the Golden Water?"

Her green eyes shone, and I tried to tear my gaze away, but it was too late. My body was compelled to tell the truth on its own as I felt my mouth was now able to move: "Somewhere ... in Everglades City ... Florida."

Even without being able to move my eyes, I could see the army of gods coming together behind Galoriah. *Angela,* I thought, *wherever you are, we're depending on you ... Sorry, Dad, this is it for me.*

Amentous flew forward. "I know you teleported the millions in the city underground from here to another country. You sacrificed yourself so that humanity had a fighting chance. Hmph, how noble of you. My father did that for our sake. But you're a fool to challenge the gods." He extended his hand to my face. "Now, perish."

A ball of yellow energy emerged from his hand and shot out. The pain only lasted for a second and darkness came.

2

I'm Dead - Angela

My eyes popped open. Then, sucking in a sharp breath, I shot up from my dream into a sitting position on the floor- and was welcomed by Florida's intense heat. My wet shirt reminded me of how hot my room was compared to outside. I wiped the sweat off my neck and my forehead, refusing to even give a second of thought to another nightmare.

Feeling an unfamiliar force tugging at me from outside. I looked out in the night sky to a red gleaming light.

"Angela, get down here!"

I sighed as Billy's crooked voice reverberated throughout the house. Exhaling out my nose trying to find a reason to live, to do my daily duties.

"No one likes you," I whispered to myself.

"Shut up," rubbing my temple. "I'm loved," I said to myself.

"No one cares about you. You're all alone, left here to die." I whispered again.

Vigorously running my hands through my hair, I shut my eyes. "Shut up!" I hissed. "I'm loved and needed." I slowly opened my eyes as I felt light headed.

"Angela Lopez get here now!"

His demand was a signal to save me from myself. I hated being by myself, it was the only time my mind ran rampant. Tired of battling myself I got up and looked at the barren room and faded pink walls. Then I drank down half the water bottle that stayed next to me before I finally headed downstairs.

I entered the living room to see my adopted parents, Billy and Lisa, sitting on the couch they'd stolen from our neighbor's garage.

I cleared my throat. "Yes, Billy?"

His eyes inspected my body. "What do you mean Billy?"

Billy continued to stare at me, waiting for a response, but I knew not to talk back.

"I'm yo daddy!" He placed the remote down on the coffee table and gave me his full attention. "You here cause yer old man ain't want you. Get in the kitchen and make me somethin' good."

Ignoring the stares from Billy and Lisa, I rushed into the kitchen. I knew what to make: what we always ate for breakfast, lunch, and dinner. Not something we loved, but something in Billy's budget that he thought would be best for all of us to eat- all the time. I turned on the stove and poured a little gold oil onto the frying pan. Multitasking, I cracked two eggs on the rim of the bowl at the same time and then poured the insides into a bowl. I threw in a pinch of salt, then began mixing the eggs with a fork. As I whisked away, I looked out the open small window in front of me, gazing at the night sky pierced by a full moon that exposed the broken home I lived in. Closing my eyes while still whisking, I took in the silent wind that blew past my face while listening to the crickets continue to call out my name.

I envied the dark purple sky every night. Outside lay my freedom, where I could run without being found. There was a certain peace to it. In the dark, you could get lost and no one could find you, no responsibilities, no feelings getting hurt, not worrying about others, and most important- not being let down. But I had no purpose or goal to pursue there- just death so that I could meet my mother again. Hearing the hot oil pop, I opened my eyes and turned down the heat on the stove and then opened the top cabinets to grab one red bell pepper along with an onion.

Hands flying back and forth, I chopped the onion and the red pepper into cubes, poured them into the frying pan along with the mixed eggs, and then increased the heat on the stove as I gave the mixture a few fast stirs. Leaving the eggs to cook themselves a bit, I turned and opened the fridge, grabbing the only consistently stocked in good supply: beer. I took out one can, then plated the bright yellow scrambled that sparkled with red and white. Beer in one hand and eggs on the other, I headed out and gently placed everything on the coffee table in front of Billy. Not waiting a moment, I hurried back into the kitchen and grabbed a fork and a knife, then ran out to the living room and placed them beside his cold beer, which had already begun to sweat from the sweltering heat.

I stood there a moment, making sure Billy didn't want anything else, but he'd already turned his attention to the meal and the TV. My new "father" loved watching sports- and shooting the endangered species in our area. He never really paid attention to me and couldn't care less what happened to me. He only wanted my undivided attention when it came to his needs.

Lisa, meanwhile, always stood-or sat by her husband's side even if he was wrong. She stayed in her nightgown all day and kept to herself while ignoring the outside world. She seemed more of a passive person who had bigger problems of her own. It didn't take me long to know that Lisa was at war with her past and her present- and that drugs kept her sane. She had her flaws but it didn't make her the worst mother. She knew she'd never replace my real mom, but she at least made an effort to treat me how she believed my mother would've wanted. That included giving me direct orders on how to survive off the land, and how to disassemble and assemble all types of handguns, along with how to shoot them. Other than that, she didn't say much of anything.

Seeing she had no use of me I walked back upstairs. Each step I took got heavier than the last. My mind reminded me of my life before being here in Florida. Remembering my friends Alice and Colvin and how happy I was tears began to come up to the rim of my eyes. Closing the door behind me. I sat back down on the floor where my sheets laid.

I grabbed at the bed sheets and covers that lay on the floor under me, looking around again at the barren room and the cracked pink walls as darkness fell outside my window. It represented how I felt: empty, lifeless, and forgotten. Seven years after moving here, I still hated where I was, and

I knew nothing was going to change. I was done pursuing this image of a happy me trying to be content with this life. After years of trying to find something to fill my broken heart, only sleep helped. Sleep was my escape to complete darkness.

Today I decided I was going to go to sleep for good.

Today would be the day I'd take my own life.

"Angela, stop!"

The small masculine voice came back—the same voice urging me for years to keep living and surviving, but failed to see my misery. I lived only to train, fight, and kill for someone who hated me. How could this voice see what I did every day and still want me to try to keep on living?

"No ..." I mumbled.

Ignoring the voice, I slipped my hands beneath the sheets I was sitting on and pulled out my mother's hand-sized photo. I flipped to the back to see her words that always pushed me to keep living:

I'LL SEE YOU SOON.

STAY STRONG.

Turning the picture back over, I locked my sight on my mom and gazed into her icy blue eyes. Seeing how happy she looked brought tears to my eyes. I covered my mouth and cried in silence. I envied her and her happiness.

Today is the day I take my own life.

I reminded myself of this again and again. Then I began shaking my head. "Sorry, Mommy, I tried," I whispered.

The more I kept saying sorry; the more tears drew down my face. I squeezed my eyes shut, and memories of me covered in my blood, fighting strangers for Lisa's entertainment, came to mind. Not wanting to give any attention or time to those memories, I opened my eyes. I looked back down and reached under my folded jacket, which I used as a pillow. From beneath it, I took out a black knife made of steel.

As I lifted the blade, the doorknob jiggled, and then two loud knocks made me jump. "Angela!" came the voice of my adoptive mom, Lisa. "Open this door now!" she shouted, the panic evident in her voice.

I focused my eyes on my arms, both covered in scars—except for the wrists. Each cut had its own story. This time, though, this would be the last cut—the last scar to tell my life story. I fixed my gaze onto my left wrist and touched the knifepoint to my skin.

Lisa's knocks became continuous slaps against the door. "Open this door now, Angela!"

Everything became silent, and nothing in this world mattered anymore.

"Come on, Angie," I whispered as I looked down at my pale wrist and the black blade touching it. "Just do it!"

"Angela, put it down," came the familiar masculine voice again.

I dropped the knife and squeezed the thin strands of hair on my head as I began to cry harder. "You don't know what I'm going through," I whispered as the tears flowed. "I'm trying."

"Stay strong. You have to keep moving forward."

"No!" I snatched the knife and again aimed its tip at my wrist.

Two more loud knocks brought me back to reality. My eyes darted to the door.

"Angela! Please!" Lisa yelled, her voice now pleading. "We don't have much time. Open this door now! Your life is in danger. We have to leave."

What? My life is in danger? I thought. *Does she know what I'm going to do?*

I got up, backed into the wall, still keeping the knife against my wrist. The bangs on the door got even louder, as it sounded like Lisa was now trying to break it down with her shoulder.

"Angela!" she cried out.

I started to breathe heavily as I clenched the handle of the knife even tighter. "I don't care!" I shouted. "My life doesn't mean anything to me. I'm going away now—for good. Just let me be, please!"

Lisa stopped hitting the door and lowered her voice. "Angela, no ... please. As much as I don't show you love, I can't let you take your own life."

I shook my head. *This is what it comes down to?* I looked at the door and began blinking hard, trying to clear my vision from the tears. What was living when every day was hell? Staring at the door and picturing Lisa on the other side, I saw what life had to offer, and I knew I had been promised only misery and enslavement. Looking down at my wrist again, I could see what death offered: the promise of peace and freedom and joy of being with my mom again.

Continuing to squeeze the knife handle, I pushed the knife down onto my vein and applied pressure. The more I dug the tip into my skin, the louder fear and death called my name. I closed my eyes and breathed even harder as flashes of my mother's face appeared to me.

I recalled a moment when I was little and had cut my finger by accident, my mother, Marie, rushed to my side and grabbed a nearby cloth from the kitchen counter. She got onto one knee and wrapped my finger with the cloth.

"Angie, stop being reckless. When you bleed, you have to quickly cover the wound."

I looked into her eyes. "Okay mommy."

Now I opened my eyes, stopping the memory, and then I dropped the knife. I let out a loud cry, falling to the floor.

Lisa finally broke through the door with her shoulder. "Oh my God!" she cried out.

She sprinted to me and kicked the knife away just as I reached out to grab it. I yelled, and before I could do anything, she grabbed hold of my wrist. She climbed on top of me, holding me down with one hand and using the other to cover my mouth.

"They're here for you!" Lisa said.

I stopped moving. Lisa turned her eyes to the floor beside my head. She let go of my mouth and grabbed the picture of my mother, staring at it and seeming to be lost for a moment in Mom's image.

Then Lisa turned her eyes back to me. "The ones who killed your mother are here."

"What?" I gasped.

Lisa got up and extended her hand to me. I knew if I reached for her hand, my destiny would take a new turn. If I went with her, I might be able to avenge my mother's death ... but still, have to go on facing this cruel world. Or I could stay put, failing to live up to my mother's word ... but be happy after death.

I closed my eyes and this time saw a memory of myself seven years ago, holding onto my mother, who was covered in her blood for three days before help arrived.

I opened my eyes to even more tears and reached up to grab hold of Lisa's hand.

She pulled me in close. "I need you to move—now."

I just stood there as Lisa strode over to the window and scanned outside. "Still clear back here, so you have to move!"

I had no idea what to do, no idea what she was talking about.

"Listen to me," she said. She turned back around and whipped out a pistol from her waist, switching the safety switch off in one smooth motion. "There are sixty rounds in here. Kill anyone near you or anyone who approaches you. Women, children, old, young, animals—it doesn't matter. Don't trust *anyone*. Kill them."

I looked at the pistol and shook my head. "What? No ... I can't do that! Why would I—"

"Listen! No one is innocent. Do you hear me? No one!" She shoved the pistol inside my backpack, which was lying on the floor.

"I ... I ..."

Before I could say anything else or process what was going on, I felt Lisa's hand slap my face, leaving a sharp pain in my mouth.

"I don't have time for you to act lost!" she said. "Just start by going to the abandoned house on the island in the swamp—you've seen it when you were out with Billy, remember? It's a hideout for the GCP. It'll be your salvation. Now put your shoes on and go!"

As I pulled on one shoe and then the other, I said, "GCP? ... The old swamp house? ... What are you talking about? Why do I need—"

"Quiet! They're coming. Survive out there ... and find George Proctor. Tell him that Lisa-Anne is at Everglades City, Florida—not too far from the hideout ... just head south and tell him to get here quick, that the gods are trying to kill me." Lisa glanced down, then looked up, catching my eyes. She seemed relaxed. "I won't survive here long, so I need you to find that house. You do that, and if I make it, I'll find you and explain everything."

I opened my mouth but didn't know what to say.

Lisa stuck my flashlight and a half-empty water bottle into the side pockets of my backpack, then threw it to me. "Too late to pack anything else. Just leave and don't come back," she said. "Go out the window and onto the porch roof, then crawl down the latticework like I've seen you done before."

I barely registered that she'd been keeping her eye on me for a long time. "No—wait," I said. "Where am I supposed to go again?"

"The house on the island in the swamp. I know you know which one it is. Take one of Billy's boats down at the river. Use the key he hid. You'll survive. Now get goin'."

I stood there, staring at her as she rushed to open the window. "Wait wait wait!" I said. I tried to hold on to Lisa's hands as she jerked me around and then put my backpack on my shoulders. "Lisa, stop it! You're scaring me!" I could feel the tears begin to fall again from the rim of my eyes.

Lisa grabbed me by the arm and pushed me toward the window. "I said, get—"

But my adopted father, Billy, burst into the room, covered in blood and holding his precious shotgun. "They're here!" he shouted. "They're controlling the locals to attack us."

Lisa nodded. "I know. But how many of them are here?"

Billy wiped the blood covering his face, and it wasn't his blood. "A whole damn army of them. This whole state is probably under attack. They started coming out of the sky like flies. I'm telling you, it's the end of the world out there." He checked his shotgun. "I'll hold them off while you and Angela head to the hideout."

"No!" Lisa said. "She has a better chance of going with you since you know the swamp so well. I'll stay here and meet up with you later."

"Fine." Billy gave Lisa his handgun. "Take them out—permanently. Don't stop when they're stone." He stepped out of the room and began shooting. "Lisa, they're inside! Take her and get out!"

Lisa grabbed me by the arm and pushed me toward the window. "Go! Get—"

She cut her words short when Billy stopped shooting and then stepped back into the room, looking directly at me. His pupils were enlarged, and the intensity he had was completely gone. Almost like a switch had been flipped, he seemed ... dead.

"Who's your mother?" Billy asked, still staring at me.

"What?" I said

Lisa glanced back at me. "Shut up, Angela! What was the rule?"

I knew all too well about the rule of this house, and that was to never mention my mother's name: Marie.

"Who's your mother?" Billy said again, louder this time.

Lisa clenched her fists. "Go, Angela! Get out of here!"

I tightened the backpack straps on my shoulders and began to crawl over the windowsill. Halfway through the window I looked back and saw Lisa wrestling with Billy. He backhanded her and she fell to the floor. Then Billy raised and aimed his shotgun at me. My breath caught, but then Lisa rose from the floor and swatted at the shotgun just as Billy pulled the trigger. A spray of buckshot hit the window and the wall around it—and then I felt a pellet tear through the skin of my upper right arm. Crying out, I fell through the open window, landing on my chest on the porch roof.

I got up, hurried down the latticework, and then sprinted into the darkness, knowing that if Billy got past Lisa, he wouldn't be far behind. As I ran from the house, I could hear fighting and shouting, and not just Billy and Lisa. *What the hell is going on?* I wondered even as I could feel more tears in my eyes.

I finally reached the river, which was just another part of the Everglades' endless waterways. I walked the short distance down the open-air dock until I reached the locked door that led inside of what was a floating storage shed where Billy kept his airboats and equipment. As I began lifting a hand upward, I heard Billy's voice in the distance, yelling my name. Ignoring him, I reached up over the doorway and stuck my fingers into what looked like an innocent crack in the wood, then slid out the key Billy had hidden there in case of an emergency. I opened the door and ran inside flipping the lights on. I jumped into the closest airboat and climbed up into the driver's seat, then fumbled around to find the key under the seat. Billy had a set of keys on his keychain but he also had spares hidden on each boat. I found the key and started the engine. I heard more shouting outside from Billy, much closer, so he had to know where I was. Seeing the remote to the garage doors on the floor of the airboat I aimed it at the doors and clicked the button watching it open. I pulled out of the shed, flipping on the airboat's headlights as I got going.

Even though my right arm throbbed with pain, I drove and drove, focusing on the water and not thinking back on all the bad memories I had from living in that house for the past seven years. I just wanted to keep driving to get as far away as possible from Billy and whatever had happened to him—and to eventually make it to the island Lisa had told me about, but the thought of what could be going on right now had my legs weak. I stopped the engine when I thought it was safe. I shut off the headlights, then fell to the floor of the boat and held on to the side as I began to cry out loud. I hated feeling this way. It made me feel vulnerable and weak. Thinking about what had just happened back at the house, I slammed my fist against the side of the airboat and accepted the situation I was now in—which meant I switched over to survival mode.

I wiped the last of my tears away, then took off my backpack and grabbed the flashlight and water bottle. Next, I took out the pistol Lisa had given me and slipped it into the back waistband of my pants.

I sat down on one of the bench seats for tourists, thinking through my situation. I knew that once the sun hit the next morning, my main concern would be dehydration, so I took a sip of the water. Then I shone the flashlight onto my right arm. I kept myself from crying at seeing how bloody the wound looked and instead grabbed the first-aid kit from under the driver's seat. I then bandaged and wrapped the wound as tight as I could. Finally, being out in the middle of the Everglades, I took a bottle of mosquito repellent from a small storage locker beneath the pilot's seat. I sprayed and rubbed repellent over all of my exposed skin, then put on a long-sleeve shirt to help further protect myself from the mosquitoes that preyed on flesh in this warm environment.

I knelt and tightened my shoelaces since I hadn't done much with them in my hurry to get out of the house, and then I noticed the sound of an airboat coming my way. Soon it came around a corner and its flashing red and blue lights lit up the area all around me.

"Yes!" I whispered to myself, thankful for my good luck as I finished tying my shoes.

The police officer's masculine voice came through a loudspeaker: "This is a Florida state trooper. Is anyone in the airboat?" A spotlight followed his voice, bathing my airboat in its brightness.

Shielding my eyes, I stood up and yelled, "Yes! Here! I'm over here." I waved my arms.

"Hold your position!" he said. "I'm coming over."

I kept a hand over my eyes and saw him pull up next to my airboat, shutting off the big spotlight and turning on a smaller light attached to the side of his vessel.

"We heard gunshots," he said. "Are you hurt? Are you by yourself?"

I held my hands up as he aimed the light directly at my eyes. "Yeah, I'm alone and I got sh—"

"Good."

Despite the bright light I managed to catch a glimpse of the trooper lifting and aiming a shotgun—right at my chest.

Without thinking I turned and jumped into the water on the other side of my boat, which was stupid since I was in alligator territory. Just before I hit the water, I heard his shotgun go off but thankfully I didn't get hit this time around. He yelled something, but I just swam forward, directly away from my boat and him. I heard his motor rev and knew he would be coming for me. In the glow of his flashing lights, I saw some land just ahead. I swam harder and scrambled up onto the shore, feeling that the ground was wet and muddy, confirming the kind of marshy territory I was in. As I stepped up onto firmer ground, the big spotlight shone near me and another shotgun blast sounded, again missing me. I sprinted ahead in zigzags, hoping I didn't catch any pellets in my back. I made it past a few trees and realized I didn't have my backpack ... or flashlight. *Damn!*

Thankfully the half-moon overhead gave me some light and so did the trooper's spotlight and flashers. And then I remembered I had my pistol. I grabbed it from my waistband and kept my eyes looking all around while running, searching for any signs of snakes and alligators, but I saw something that scared me more: my eyes caught sight of silhouetted people running toward me. It hit me what Lisa had said about not trusting anyone, so I cut to my left and ran on, ignoring anything behind me.

While sprinting through a marshy field, I looked to my left and saw a narrow riverway leading to more land. I scanned the water for movement and saw none and it didn't look like the trooper—or whatever he was—had come to this direction. Hearing the people behind me in the field, I made a sharp left and leaped into the river. I swam the few seconds it took to get to land and charged ahead to where I saw multiple trees.

Running onward, I could hear multiple splashes in the river. I found refuge behind a large tree and stopped. I peered out, thinking of what to do next. I knew my surroundings decently well, having lived in the area for a while now and exploring the swamps with Billy on his airboats. Plus, I'd spent seven years plotting my escape, and so I'd mentally explored all kinds of possible ways to leave without being detected by the police—or running into animals who don't mind eating you ... if bothered.

I saw movement and looked at the people lurking in the night, hunting for me. Something told me that whatever had killed my mother was here to kill me. The longer I waited, the higher probability they were going to find me. Not giving much thought to my next move, I dashed off to the next tree. I exhaled as I nervously tried focusing on the tree, but from my peripheral, I could see the figures now running after me as if their life depended on it.

I continued to run, past all the trees and back into the open—until someone grabbed my shirt and yanked me down, causing me to tumble forward and land face-first on the ground. I looked up and in the moonlight could see that this figure looked like a man—a very dead man. He lunged toward me. I rolled forward, throwing all my force into elbowing the side of his face, knocking him to the ground beside me.

Not wasting time to fight—or shoot, since I didn't want to draw more attention to myself—I jumped up and ran, tasting a mixture of dirt and the metallic tang of blood. But after running for only a few seconds, something tackled me to the ground and I felt a sharp pain in my back. Losing my pistol as I hit the ground, I landed on my stomach, then screamed and rolled over to see that this time it was a lady who looked almost elderly—and also very dead. The lady shrieked like a feral animal and lifted her arm. I saw the glint of a knife in the moonlight. Before she brought it downward at my chest, a gunshot went off from behind her. I felt her blood splatter onto my face, and then she fell to the side. Two more gunshots sounded from somewhere close by, thudding into the woman lying next to me, but I felt only the stabbing pain in my back and my heart beating against my chest. I didn't want to risk the chance of getting shot, so I stayed on the ground, rolling onto my side to reach toward my back. I felt two small daggers stuck there. I decided to leave them where they were, for now, then I reached out slowly to pick up my pistol, which lay on the ground near the lady's head. I coughed and felt more blood in my mouth. I rolled onto my stomach and lay still to assess the situation as another three shots rang out in succession, but they didn't hit the lady next to me this time—or me, thankfully.

Damn, this is not good. I was in an open area of the Everglades, so running wasn't a wise idea—or maybe even possible given my current condition. My only option was to play possum. I slowed my breathing, inhaling, and exhaling through my nose. I closed my eyes, putting all my focus into my hearing.

After another two shots the gunfire stopped and then I heard footsteps—coming my way. I held tight to my handgun as the footsteps continued to get closer and closer.

They stopped and I felt a hand cover my mouth. Then came a quiet voice: "Shhh."

I rolled quickly and raised the pistol, ready to shoot whatever was standing over me—until I could see Lisa's face right in front of my eyes.

"Let's go!" Lisa hissed.

I sat up and whispered, "Daggers in my back—two of 'em."

She nodded, then I felt her yank the pair of blades from my back. I grunted at the new sensation of pain, but Lisa just grabbed my hand to help me up, and then she started jogging back toward the main riverway.

After sucking in a deep breath to fight the pain in my back, I followed her as she ran on. Coming to the shore, I saw three airboats: the one the trooper had been in but was now empty, mine, and a third that had to be Lisa's. She jumped into that airboat and sat in the pilot's seat. After I got in and sat on one of the bench seats, she drove off, heading north to follow the river's path that would lead us to the abandoned house.

With the airboat propeller so noisy, I stood up and held onto the bench seat, then turned toward Lisa and said in a loud voice, "You have to tell me what's going on!"

She shook her head. "I'll tell you later. Sit back down!"

"No, I need to know now!"

Lisa shot a glare. "For now, I just need you to listen when I speak and do the things, I tell you to do!"

I frowned and sat back down. We drove on in silence until we made it to the island Lisa had told me about. A few times I had looked behind us, but no one was in sight.

Lisa stopped the boat and turned off the engine. "We need to get to the safe house just up that rise." She pointed out that way.

I glanced up at the old house, but then stared at Lisa as she jumped from the airboat onto the shore. "Why do you treat me like this?" I asked.

"Angela, we have to move! I don't have time for this."

I stood up and stepped onto dry ground. "No! You treat me as if I've done something bad to you. Everything you ever told me to do, I did. I never argued with you. Why did you take me in if you never wanted me? Why punish me?"

"I treat you how your m—"

My eyes popped wide open as I interrupted, "How my mother would've wanted? You never knew my mother."

Lisa just shook her head and looked at me like I had no idea what I was talking about. "Marie ... as in, Marie *Proctor*?" she said.

When I started shaking my head because that wasn't my mother's last name, Lisa raised a hand and went on, "The one who had you at seventeen? Yeah, she lived in Closias, New York. You knew her as Marie Lopez, the caring mother who moved here for work. Yeah, I knew her, but I also knew the *real* her—Marie Proctor, the merciless killer who did everything in her power to protect you. I've known you both very well. You're perceiving me all wrong. ... I do care for you."

I felt so confused, but my anger cut through it all and erupted. I stepped up in her face and almost shouted, "You care for me? Then tell me, when's my birthday? When's the last time I had a real meal? The last time I slept on a bed? The last time I laughed? ... Hmph. Don't say you care for me!"

"I gave you everything I had." Lisa offered a tight smile. "I gave up my life and hid from the world to protect you. How many seventeen-year-olds do you know who could've done what you did today? To defend yourself, to attack without hesitation—and judging from your wet clothes, you swam with a wounded arm and went into hiding. You know how to cook, clean, hunt, and survive on your own. You should be thanking me."

My mouth fell open. "You turned me into a killer!"

"I turned you into a woman—an independent one."

I removed the long-sleeve shirt I was wearing and showed her one of my arms. "Not all these scars are from self-inflicted wounds. When you were unconscious from the drugs you took, I had to defend myself from Billy." My stomach churned just thinking of the past and my experiences with Billy—and Lisa too. "Yeah, I know how to defend myself from the outside world because I've dealt with it inside of that house."

Lisa took a deep breath. "You are the last generation of the Proctor family. I need you to know that it's genetics that makes you special. Although you're the last, your blood reaches other planets, and that gives you the advantage to make a difference."

"What the hell are you talking about?" I said, feeling my anger rising again.

She shook her head. "You'll find out soon enough. But never feel like you're alone. You have a bigger family than you think. You have to find an outlet for your anger. Don't let it get the best of you, and most importantly don't hurt yourself. Channel the hurt, the hate, and the anger toward your enemies and don't hold back when you do. I've never babied you because I know you can handle any challenges that life throws at you. And ... I'm sorry I couldn't protect you from Billy, but right now we're almost to your mother's safe house. The ones after you are gods, and I'll tell you more about that, but right now you'll be—"

"Dead," came a female voice.

Lisa and I both turned to see a lady walking toward us. Her dark-green eyes glowed in the night as she came from the direction of the house. The breeze caught her long, wavy black hair.

Lisa started to say something, but the woman went on, "I dreamed of this moment," she said, looking right at Lisa. "To watch you die in front of my eyes."

I saw Lisa's eyes dart around nervously, and then she quickly pulled me behind her as a horde of others came from amongst the trees around the house.

Soon we found ourselves surrounded, with guns pointed at us from every direction. These were people who lived in this city. They all looked out of it like Billy had ... and the guy and woman who attacked me—dead. I figured they had to be controlled by this woman.

"Where's the Golden Water?" asked the woman with the green eyes.

"I'll tell you," Lisa said. She grabbed my arm and walked to the airboat, pulling me behind. "I'll even show you, but it'll only be me. The girl stays out of this."

The lady eyed me. "Who is she?"

Lisa shrugged. "No one important."

And just like that, the woman appeared right in front of Lisa, standing on the front bench seat of the airboat. My breath caught, and I backed away.

"Then you don't mind me killing her?" the woman said, stepping down off the bench seat toward us.

Lisa pulled out her handgun and aimed it at the woman. "Aerozayle," she said, "I don't fear you."

The woman—Aerozayle—kept her eyes on me as she reached out to grab hold of Lisa before Lisa could make a move. A moment later Lisa was hurled into the sky out over the water.

"Lisa!" I yelled.

Aerozayle looked at me. "Where is the Golden Water?"

I backed away slowly, knowing I had nowhere to go. "I-I don't know. I don't even know what it is."

Aerozayle smirked. "Wrong answer."

Her hand came up from her side so fast that I barely saw the motion. But I did see the blade as her hand returned to her side—and then I felt a hot, piercing pain in my throat. She reached out and took the pistol I'd jammed into the front waistband of my pants.

I staggered back, holding my throat as blood began pouring through my fingers.

Next, I heard the sound of a click as my eyes went downward, my hands still trying to contain the blood from flowing out of my neck.

The loud sound of a gun followed and everything went black.

3

Dead End - Colvin

Having my eyes closed I thought to myself, *328 confirmed kills today and 6,589 kills to date. I hope I made you proud, mother.* Kneeling on one knee and holding on to my scythe, I looked ahead at the plain field. The grass was tainted with blood and debris from the gods. Corpses of Protectors spread throughout the field as I looked around. The gray clouds blocked the sun and the wind blew hard. Screams of agony and the crowing of crows were the only sounds that filled the air. I wiped the blood of others off my face as I scanned the area for American flags but it was pointless. Flags that were implanted into the ground stuck into the bodies of fellow members. Some were torn apart and others still waved in the air. Nurses and doctors walked around with clipboards checking for the wounded and counting the dead. I closed my eyes again remembering all the screams and explosions.

"Good job," A hand from behind tapped my shoulder. "328 kills today. 560 yesterday I'm proud of you."

"Thank you Adumay but we failed." I looked back at my Guardian. "It's far from over." I got up on my two feet and saw the same stern look from him. His white and blue steel plated armor shined. There was no sweat on his bronze face, no blood nor did he carry any wounds. This was nothing more than practice to him. "Get in contact with these nurses and find out how many of our Protectors we lost. Then send three million to their immediate family."

Walking I could feel the pain I had in my ribs and chest from the first day of this mission. From my peripheral, I could see Adumay's eyes studying me. "You can ask you know."

"Right now you're reminiscing on the moves you executed, should've executed, and the outcomes. How it affected your victims, how long it took to kill them, why you were able to get touched, every single move. Don't push yourself too hard."

I stopped walking and studied the mass murder that just took place. "How do I explain this to Washington?" I turned my head back to my Guardian.

"You're not the savior of this world. No matter how many gods you kill or humans you protect there's no denying the inevitable." He faced me. "People will die, chaos will emerge, and you can't save everyone from what's now about to happen."

"So what? We sit down and let our actions take its course."

"No, you do the best you can but you aren't God. You were called to help protect the world, prevent its destruction, not make it perfect and peaceful. Such goals aren't real, don't seek for perfection, only the North Creator can achieve that when he returns. Let's accept what has happened here today and prevent the entire universe from meeting its end."

Now feeling an ache in my knees, I limped up the hill towards the Great Proctor Castle where all the commotion took place. Walking over the dead bodies, I saw the faces of Protectors under my supervision.

Manhattan opened his mouth in shock. "Captain!" With open arms, he ran to me. "We thought you were gone!"

I lifted my hand signaling him to stop running. "I'm fine, spread the word we're heading home."

Switching my focus up at the castle where people were coming in and out with medical supplies, Wales trudged forward. Straightening himself, he stood still and everyone on the field took notice and stopped what they were doing. I could see his red eyes from where I stood, he had finished crying. His short blond hair was drenched in blood as well as his navy blue uniform. "Mates, it comes with great sadness that our supreme leader George Proctor code name United Kingdom was KIA earlier today. I fought my best but to no avail could I have stopped Vera who took the Golden Water."

For a moment it was silent as everyone tried to digest the news then realization hit and cries filled the air. I watched everyone cry out. My eyes caught England's lifeless body. I walked over as London fell to the floor in defeat and began to cry his eyes out for his dead sister. Scotland and Northern Ireland walked over in shock as all heads turned to the scream of London.

"I'm sorry for your loss," I watched as he hurled his sister's body into his arms and began kissing her head as tears fell onto her forehead. His eyes stuck onto mine as he squeezed her body. "This is your fault; you were supposed to protect her." He removed her blue diamond headband which kept her long brown curls in place. "How do you propose to her and let her die?" He shouted.

Having her headband removed, her armor shined and her red glossy dress appeared on her. The dress she wore to our date right before she was called to this war. I promised her I would assist seeing how scared she was to the call. Closing my eyes, a flash memory of being separated from her during the fight came to mind. Seeing her body, I didn't cry, nor was I heartbroken.

"I don't know how I feel," I said to myself as I looked to Adumay searching for an answer. "I don't know if I even loved her, I can't even cry for her."

"You never loved her, you loved what she provided and that was affection. Something your mother never gave you. She never showed you love and you yearned for it from her. That human was the love you envied from your mother."

Not wanting to think about my childhood, I switched my focus. "Malachi Walker is alive in that castle; Wales is investigating him at this very moment. I can sense Malachi confined behind those walls."

"You investigate and I'll head home with the rest of America," He closed his eyes listening to a voice I was unaware of. After a few seconds, he opened them with a concerned look. "The gods landed in New York and Florida," We shared a look and he knew what to do. "I'll let you know if things get out of hand."

"Same here," I turned and headed to the castle where heads turned to me. Everyone remembered me entering the war and leading them. When all hope was lost, I broke through enemy lines and gave humanity a fighting chance. Catching their eyes, I nodded my head greeting them. I didn't have to know their names but fighting beside a Protector, you form a bond that can't be explained.

As I walked through the large steel gates, more bodies of the injured were on the ground with Guardians holding onto their hands giving support as nurses began healing the wounds. Complexes of buildings within the walls were half destroyed. Ascending in the sky, I flew over to the headquarters where it was heavily guarded. One Guardian who watched over the entire castle stopped me. "You aren't permitted any further, no one flies in the air for safety precaution either."

Ignoring his orders, I closed my eyes and teleported to where I sensed Wales. Being in a dark room I saw Cardiff, Bangor, Swansea, Newport, Barry, and Conway surrounding Malachi who was chained to a chair.

Wales turned to face me. "You shouldn't be here. Your part in this war is over."

"It won't stop here, let me investigate." I took a look at Malachi who was severely beaten, but I knew he hadn't talked. He was loyal to the Zaygaian Gods. "He'll only talk to me."

Wales looked at the other Protectors and they took a step back. "He's your cousin, I hope he does talk or I'm taking his life."

I nodded and walked forth. "The Walker family gave up their very lives for a single cause. Today Malachi accomplished his part, death doesn't fear him." Kneeling I faced Malachi and looked into his red pupils. "What happened here?"

"What do you think our Creator is fighting out there that he had to leave Heaven?" Malachi looked at each of us in our eyes. "What is out there that killed the South Creator? The gods need their leader, Genesis.

Whatever is coming is coming soon and we're sitting ducks. The Walker family for generations has sided with Ominous because he can save us!"

"We put our faith in the Most High," said Cardiff. He walked to my side. "We'll wait for the North Creator, the king of the universe who reigns over heaven and all-"

"Are you not hearing me? He hasn't returned. Planet Zayga has never lost a war, they're our best bet. What we're doing is pledging our trust in them. We die now but we come back resurrected with the power of the gods and we save the four universes."

"You think you're justifying your actions and that you're doing this for the greater good. All you did was kill your race and betray the North Creator."

Malachi smiled, "Say what you want but the time has come. Vera will destroy Earth and save the universe. You can fight and die or surrender and fight the more important battle."

A bright light shined behind me. I turned to Adumay who had Alice by his side. "What is she doing here?"

Worry covered his face. "We need to head home now."

Alice ran and hugged me, pulling back I saw tears falling down her face. "They came to attack us. Cade tried to fight but he couldn't-"

"What is she talking about?" I switched my gaze to Adumay.

"The city was put underground by Cade according to Moses and he was taken. Whether or not he's alive we don't know. He's currently missing."

I touched my Kurai necklace. "My item is supposed to shine if Cade is severely injured or if he's dead. It didn't shine."

Malachi set his eyes on me and began to speak telepathically. *"Baby Cousin, all things that Ominous told us will come to pass. Thank you for helping in the resurrection of Vera. If you want to save your mother, kill Gabriel and Cade."*

I turned to Malachi and responded the same way. *"When you see Eve tell her I love her and I'll bring her to the Afterworld."* Opening my hands to my scythe I swiftly sliced his neck putting an end to his life.

"Why'd you do that for!" Wales walked up to me.

"Dead end," I turned to Adumay. "Let's move."

"Dead end," I turned to Adumay. "Let's move."

4

The Truth Shall Set You Free - Angela

Everything appeared so clear and vivid. I was ten and we had just buried my mother. My room seemed empty and lifeless. The toys that crowded my room didn't look like toys anymore—just objects. I still felt the cold streaks of dried tears down my face. Screams and curses were the only sounds that rang throughout the house. I got off the bed that I'd lain in for the past twenty-four hours. My feet pressed against the cold wooden floor, and I held onto the corner of my bed for balance as I began the walk to my door. I couldn't remember the last time I'd eaten or showered.

The heavy curtains in every window throughout the house blocked any light from penetrating inside. I walked toward the loud noises—coming from the master bedroom. At the entryway, I could see movement beneath the door: the shadow of my father wrestling with his demons. As I got to the door, which did nothing to block his screams and curses, fear crept up, telling me to stay away from the barrier separating me from my father.

Leaning forward, I pushed the door open and peeked inside to see him digging his fingers into his head as he cursed into the air.

"Daddy ..." I whispered.

He whipped around to face me, and the intensity of his dark black eyes startled me as they locked on to mine. Drool hung at the corner of his mouth.

"What do you want from me?" he yelled.

I saw that he still had on his military uniform from the funeral, although it had now lost some of its badges and medals.

I inched away as he started to approach me.

My father clenched his fists. "What do you want from me?" he repeated.

"Stop it!" I shouted, then ran back to my room and locked the door.

As he tried to break inside, I backed away from the door and covered my ears.

"Stop it!" I shouted again. My heart thumped against my chest. "Stop—"

"Stop what? Angela!" He continued to punch the door.

I could hear the heavy breathing and grunts through the corner of the door.

"Hello, ma'am, are you able to say something?"

This new voice seemed distant but clear. Everything turned bright.

"You're going to go through a little shock now. Please forgive me."

"Angela!" my father yelled—but it wasn't my father's voice this time. "Angela!"

An electric sensation went through my chest. My eyes popped open. Sucking in a sharp breath, I shot up from my dream into a sitting position on the floor. "Ouch!" I gripped my chest as I looked to my left.

A man with dark, gelled hair and neon-blue irises stood over me, looking into my eyes. He backed away, and I saw that he wore a black suit.

"Sorry for the shock," he said. "Correct me if I'm wrong, but you're Angela Proctor, correct?"

I looked around to find myself in the darkness of someone's home. A streak of sunlight broke through a filthy window off to my left, revealing dust swirling in the air. Everything looked lifeless and dirty. I saw broken glass on the carpet. The couch was broken in half, showing the insides. Empty cups, along with crumpled paper, laid everywhere. I turned to my left to see a marble counter; behind it was the kitchen. The stainless-steel refrigerator had a huge dent on the doors. The area started to look familiar to me. I continued to observe every inch of my surroundings when it hit me: *this was where my mother died.*

I looked back at the man who hadn't moved. "What am I doing here?" I asked. "I thought I died." I slowly clenched my fists and then placed my feet firmly on the floor, testing the control of my body. I stared at the man. "Who are you ... and how did I get here?"

"My name is Mandroid. You're with Lisa Proctor, correct?"

I gave a slow nod. "Yes, my name is Angela ... Lopez." The memory of Aerozayle came to mind and then hearing a gunshot turned everything black for me. It reminded me where I should have been—six feet underground. "I shouldn't be alive."

"Well, ma'am, your life is still in danger as we speak. Not only are your back and arm still wounded, but I can sense a large group of gods now spreading out around the Everglades. You need to follow me immediately."

I rose, still not sure what in the world was going on.

Mandroid turned and started to walk down the hallway saying, "I know you must have a lot of questions. I'm an advanced machine created to assist your mother. I was put into shutdown mode because of the Third Great War, and now it seems this place has been deserted. A lot must've happened in the past seven years. I've been programmed to retrieve you if the gods ever came to the Everglades, which is what reactivated me."

"Whoa whoa! What are you talking—" I stopped in my tracks when I saw Mandroid's skin and hair slowly turn to steel as his suit became part of his body. "You're a robot?"

Mandroid looked around. "Yes, an advanced machine, as I said. Please follow me, ma'am. I have to reboot this entire island because we're defenseless as of right now. Where is Florida?"

"Florida? I'm sorry, I'm not following you. We're *in* Florida. It's next to Georgia."

His eyes shone bright and then blue lasers came forth his eyes as he scanned the entire house with his eyes. "No," he said. "Florida was murdered."

Before I could say anything, he opened the door at the end of the hallway and ushered me into a fully furnished bedroom. Everything was neatly in place. The queen-sized bed had two big pillows and white silk sheets. I turned toward the black-wood dresser to see that dust covered it. I took a few steps forward to find framed pictures of me on top of the dresser. It felt like walking into a nightmare as I began remembering every inch of this place.

My legs trembled, so I held onto a tall ebony wardrobe right beside me. The wardrobe started to illuminate a blue light at the pressure of my fingertips. I drew back as the bed began to split apart, right down the middle. The silk sheets sank in between the bed halves, unveiling a stairway that led to a lower level of the house.

Given my current emotional and physical state, I knew I'd soon fall unconscious.

Mandroid must have realized this as well. He looked at me and said, "You're losing blood from that arm wound, and your back is still damaged." He studied me for a second and concluded. "Also reading you're dehydrated. Quickly, follow me and I will heal you." He turned and walked down the middle of the split bed.

I stumbled forward and followed him down the stairs.

"Mostly everything in this house has a hand scanner," Mandroid said as the lights came on along the sides of the stairs. "The one you accidentally touched on the wardrobe gives you access to the most important part of this house: the underground base."

I followed him to the bottom and the stairwell disappeared behind us and closed up into the ceiling. Overhead LED lights switched on overhead, exposing a large oval room. The lights revealed all sorts of high-tech weapons hanging on one section of the wall. Directly in front of me stood an enormous computer that almost touched the ceiling. Aside from the wall section that featured the exotic weapons, a series of black metal doors stood all around the oval room.

The room ... the scent of metal ... the cold temperature—all of it awakened a memory that came alive in my mind and imagination. In the memory, I was holding on to the door with my heart beating fast. I could hear the grunts of my mother and a man fighting out in the middle of the base as I hid in one of the closets. As much as I wanted to help her, she was protecting me. My mother was strong but this time I was scared for her. Hiding in the closet, I slowly locked the door as fear crept inside as my mother screamed in pain. Hearing her scream, I peed myself and began to tear up hearing my mother yell for help. When the noise finally ceased, I pushed the door all the way open and was welcomed by complete darkness. I closed my eyes, embracing the dark. A few seconds later a dim light came on overhead sensing movement, the light allowed me to see what was left of my mother.

Crying, I fell to my knees on the cold metal floor as my mother's blue eyes shone through the blood that covered her face. She used her remaining strength to crawl toward me. My tears came harder as I realized that my mother wasn't my strong protector anymore. Every inch she got closer to me, the closer depression and anger approached to take over my life. The closer she got, the more my heart was getting ripped apart—the more my happiness in my life was being killed off.

Finally, she could go no farther. "My baby, come and hold me," she whispered as tears fell down her face.

As I reached my mother, she placed her head on my chest. My tears spilled down onto her face as she looked up and spoke her last words: "Kill him for me."

I held on to my life, my purpose, my happiness, my mother for hours, hoping, wishing, and praying I wasn't experiencing this hell. That this wasn't real.

A cold hand touched me, bringing me back to my current reality. I turned and saw Mandroid's bright blue eyes staring at me. A wave of light shone through his metallic hand as he touched my injured arm. He placed his other glowing hand on my back. Within a few seconds, my back felt normal, and I looked down to find my arm completely healed.

Then a voice from somewhere said, "Angie ... Angie."

I paused and my eyes widened. I knew that voice, even after all these years. And there was only one person I knew who had ever called me "Angie."

My mom.

Feeling fear rise within me, I slowly turned around to see the face of my beautiful mother, Marie, on the enormous computer screen, wearing some kind of bodysuit. Her dark brunette hair was just how I remembered it: long and beautiful.

I kept my focus on her blue eyes. "Mom … is … is that you?" My voice started to crack.

"This is a recorded message and if you're watching this, then it must be you, Angie. Right now, we're on the brink of another war. If I'm dead, then the fight between humans and the gods is continuing. You are chosen to be the next Protector after me, and if you're in the underground base now, then Lisa must believe you are old enough to do what's necessary as a Protector. I had a dream you would be hereafter the gods arrived and attacked you. Two things are going to happen. First, a Guardian by the name of Clark is going to come to help you if you summon him. Trust only him and a robot named Mandroid if you have any questions. Both will tell you everything you need to know, and they'll protect you. You must always stay close to Clark. Second, a group of gods will come and demand the Golden Water. They'll kill anyone who stands in their way. Don't underestimate them and don't go in public if you see them; you'll only make the situation worse."

My mother stopped talking and turned in her chair to look back at a girl who could've been in her teens, with light brown skin, scarlet-red eyes, and dreads that stopped around her neck. "Addis," my mom said to the girl, "protect your sister at all cost. I can sense someone coming." Addis walked up toward the screen as Mom continued speaking to her: "We can't stay here. I'll protect Angie, but we would be exposing this base."

Then my mother turned back to the screen, focusing on the camera again. "Angie, the Golden Water is a revitalizer. It can give life to the dead, heal the injured, and increase the power of anyone who drinks it. The gods that are after this item—Aerozayle, Galoriah, and Lucius—are ruthless killers and will do anything to get what you have. They plan on reviving their king, Zulu, and if he is revived, he'll try to end this universe by resurrecting Genesis. As a protector, you must never drink the Golden Water, only protect it. Your job now is to make sure they don't get their hands on it, even if it means defending it with your life. At this very moment, they're plotting against you. The most important thing for you is to have faith. Believe in Clark and call him and he'll appear. Until then be cautious of your surroundings. Some gods will come in plain sight; others will be hidden, blending in. I don't have much time. Well … bye. I love you, Angie."

She turned back to Addis and then got up from her chair. "Let's move. I'll fight and you protect Angie."

The screen turned black, and Mandroid walked over to the computer. I watched as he lightly tapped the side of the screen and a small chip popped out. He inserted the chip into his left temple and focused on the screen.

"I'm confused," I said. "What did I just watch?"

I closed my eyes, recalling everything that had happened over the past several hours, and what I'd just seen and heard in the video from Mom. "I don't remember anyone named Addis protecting me. Who was she?"

I took a deep breath and focused my attention. "I … I need to find Lisa—Oh, and how do I get in contact with George Proctor … whoever that is?" I asked.

Mandroid kept his attention on the computer screen.

I walked up to see that he looked like he was zoned out. "Do you not hear me?"

"I'm receiving every bit of information this computer has collected from the various GCP headquarters over the last seven years." Mandroid met my eyes. "In a few seconds, I will be able to answer all of your questions."

The letters *GCP* appeared on the screen, and a search engine popped up.

I again asked, "Can you find or get in contact with George Proctor?"

Mandroid walked away from the computer, and I could tell he was still in his world. After a few seconds, he looked around the room. "We can't put up a force field. The US headquarters of the GCP intercepted every Guardian power source to protect Closias. They don't even know we're here now." He turned and raced back to the computer to begin typing. "Right now Earth is only a few hours from being controlled by the gods. This George Proctor you speak of ..." He looked over his shoulder at me. "He's dead."

I frowned, but I couldn't feel sadness at the moment because I didn't know George Proctor and I had no idea what was going on and felt like an emotional train wreck.

Mandroid went on, "The nations of the United Kingdom have already fallen." He started typing again. "The GCP members here in the US have abandoned our headquarters after moving it underground. The city—Closias—they left is now completely out of power, which is why the gods are now here looking for the Golden Water. This very well may be the end."

Mandroid stopped typing and pointed to the image of a large city on the screen. "That's the city of Closias, where the GCP US headquarters is located. As I said, right now that city is empty and powerless, which means it is no longer a good option for me to take you to, so I need to get you somewhere safe. If the gods are in this area, it's only a matter of time before they find us. Allow me to teleport you to another location now."

I raised my hands and shook my head. "Hold on, hold on! You're going way too fast. I'm not going anywhere. I need to know what's going on first, okay? I just watched my mother talk to me about these gods that you mentioned—and Lisa too. And you're telling me this George Proctor person is dead? And I keep hearing the name Proctor, so what's up with that? And earlier you asked if I was with Lisa but you said you were shut down seven years ago?" I shook my head again. "You better start making sense, like who this place belongs to and what's going on."

"This base belonged to Marie Proctor—your mother. She was a member of a secret international organization called the GCP. The GCP stands for 'God's Chosen People.' The people selected to be in the GCP are chosen by Elohim, the creator of this universe. The last living Angel, Gabriel watches over this organization. You were also chosen to be a Protector of the GCP. There's no option in deciding if you want to be a GCP member or not. Once a member, you're partnered with a Guardian."

I still had no idea what he was talking about but figured I should keep listening.

Mandroid again pointed to the computer screen, and an image of people with shining skin appeared. They all had different colored eyes that shone. Some of their eye colors were irregular, but they all looked angelic.

"Guardians are a species created to assist humanity and protect this universe. They are supernatural beings with unparalleled power and intellect living in the cosmos in their home planets. Some live here to protect those in the GCP. The gods are after items that could cause universal destruction, and you as a GCP member now must help protect them. As your mother stated, you're responsible for protecting the Golden Water because it had previously been entrusted to her. She made that message for you because seven years ago she had a dream of your arrival here as an older individual."

Nodding slowly, I looked around and knew this was the place where she died. I could never forget the scent of blood that filled the air. I looked at Mandroid and said, "My mother's name was Marie Lopez, not Proctor. And I don't see how she could have been some protector for this Golden Water stuff. She was a journalist and an explorer. We're talking about two different people."

"No. She would make many trips to this very location. I specifically remember your mother bringing you here. You couldn't have been more than a year old, and she uploaded your handprint to every hand scanner so that you would be able to gain access here. Only three individuals can enter this secret place as of right now: your mother, Clark, and you. Your mother also used this location to train a few other GCP members. In the past, she trained New Jersey, New York, and Addis. Addis is currently the Protector of Ethiopia and was adopted by your mother at a young age after the gods murdered her parents. Addis watched over you from afar."

"What are you saying? That my mom lived a double life and adopted some girl and so she's my sister?"

"Correct, ma'am, and right now your aunt and yourself are in danger."

"I don't have an aunt! You're saying things but with no proof. You're saying 'Proctor' as if I'm related to Lisa."

Mandroid pushed a button on the side of the keyboard, and a metal chair rose through a hatch in the floor. He sat down and turned to me. "I'll show you." He turned back to the keyboard and started typing.

I saw multiple pictures of people pop up on the screen.

"What you're seeing ma'am, are generations of the Proctor family that originated from England."

A larger picture appeared on the screen: a man with short brown hair and brown eyes.

"That, my dear, is William Proctor," Mandroid said. "He's the older brother of George Proctor. William Proctor was your grandfather who traveled to America. He fell in love with Elizabeth Mendoza. Elizabeth had become the GCP Protector of Florida after her brother was killed. Even as a young orphan, Elizabeth worked within the GCP, then rose through the ranks and became the first female leader of the organization. She neglected her children to protect them. That's her on the screen now."

I looked at Elizabeth's image. Her hair was long and black, and she had full lips and a smooth face. I couldn't help but notice that she looked like me.

"Elizabeth led the GCP during the Second Great War, protecting her two kids—Marie Proctor and Lisa-Anne Proctor. Marie, the older sister, raised Lisa-Anne when their parents couldn't. William tried to but he was murdered in a home incident by the gods. Shortly after, Elizabeth suffered the same fate in the Second Great War."

I slowly backed away, gazing at the resemblance of Lisa, Mom, William, and Elizabeth. "No ... no no," I mumbled. "You're—No, Lisa can't be my aunt."

Another chair came up beside Mandroid. "Ma'am, please sit." He opened his hand toward the metal chair. "There's more you need to hear."

Feeling numb inside, I sat down and watched as Mandroid opened dozens of video files. He clicked one of the last videos.

The large screen turned black and then the video started.

It began with Lisa crying in the living room of this house before it was abandoned. She looked in her early twenties, if not her late teens. My breath caught and my eyes opened wider when I saw that my mother sat across from Lisa. Mom again looked so beautiful with her long hair, blue eyes, and that same form-fitting bodysuit she'd had on in the other video.

"This isn't right!" Lisa said. "You ... You can't decide to leave and just drop her on me." She covered her face and tears escaped from between her fingers.

My mom kept a straight face. "This isn't easy for me, okay? It's my only option. It'll be risky to have Antonio take care of her. Aerozayle will come after him when I'm gone, and then the gods or Gage will come after her."

Lisa continued to cry. "I lost everyone! Everyone we ever cared about is dead, and now you're going to do the same thing to me as Mom did to us. It's so selfish!"

Mom got off her chair and crouched down in front of Lisa. She gently pulled Lisa's hands away from her face and placed her own hands on her cheeks, wiping off the tears. "Take care of Angie for me, Lisa-Anne. I need you to take guardianship. Train her as I trained you. Teach her how to survive and show her the realities of life. Do what I couldn't do. Protect her and guide her."

"No," Lisa mumbled. She moved my mother's hands from her cheeks, revealing the redness that covered her face. "I already lost a child not so long ago, and now you're asking me to take care of yours?" She shook her head. "You know it's going to open up emotional wounds. How ... How could you ask me to do something like this?"

Mom deeply exhaled. "I know, Lisa-Anne, I know. I lost a newborn as well. I know how it feels and I'm sorry I wasn't there to protect you or your child from the gods." Tears started to fall down my mother's face. "An entire species is betting on the death of my child. I have a feeling Gage will be the one to kill me. If he doesn't get to me, maybe Aerozayle, Lucius, or Galoriah will—*if* Angie stays with me. That's why I need you to save my child."

"I can't, Marie! I'm ... I'm sorry but—"

"Please, Lisa-Anne. For me ... please."

"I'm not stable enough, okay? I—"

Mom wiped at her own eyes. "Save my baby please, Lisa-Anne. I know you're not stable and you never asked for this life. I've felt dead inside too since Mom and Dad died. The only light I have left is inside that child."

Lisa gave a deep sigh and finally nodded. "I'm going to die if I take care of her ... but I'll do it." She looked away, biting her lower lip, then shrugged. "Screw it. This life is meaningless anyway."

My mother smiled through her tears. "Thank you, Lisa-Anne. Thank you so much. I love Angie with all my heart, so please don't let anything happen to her." Mom looked down and then her head popped back up as she'd thought of something. Whatever it was, it made her smile even wider, and she looked Lisa in the eye as she took her hands into her own. "Angie is special. She just doesn't know it yet."

Lisa nodded, but then said, "This is going to ruin her. She's going to go through a lot. Are you prepared to let your daughter go through that? She needs you."

Mom put her hands on Lisa's shoulders. "She just needs guidance. I'm entrusting you to do that. I weighed my options with this war coming up. If things don't go right, the gods will get to her sooner or later, and with Genesis soul inside of me, I've dreamed of my death ..."

As Mom's words trailed off, Lisa looked the other way. I watched as she squeezed her eyes shut and more tears began falling down her face. My mother hugged Lisa, and Lisa hugged her back tightly. The video stopped suddenly, and the screen turned black.

"What happened?" I asked, feeling tears in my own eyes. "Where's the rest?"

"Those three gods your mother mentioned in the video—Aerozayle, Lucius, and Galoriah—I can sense them heading here," Mandroid said, "so we need to evacuate to safety immediately." He looked down at my thigh, where a small object created a bump in the fabric of my pants. "I see you have the ring that contains the Golden Water. We need to leave before we're seen."

I started to say something about the ring being a special memory of my mother, but then I realized why Lisa had given it to me all those years ago, telling me to always carry it with me.

I stared at the black screen. "I'm not leaving here without Lisa." Closing my eyes hearing my mother saying she lost a child too brought up multiple questions. Knowing the current situation this wasn't the time to dwell in the past.

"Ma'am, you don't have the proper training to get into combat with these—"

"This isn't a debate!" I looked over at Mandroid. "Show me those three who are making their way here."

Mandroid typed on the keyboard quickly, and the computer showed the images of three gods: two men and a woman. The first man—identified as Galoriah—had a full beard and long black hair. He wore some kind of armor that covered everything from his neck down, except for his arms. He looked really large in stature. The other male—Lucius—was slimmer and looked to be of average height. He had shoulder-length hair, blond with brown highlights, and had a light beard. He wore all-black clothing: a long leather jacket, tights, and boots. The last in the group I recognized from meeting her in the swamp: Aerozayle, who looked the same as when I'd seen her—dark, rosy lips and those bright green eyes. She wore the same black, long-sleeve shirt, protected by a thin vest of armor, along with black pants and high black boots. Her long black hair curled at the bottom.

Mandroid said, "This notorious group is well-known among the GCP. They are highly skilled in combat, using their abilities and any weaponry they obtain. They are not average gods. They're at their strongest when they are together. As I said, I would avoid any fight with them."

Ignoring him, I said, "Tell me their abilities."

"Very well. Galoriah is the strongest of them. His abilities are telekinesis, pulse wave, and flight. He's also the largest among them. He's a god who enjoys delivering pain. No Protector has ever beaten him. They say it's scary fighting a monster like him because he kills slowly."

"And what about the blond guy?" I asked.

"Lucius—fighting him alone is more than anyone can handle because he can duplicate himself using other living bodies."

"What do you mean—like he can make clones?"

"Not exactly. He can turn any human into a replica of himself. All he has to do is touch someone with a single finger. Once touched, the person will look and act exactly like him, and follow his plans. It only takes a second for him to transform someone. And the person who's been touched will be stuck on the inside because there's no reversing it."

"So how can you ever know if it's the real him or not?"

"The only way of identifying if it's him or not is by killing him, and if it's a replica, then it will reveal the body he touched."

"Okay." I pointed at the screen. "And that god is Aerozayle."

"Goddess, you mean. She's Lucius's lover."

"Well, at least we know Lucius's weakness."

"I wouldn't say that. To have the power to never be refused makes her quite a contender. If she can lock eyes with any human or animal long enough, they will obey her commands without question. It's her greatest ability, and she also has the power of fire, which is like no other. Once this particular fire makes contact with a living being, it can't be extinguished—until the corpse has turned to ashes. These gods should be fought in a one-on-one manner and never three-on-one."

I got up and looked down at Mandroid. "Can you find Lisa?"

"Yes," Mandroid answered. "I will locate her now."

He started typing, and I saw the screen view begin sweeping across the entire Everglades. After a few seconds, it zoomed in on my "prison"—the place I lived for seven years.

"So, she went home?" I asked.

"It appears so, but that could only be because the gods allowed her to go back there. They're expecting you to go after Lisa-Anne, and so it will be an ambush, but you're unprepared," Mandroid said. "You need to seek refuge in the GCP of Ethiopia. It's where the rest of the US-based GCP is hiding."

"I'm not letting the last person whose family to me die! Not when I have a chance to do something!"

The computer screen switched back to the three gods.

I glared up at their faces. "They're the ones responsible for everything bad in my life. My mother told me to kill him. I don't know who 'him' is but it has to be Galoriah, Lucius, or Gage."

According to the GCP files Gage was KIA, he's the father of Colvin Walker, currently New York. I don't think it was Gage Walker."

"Then it's the gods that'll be here any minute. I'm taking them out and saving Lisa." Colvin came to mind, a family friend, the only person that came close to a sibling beside Alice.

"Very well. If that's what you want, then I'll have to comply." Mandroid looked back up at the large screen as he said, "Summon the suits."

Behind us, the floor opened up, and two glass cylinders rose and revealed a pair of full bodysuits on mannequins. Mandroid stood and walked forward to touch both glass cases, which opened up to better show the outfits.

I found myself drawn closer to the outfits, almost as if they were calling my name. The bodysuit on my left was a shiny white one-piece with gold trim from the neck down to the ankles.

"If you're going to battle the gods," Mandroid said, "you'll need to wear armor. Now the outfit you're looking at resembles white latex, but it's a one-piece made of what we call 'Guardian material.' The gold trim from the neck down to the legs signifies the Golden Water. This outfit comes with a shoulder holster and a leg holster. The pistols you see on the wall are equipped to fit into the holsters and they are no ordinary weapons. The pistols are state of the art, made and used by the Guardians in their world. There's an infinite amount of ammunition contained inside each pistol. The bullets have been tested to go through any material on this planet. They are made to pierce a god's skin because Earthly materials—from firearms to heavy artillery—are useless against the gods."

I walked around the mannequin and could only think of my mother, who had worn something similar in the videos I'd seen. "How do you know it'll fit?"

"The suit adjusts and remains your size whenever you wear it. There's a zipper starting from your stomach and stopping at your throat, and once zipped, the zipper disappears." Mandroid nodded at the white suit. "This combat suit is called the 'White Stallion.' It comes with those boots." He pointed at the boots the mannequin was wearing, the boots had gold lining designs on them. "The White Stallion comes with those gloves that allow you to touch any object, no matter how hot or cold; temperature is nothing but a number with the gloves on. And both of these combat suits are not only weatherproof but also shockproof and impervious to cutting or tearing. Next, the utility belt has features to help you survive almost any attack and also aid you in battle. Always keep the belt on."

"And what about powers? Does it give me any?"

"Well, the boots give you super speed, and the gloves give you super strength. The armor itself gives you the ability to fly. Once you have everything together, you'll be given the talent of becoming an outstanding marksman, and all of your senses will also be enhanced."

Mandroid reached out and removed the gold watch from the mannequin's left wrist. "The most important part of the outfit is the watch."

The gold watch had a white face, and it shone brightly—and looked expensive.

"To wear either of the suits, you must wear the associated watch and think about the suit, and then it will appear on you. Simple, right? The original watch is still on your mother's wrist. She requested this if she was to ever die."

I gave a grim nod.

Mandroid stepped over to the second outfit in its glass case. "Two ways to take off either suit: you can either think it off while you're wearing the matching watch and it will disappear, or you can simply physically remove it."

The other mannequin was wearing a black one-piece. I couldn't take my eyes off of it. It was almost identical to the White Stallion but black and gold instead. That suit's watch was black, and its dial shone gold.

"I call it the 'Black Beauty.'" Mandroid smiled at the sight of the combat suit. "Your mother thought you would look flawless in black. She said it was your favorite color right after green. So wear it proudly."

I took the black watch and visualized myself wearing the Black Beauty—and suddenly found myself clothed in the suit, which fit well.

The computer beeped, then the screen lit up and showed Aerozayle, Lucius, and Galoriah flying toward this island. The computer's mechanical voice said, "Arrival time expected in twenty seconds."

I pulled my hair into a ponytail. "No one gets in here except me. Got it?"

At my side, Mandroid also looked up at the computer. "Yes, of course, ma'am," he said. "And I knew of Lisa. She sacrificed everything—if not the same as then more than your mother. Lisa had a full life ahead of her but put you first and hid from the urban world to live out by the swamp near Everglades City. She lost everyone you lost and even more since she's been living longer. It's the reason why she's in her current state, and even now she protected you. Do you honestly want to risk your life going back for her? She wouldn't want that."

"I've been training for seven years, putting my body through physical pain to find some meaning in this life. Even hated myself for not being able to save my mother, and she was right there. I fought so that Angie wouldn't exist. She's dead and now I'm ready to fight." I looked over at Mandroid. "Now how do I get out of here?"

Mandroid said, "You need only to say, 'Open base,' since the computer is programmed to recognize and respond to your voice."

"Thanks," I replied. Then, looking to the ceiling, I said, "Open base."

One section of the ceiling opened up, and the stairs reappeared. I headed up into the house and then to the front door. With the Black Beauty combat suit on, I felt almost naked, it was so light and form-fitting. But I didn't feel stronger or faster or any better. The only thing that seemed different was my mind being more alert. My thoughts felt ... enhanced, as if I was using a hundred percent of my brain at once. I guessed that it was the feeling of my mind being connected to the suit.

As I went for the front door, the house shook from the gods landing outside. I rushed out of the house to find the wind gusting. The skies turned dark, and clouds were forming, covering the sun.

I looked to my right and saw the three gods. I glanced back at the safe house to see it thankfully hadn't been affected by their landing. Turning back, I saw the three gods standing side by side, looking just as they had appeared on the computer. Galoriah was in the middle. Aerozayle was on his right and Lucius on his left.

Aerozayle stepped forward. "I got this one."

Frowning, I walked forward, feeling nervous but even more determined. "You're all dead."

5

Fight For Life - Angela

I flew up and could feel how awkward it was to be in the air, but by the time I got close to Aerozayle, I felt a little smoother. She'd just launched herself into the air, but I was already throwing the first punch as she came near. She easily moved back and moved aside, dodging my attack. I turned around for another punch, but this time she ducked and then palm-punched my chest. I sucked for air as I flew backward into some trees, feeling the impact of the branches. It *hurt,* and I figured I broke some ribs, but at least the suit wouldn't rip. I struck the ground and opened my mouth as I tried to take a breath. Looking up at the sky a hand grabbed me and picked me up by my hair, then I felt an impact on the jaw. But Aerozayle continued to hold on to my hair, so I didn't fall. I groaned, and she elbowed me to the jaw, then repeated this time to my temple, sending me flying into the air again, only to slam back into the ground.

Gasping for air, I got on one knee and watched as Aerozayle slowly flew my way.

"Hand over the Golden Water," she ordered.

Ignoring her demand, I flew up and went for a kick. Blocking my leg with her forearm, she kneed my stomach, leaving no space between us, then elbowed the back of my neck, sending me to the ground yet again. Teleporting next to me, she lifted me into the air by my throat.

"I hope for your sake you're not this slow. But ... seeing the rage in your eyes, you seek my death, don't you?" Aerozayle locked a tighter grip around my throat, then tossed me aside.

Rubbing my neck, I looked up. "Shut up!" I sprung up and rushed in.

I went for a punch, but then I saw Lucius appear to my right. I focused on him all the while executing a punch to Aerozayle. I knew his intentions and used every muscle to quickly move out of the way and time slowed down, as I could see him attempting to punch my face. It had to be my super speed. After backing up to avoid his punch, I stopped and time resumed—just in time to be kicked in the chest by Aerozayle, sending me to the ground one more time. Not hesitating, I got to my feet as Lucius and Aerozayle flew toward me. I welcomed their attack, flying at Aerozayle and throwing a punch, only to have it dodged. Then Lucius disappeared. Sensing him behind me, I turned and performed a roundhouse kick. He ducked and tried to jam a dagger into my knee. I yelled at the pain of the impact, but thankfully the suit was as impervious as Mandroid had said.

"Won't tear, eh?" Lucius said with a smirk. "Whatever."

He moved forward to tackle me to the ground, putting me on my back. The only thing I could see was the tip of his dagger coming down straight at my face. Without thinking, I blocked the strike with my hands, and his dagger struck me in the palm of my left hand. Not being able to pierce through the gloves, I used my good leg and went for a kick to his face. But Aerozayle caught my foot, slamming it back to the ground. Lucius drove his dagger at my face again, seeing what was coming I grabbed his wrist and shoved him aside. Trying to get up, Aerozayle immediately grabbed hold of my other leg and pinned both legs down as Lucius scrambled halfway up and attempted to jump on top of me. My sixth sense forced me to look up and saw Galoriah standing overhead. I watched as he lifted his war-hammer over his shoulder and aimed it for my face. Seeing what was to come, I moved at super speed to slow down time.

The war-hammer flew through the air toward where I had been laying as Lucius continued to move slowly in the air trying to pin me down. Continuing to move at super speed, I pulled out one of my Guardian pistols from my holster and shot Galoriah in the shoulder. I stopped moving and time resumed. I saw Galoriah jerk back, his hand going up to hold his wound. I moved in just in time to head-butt Lucius, sending him crashing into Aerozayle. Seeing my opportunity, I exploded into the air, keeping my eyes on the gods. I could feel my bones restructuring themselves and my other wounds mending. I couldn't remember Mandroid saying anything about the suit having special healing powers, so maybe it was the belt he'd mentioned. I descended a little to see Lucius and Aerozayle also take to the air.

Then I suddenly heard Mandroid's voice in my head: *"For a second I thought you were a goner, ma'am."*

"What?" I said out loud. "How are you talking to me?"

"The suit allows for telepathic communication, so you don't need to speak out loud to communicate with me. Just think it back to me."

"Really?" I flew backward in the air to put some distance between me and the gods. *"Well, maybe I should have let you tell me more about the powers of the suits."*

"It's okay. If you hadn't left when you did, they likely would have discovered us. Also, I'm proud of you for showing such bravery."

"It's still too early to be celebrating," I said as the three gods flew toward me. Even from a distance, I could see the anger in Galoriah's eyes.

Galoriah lifted his hands and faced his palms at me.

"Move!" Mandroid shouted in my head. *"That's the pulse wave I told you about."*

But it was too late. Even as Mandroid finished speaking, a pulse wave shot out of Galoriah's hands, hitting me square on. I shot through the air, arcing downward before I finally crashed into some trees again. I looked up in time to see Aerozayle hurling fire into the trees surrounding me. The fire began to spread fast.

"Quickly, you must leave!" Mandroid said.

"Oh really?" I said sarcastically. I looked around and began running toward the sound of water.

This fire was different though. It was as if it had a mind of its own. It began to follow me like it wanted to burn me alive. I kicked it up a notch using my super speed. The air around me got hotter and filled with smoke. As I continued running, I could tell that all of my senses had been enhanced, just like Mandroid said they would. Farther ahead I could hear the sound of water—and a motor.

"Mandroid, can you see what's ahead of me?"

"Tourists—they're trying to leave the area on airboats. Probably saw the smoke."

I covered my nose and mouth with a hand, trying not to breathe in the toxic air. But every second that passed, my environment became more unbearable to see or breathe, and as I drew near the water, my enhanced hearing picked up the shouts and cries of the fleeing tourists. I finally flew above to escape the smoke—only to find myself face to face with Aerozayle. The screams from below made us both look down. The airboats had gotten ahead of the smoke, and now many of the people aboard were looking up at us, pointing in astonishment.

I looked over at Aerozayle. Seeing the fleeing, frightened tourists made her smile.

"No!" I looked back down and caught the eyes of the nearest boat driver.

"Move!" I shouted down at the tourists.

But Aerozayle launched her scorching flames at the airboats, all filled with men, women, and children. The flames caught and consumed all five of the boats. I turned back to see Aerozayle staring at me as all of those lives below were being snuffed out, with many of them screaming in pain.

I saw what I figured to be a family of three manage to escape and swim to land. The father held on to his daughter and wife.

But then Lucius flew down and walked toward the family.

"Look out!" I yelled.

As I flew down toward the family, I heard a child's cry: "Mommy!"

The little girl on land stood still as her parents transformed into clones of Lucius.

I turned my attention back to the girl, who couldn't have been more than five. The two clones flew toward her. Using my super speed, I ran to the little girl. Wrapping my arms around her from behind, I flew off with her, not looking back.

While flying away, the girl began to scream and cry even as the clones were tailing me. "Mommy! Daddy!" she wailed.

"Just stay still!" Holding tight to the girl, I knew I had to take her to a safe location, but it was impossible with two clones tailing close behind me.

As I headed toward the ground, a force took control of my body and I found myself flying full speed directly at the ground, losing grip of the child as I got closer.

"Mandroid, get the girl!" I yelled out loud.

"Ma'am, I'm not allowed to leave—"

"Get her now! That's an order."

Mandroid teleported by my side, caught the girl out of the air, and then disappeared with her. I closed my eyes as my body ripped through the air, only hearing the wind I prepared for impact.

Crashing hard into some trees, I could only lie there on my back and look up at the sky, as I felt completely numb from head to toe. Smoke continued to fill the air and it became unbearable to breathe as I heard more screams. I realized I couldn't move at all, and I knew my injuries had paralyzed me.

I could hear the gods approaching and my heart started to beat fast. *"Mandroid why isn't my body responding. I can't move!"*

"Such an injury is going to take some time. Ma'am, you need to think of something if they get to you while you're still in that state."

Aerozayle, Galoriah, and Lucius—along with his two clones—came my way, all smiling.

I could only groan as I waited while Black Beauty began healing my injuries.

Lying there, I fought to keep from passing out, blinking repeatedly. "C'mon! Kill me ... kill me!" I shouted. "I'm not scared of you."

"Your belt should contain small beads in the left pocket," came Mandroid's voice. *"Throw one in the direction of the gods and plan your escape."*

Feeling my hands again, I pushed my body off the ground and flew backward just above the ground. As I passed a large fallen tree, I hoisted it up, amazed at the feeling of my super strength, and then hurled it in their direction. I followed up by throwing five of the beads. I waited just long enough to see the beads begin to explode all around the gods. A bright light came from the explosion, I turned and flew off, but a powerful surge of air from the explosions knocked me back into some more trees. Unable to control my body, I found myself crashing into the ground, and I could feel unbearable heat on my face as it touched the dirt. The sky brightened and my surroundings began to shift as if an earthquake commenced. I stood up and turned back to see a mass of energy consuming everything in its path. I flew up and farther away to a safe distance to see parts of the Everglades completely wiped out. The energy explosion had caused the air to fill with dirt and the temperature to rise. The Black Beauty suit began to shine, keeping my body cool. I flew back and didn't find any human scattering or animals which was weird. I had a feeling that it wasn't just the Everglades that was being attacked. As I continued flying toward the house where Mandroid was hidden, it was surprisingly the only place not destroyed in the immediate vicinity.

I descended to the safe house. *"Mandroid, are you alright?"* I mind-spoke to him as I scanned the island, but everything looked normal.

"Yes, I managed to gather enough power here to raise a force field to protect the island from the explosion you caused. I did say to only throw one of the beads, ma'am."

I heard laughter from behind me, and I turned to see Galoriah and his followers walking toward the safe house.

"How ... How are you still alive?" I said. "That's impossible."

Galoriah opened his arms toward me. "Naturally it could've killed us, but we sacrificed Lucius's two clones, which gave us enough time to move at the speed of light. You might be the fastest human, but you're not the fastest in the universe. There's no point in keeping you alive. If you keep fighting, you'll only make me stronger. I'm superior to you in every way. Your healing won't mean anything, and there are other gods anxious to get a piece of you."

Galoriah and Lucius hung back as Aerozayle walked toward me. I hated myself because even with the power I had, I felt weak and my body started to tremble in fear, with my heart beating rapidly.

Before Aerozayle could get any closer, I flew up into the sky and took off toward home. As I sped through the air, I looked down at the destruction. The explosion had even reached the outskirts of the city. I continued to fly toward home but then I sensed Galoriah, Lucius, and Aerozayle following me. I looked back and saw that they were still far behind me, so I sped up.

I stopped in midair when I saw a police force in front of my house.

I flew down to one of the police officers. He'd already had his weapon drawn and aimed it at me. "Hands up!" he shouted. "Identify yourself!"

"Whoa whoa whoa!" I said, raising my hands high. "Captain Morgan, it's me, Angela Lopez. I'm here to help ... and this is my house."

"Very good, ma'am," came Mandroid's voice. *"Be calm because they are on guard right now, not knowing who they can trust."*

"In a few seconds, they're going to be casualties." I watched the sweat come down their faces and some were covered in blood. I knew them all but their eyes told me I was someone new to them.

"I'm reading a body report on the officers. They're traumatized, they've had to endure killing their men and the citizens you came across that attacked you earlier. They were all under Aerozayle."

Some of the other officers had also turned to point their pistols at me. Captain Morgan aimed his pistol to my head as his hands shook in fear, "Just stay where you are!"

Just then Lisa and Billy came running out of the house.

"Angela!" Lisa yelled. "Oh my God! Thank God you're alright! I thought you died."

"Stop right there, ma'am, sir!" Morgan shouted at Lisa and Billy.

Lisa was close enough to grab my arm and start pulling me into a hug, but she stopped and looked at my outfit. "You're a GCP protector."

I grabbed her hands and didn't see Lisa but my aunt. "I saw you thrown into the sky," I looked at her legs. "You look fine." My mind automatically went to Galoriah, he must've been around and stopped her from falling to her death.

A shadow hovered over us which sent a chill down my spine. The sun wasn't shining bright anymore and my senses heightened, wanting me to focus above. I looked up to see multiple cars levitating around the gods.

"Incoming!" one of the police officers yelled. "Overhead!"

Lisa tugged on my arm to draw my attention back to her. "Why haven't you summoned Clark?" she said. "You're putting millions of lives at stake doing this yourself."

I started to say something, but then Lisa, Billy, and I all jerked back at the sight of every police car in the area lifting off the ground to float in the air.

"What the hell?" Billy said.

A moment later, one of the cars launched itself at a group of three police standing nearby, slamming into them and then crushing them under its weight.

Captain Morgan shouted, "Open fire on targets overhead!"

At his command, every remaining officer unleashed a barrage of bullets. Galoriah made a horizontal shield with the levitated police vehicles. One bullet, though, managed to slip through and hit him in the head, which made him smile. With the bullets mostly hitting the cars, several of them exploded. I stood in awe at the gods as they stood amid the red flames. The fire that caught on to their skin and hair immediately disappeared inflicting no damage.

"Get inside with Lisa and Billy!" Mandroid said.

I grabbed Lisa's hand and ran inside with her and Billy as the sounds of screaming rang in the air.

"I shouldn't be in public. I'm so stupid!" I said as I shut the door, then leaned against it. I looked at Lisa. "I can't summon this Clark you keep talking about. I don't even know how." I hit the door in frustration.

"Ma'am," came Mandroid's voice. *"In the video, your mother said that Clark would come if you—"*

"Be quiet for now, Mandroid!" I mind-spoke, trying to think of a plan. I knew it would be suicide to fly away with nowhere to hide. Being out in the open with those three was suicide. I could be stopped by his

telekinesis, my aunt and Billy could get touched by Lucius, or fall under Aerozayle's words and I have to end up fighting my only relative alive.

Lisa looked down, regret in her eyes. "When you find out who I am, know I didn't do this because I hated you. I acted the way I did because it was my job to do so. Know that a certain someone told me to act this way toward you."

Remembering the video I'd seen of Lisa and Mom, I squeezed Lisa's hands as I moved in closer to her. "We're family. I won't let you die here. I promise."

Hearing footsteps outside, I backed away as I kept my attention on the door, keeping my aunt and Billy next to me. A second later Galoriah kicked open the door and entered as we continued to back ourselves into the living room.

A wave of energy shot out of Galoriah's hand, separating me from Lisa and Billy.

"No!" Billy shouted.

He charged at Galoriah, who just laughed as he swung his war-hammer and caught Billy in the head. Billy collapsed onto the floor, lying still and bleeding hard from where the hammer had crushed his skull.

"Billy!" Lisa shouted.

"No!" I cried out.

Aerozayle flew in behind Galoriah and eyed Lisa. "I'd been waiting to kill Marie but lost the opportunity," Aerozayle said. "But killing her younger sibling is the next best thing."

I clenched my teeth at the sight of Lucius entering and standing beside Galoriah. I got ready to attack them, but then Aerozayle landed a few steps in front of Lisa and flashed an ebony blade, throwing it to her.

"Let's see if you still have it in you," Aerozayle said. "Let's play."

Lisa leaped to grab the blade out of the air and then charged right past Aerozayle, headed straight for Galoriah. In a blur, his leg came up and he kicked Lisa in the chest, sending her across the room and crashing into the wall.

"No!" I shouted. "Lisa!"

I saw blood trickling from her forehead where she lay in a heap on the floor not far from Billy's body.

Turning my eyes back toward the two gods by the door, I hurled myself at Galoriah—but Aerozayle crashed into me from the side, putting me into a chokehold. She held me tight and forced my gaze to where Lisa had now risen to her hands and knees. Galoriah and Lucius approached her.

"Let ... me ... go!" I grunted.

But Aerozayle just tightened her grip around my throat.

Galoriah looked down at Lisa. "How dare you try to attack me first. Don't you know who I am?" He revealed his teeth smiling wide. "I've been praying to find someone to take me out. I guess your God is scared. Praying won't save you, I challenge your God!"

He pressed a foot down onto Lisa's right shoulder, pushing her back onto the floor. She groaned but tried to fight against him. Galoriah, though, just jammed his foot down harder, and with my enhanced senses, I could hear the sound of her bones being crushed, and then she began to scream and spasm.

"Yes, scream in pain!" Lucius said. "Call for help!" He smiled and kicked her in the ribs.

The sick snapping sound I heard made my stomach lurch, and in rage, I tried to shout but Aerozayle's grip was cutting off any sound in my throat.

"What will you do now, daughter of Marie?" Galoriah said to me as he walked behind Lisa.

She now laid still on the floor, frozen in place due to his telekinetic ability. Galoriah looked down at her and then into my eyes as he reached down to gently grip both sides of Lisa's head, lifting her off the floor. He began to squeeze her skull. Lisa started to scream again.

A mix of emotions surged through me: anger, sadness, hate, love. But as much as I wanted to do something—anything—I couldn't move at all.

"Enough!" came a strong male voice that I didn't recognize.

I moved my eyes and could just see that someone else had entered the house. He wore armor similar to Galoriah's, except his was gold and covered every part of his body from the neck down. He looked as if he was in his early thirties, with shoulder-length blond hair.

Galoriah dropped Lisa, and she collapsed to the floor. It only took her a few seconds to react to this new god. She slowly rose to her knees, looking shocked as she pointed at him. "You ..." she said in a hoarse voice. Her eyes looked terrified. "You ... you killed her!"

For the first time, I saw tears come down Lisa's face. She was no longer the strict lady who raised me. She looked young again. She looked like her younger self when she talked with my mother in the video.

"You killed my sister!" Lisa shouted. "She trusted you!"

My eyes opened wider and I felt my heart pound even harder.

Lisa looked at me. "This is the god that killed your mother—Amentous."

I turned my eyes back to this Amentous. His irises shone gold as our eyes met.

Amentous faced Galoriah. "This is the human that'll put an end to our existence. Prepare her."

A chair levitated from the kitchen and made its way into the living room. Aerozayle shoved me down onto the chair, and I was held in place by Galoriah's telekinetic power, even as Lucius held Lisa in the place where she knelt. Even having healing abilities, I still feared what was to come.

Amentous stepped forward and touched Galoriah and then Aerozayle on the shoulder. Then Amentous raised his left hand, which he'd touched Galoriah with, and all the furniture in view started to float. Then black fire appeared in his right hand, the hand he'd used to touch Aerozayle's shoulder.

"Amentous can borrow the powers of other gods and bestow them on anyone he chooses," Mandroid communicated to me.

"Yeah, thanks," I replied, keeping my eyes fixed on Amentous.

My body froze in the place where I stood, but I could still move my head.

Amentous walked toward me. "I'm going to give you the power of god fire. It hurts a lot more than the fire you experience here on Earth."

He glanced toward Lisa, who could barely stand or move from the injury she sustained. He then turned to look at me again.

"No! No ... don't!" I knew exactly what he planned to do. "I'll give you the Golden Water, all right? Just cool it!"

He shook his head. "Don't take me for a fool."

The closer Amentous came to me, the more rapidly my heart thundered within me. He used his newly obtained telekinesis again to lift my right arm. Then he transferred the obtained power of god fire to me by touching my shoulder. I could feel the heat flow through my veins as he laid his hand on my shoulder.

"No!" I shouted.

I tried to resist, but my right arm obeyed the will of Amentous and soon my hand was aimed at Lisa.

"No!" I cried out again pleading for my body to listen to my voice.

I willed my arm to go down but it didn't move. Galoriah kept her in place with his telekinesis. Lisa's eyes found mine and I could see tears welling up.

"It's okay," she said. "It's okay, Angela."

"No ... please!" I whispered.

My hand opened toward Lisa, and I felt an immense heat from my palm that reached into my fingertips. Then black fire erupted from my palm and shot out, going straight to Lisa. As the black flames began consuming her, Lisa screamed and shrieked in agony—and my heart dropped. I completely lost it, crying and shouting and fighting against the telekinesis holding me in place to no avail.

Amentous, Galoriah, Lucius, and Aerozayle just stood there, watching. Lisa stopped screaming, and the fire turned her body into ashes within a few seconds, then the flames disappeared on their own.

The stench of burnt flesh made my stomach lurch, and I couldn't stop myself from vomiting on the floor in front of me.

I felt like I'd just died from the inside watching Lisa perish in front of me. I could feel my heart turn black and hard.

As I spat the last of the vomit from my mouth and licked my lips, I saw Aerozayle to the side of me. She turned my body toward herself and grabbed ahold of my face, looking into my eyes. "Give me the Golden Water," she said.

I couldn't fight her command and knew I had to obey. I thought of the ring in the pocket of my pants, and the Black Beauty bodysuit instantly disappeared as my mind pictured my previous attire, which I was now wearing again. My hand dug into the pocket and then handed the ring over to Aerozayle.

Galoriah walked over and grabbed the ring, slipping it on. He lifted his hand into the air. "Release!"

Eleven cylindrical silver containers appeared out of nowhere and floated in the air in front of Galoriah.

He grabbed one of the containers and looked at it. "They're full," he said, looking around at the other gods. "We've done it."

"Put all of it away and let's go," Amentous said. "Vera is waiting at Death's Temple and she doesn't want any more casualties." Pointing at me, he said, "That human can live, since she isn't a threat," then he teleported away.

I stared down at the wooden floor, not saying a word. Moving my thumb, I was set free but I didn't care. I was done fighting.

Aerozayle eyed me. "I won't let you live. None of us will allow that to happen. Our King is Zulu, not Amentous."

Galoriah levitated my body, slamming me against a wall and holding me there. "This is for the gods your mother killed," he said.

Aerozayle opened her hand and a fireball emerged from her palm. She aimed it at my head, then sent it slowly forward for the kill.

As the fireball floated toward me, I knew this was it. At that moment, I knew what death was. Nothing else mattered. The only things that seemed alive were me and the flames.

I remembered how Mom had once told me that when death approached, that's when a sign would appear. I looked around. No one was coming for me, and nothing was stopping those flames. This was it for me.

I closed my eyes and stopped resisting, thinking of my so-called

Guardian Clark. "If you're out there ... then save me," I whispered, giving in to whatever luck, the universe, or Superior being was listening.

A brightly glowing back appeared right in front of me, taking the fireball meant for me. Everything flashed bright, and something told me to let go—that everything was going to be alright. And that's what I did—I gave in and fell into a deep sleep.

6

Declaration Of War- Cade

I popped open my eyes to find myself lying on the floor. The battle outside of the headquarters played in my head. I sat up, then looked down at the floor and saw that I was at the front of a church in near darkness. The place was filled with gods sitting in the rows of seats before me. The scent of smoke clogged my nose, and the dancing light on the walls told me that the only light was coming from fiery torches held by the gods. I noticed that the windows were covered with wooden boards, preventing any light from entering.

Realizing that I wasn't tied up at all, I tried to stand but barely managed, with my arms and legs shaking. "What ... What did you do to me?"

I saw I was wearing my sneakers and it hit me: I wasn't wearing my armor. I reached up and touched my neck. The Karui necklace was gone.

"I have what you're looking for," came Vera's voice from the first row. She sat there with her legs crossed in front of her. "I needed your undivided attention so I took it."

She let the silver-chained necklace dangle in the air as it hung from her fingers. The Karui sparkled white, wanting to make its presence known in the dark.

"Don't worry," she went on. "I won't keep this. I have no use for an artificial half-powered necklace." Vera got up from her seat and started making her way to me. "But to answer your question, I took a good portion of your life force to steal your knowledge."

I looked around again, closer this time, and finally understood that I was not in a church but rather Death's Temple—the place where people could sacrifice someone precious to them in honor of Ominous. The person who made the sacrifice could be converted to a demigod, having Zaygaian power, or could receive Ominous' blessing in exchange. This, I knew, was how the Walker family had obtained their wealth.

"What... what do you mean?" I said, my voice was weak. My body couldn't physically stand any longer, so I sat back down. "What exactly did you steal?"

Now standing in front of me, Vera said, "When I take someone's life force, I don't just receive an abundance of health and power. I also gain access to their memories, who their ancestors were, what they're feeling, and their knowledge. When I stole your life force, I know all about you." She looked down at me. "And with what I took from you, nothing is hidden. I know that Alice Lombardo holds the soul of my Creator and that my father Ominous is imprisoned beneath the GCP headquarters in Porto-Novo." She paused and then stared into my eyes. "And I also have the Golden Water in my possession." Vera held up her hand to reveal two rings that shone gold. "Release," she commanded.

The rings projected a transparent light in the darkness, and in the light, I saw a host of silver cylinders slowly appear and float in the air. Vera grabbed one of the containers and moved the cylinder around.

"They're all full ... but I count only twenty-three cylinders. I foresaw this and allowed it to be so. The last one is still with Angela, although she may not even know it." She crouched down in front of me. "Here are your options: You hand over every holy item the GCP is hiding, along with Alice and Angela, and you bring me the last of the Golden Water. Once this is done, I'll see to it that we simply enslave this universe rather than put an end to this wretched place you call home." She stood up and looked down. "Your other option is refusing, and that's when I wipe out everything."

I shook my head. "You're not getting anything." I moved back while still on the floor, trying to keep some distance between us. "I won't let you have your way; I promise you. My father dedicated his life so this wouldn't happen—to make humans kill the people they love to benefit yourselves. How do you justify that and think what you're doing is right?"

Vera shrugged. "To give one's life for the greater good ... that's our Zaygaian belief. You humans do it all the time. The moment I was resurrected, I came to realize that my entire planet—gods, goddesses, animals, and every living thing—had sacrificed its life for a purpose. They did it so I could do what many in the past failed to do, and that saved the South Universe." She looked off to the side. "I meditated, only to find out that everyone I'd ever known was dead. So, they entrusted me to save every planet in the South Universe. The longer we wait, the weaker the gods get without their Creator. Soon our sun will die out, and it'll be the extinction of the gods."

After a pause, Vera turned back to me. "Then I realized my Creator's prophecy has begun to be fulfilled—the First Resurrection, the foretelling of when the new queen of Planet Zayga is awakened and she resurrects her father and he brings calamity against his foes. By this, he will bring the gods a step closer to reviving Genesis, our forefather. The Walker family aided in this prophecy. They knew by giving their lives that it would be a beneficial cause toward future peace."

"So that's your plan."

"No, child, it's part of my planned destiny. You're half Avian—can't you sense the truth I'm speaking? Victory is on my side." Vera threw the Karui at my feet and walked off. "The next time we meet will be on a battlefield for the survival of our race."

"It won't get that far. You're not touching Alice or any other items. It ends here with you and me." I put on the Karui and my GCP armor appeared. "There were thousands of planets in the North Universe and your kind killed off every planet. Mars, Saturn, Jupiter, and other planets ... all empty now because you killed off the species there. They now live in the Afterworld in peace. I won't let you do the same with Earth."

Vera stopped to turn around and look at me but said nothing.

Then I heard a familiar voice in my head, coming through my subdermal communicator: *"Cade, can you hear me? It's Alice. I have your location. Are you okay?"*

"Alice, call reinforcements now," I replied.

Then I got up and looked at Vera. "Even if you're right, you won't live long enough to see the First Resurrection come to fruition."

An Avex appeared by my side. I pulled out my bow as every god stood up from their seats. "I'm Cade Walker," I said. "You should've killed me with the rest of my family." I looked over at the Avex. "Let's go."

Vera waved a hand toward us. "Go home, child. Your bravery won't accomplish anything. I have an army of gods who can wipe out this planet in seconds. At this very moment, war is being waged for my father."

Now she folded her hands, and Galoriah, Aerozayle, and Lucius appeared out of the darkness in the exit of Death's Temple.

Vera pointed at them. "Those three are just a few of the gods who have been here for centuries and haven't been killed. I also have Amentous, a royal god like me and one who goes by many names—the last son of Genesis, the savior, and the king of Planet Peace. It's said, he alone almost won the Second Great War. As for me—I almost took out this planet years ago. I can do it now but senseless killing isn't what I was raised to do. Now go home. I have foreseen the end. Love that human while she's still alive."

"Can't you see what you plan to do? You say you weren't raised to kill in a meaningless way, but what do you think you'll be doing by awakening every god?"

"Tell me, what am I?" Vera studied my face. "I want you to think about this question."

Having studied every god and Protector my father fought; I knew everything about Vera. "I know you weren't born but created. Genesis created you to restore balance in his universe. You were created to be the second Evrakra.

"So tell me, what exactly is an Evrakra?" Vera's eyes glowed red as she smirked.

"An Evrakra is the left hand of the king. With that title, a person holds the honor to scout planets and make their presence known upon invading. Once they overtake and rule a planet, it's offered to their king. Kanos was the first Evrakra, left hand to Genesis. He was created with immense power and obeyed the orders of the South Creator instead of Genesis. He waged war against Heaven and the Heavenly Host. He fought his way to the entry of Heaven but died against archangel Michael. Elohim, The Creator of all creators rose from his throne and put the South Creator to sleep as well as Kanos, who was turned into stone. This left multiple gods creating their own planets and there was no order. Super gods fought for leadership and that's when you were created by Genesis."

Vera clapped her hands. "Let me finish the rest for you." She sat down. "I was created shortly after becoming the daughter of Ominous. I was created loving my father and Genesis, and six days into my existence, I conquered all planets in the South Universe. I killed every super god, and Genesis created the gods you fight today. The difference between myself and Kanos is that I have a hundred percent chance of winning any war, created with loyalty and determination to complete the plans of Genesis, and the wisdom to plan correctly. Let me tell you this: I do not lose. I'm faced with another problem and I will restore my universe for my Creator and see to it that my gods are resurrected again."

Vera extended her hands toward me and I disappeared.

7

∿

Extinction Or Survival - Angela

I felt cold when I woke up. I could hear birds chirping and cars passing by. As I blinked a few times, sunlight poured into my eyes. I sat up straight in an unfamiliar bed, using my forearm to wipe the dry saliva from the sides of my mouth. The muscles in my body ached as I turned to each side, trying to stretch my back. My right arm felt numb, so I tapped on that forearm a few times.

A gust of wind blew through the room and made me feel exposed. I looked over to the open window and then began rubbing my eyes to get my vision straight, hoping everything that had happened was just a horrible nightmare. I looked at the bedroom door and then around the room. The cheap blue paint did no justice in hiding the crack marks on the walls. The uneven wooden floor of the small room showed visible chatter marks. Turning to my right, I saw the Black Beauty bodysuit folded on a chair, with the black GCP watch lying neatly on top. I stared at the combat suit, and it all came rushing back to me at once: everything from fleeing from home and running in the swamp to the safe house and almost dying ... and then seeing Lisa die. It all played out in my head. I squeezed the thick covers, angry at myself, angry at the gods, angry for getting Lisa killed—Billy too. As tough as Lisa had been on me, now I understood

76

that she'd done it out of love—and because of a promise to my mom. I felt overwhelmed that I'd never been able to forgive myself for having a part in her death.

I covered my face with my hands, and I could almost feel myself crying until it finally hit me: I was in someone's home.

A few moments later, I heard footsteps drawing closer to the door. I slipped out of the bed as quietly as possible and grabbed my watch. Just as I was about to strap it onto my wrist, the door opened to reveal a man in a blue suit, holding a folding metal chair.

"Please sit," he said. "You've been asleep for some time."

Still holding the watch in my hands, I didn't move. "I'm fine standing. Who are you?"

"I represent the GCP." He unfolded the chair and took a seat by the end of the bed. "Where's the Golden Water?"

Remembering the fight with the gods, all the other details came back. "I ... don't have it. They managed to take it from me."

"Hm, that's not good," he said to himself. He rose and walked back toward the door, but then he stopped and turned toward me again. "Are you with the GCP?" He nodded in the direction of where Black Beauty lay on the chair.

I knew what he was asking. I knew what my choices were. But it felt like I had no choice at all. This was now part of my destiny—a destiny that had begun the moment I grabbed hold of Lisa's hand in my bedroom. There was no going back.

"If it means killing the gods," I said, nodding, "then, yeah, I'm with the GCP."

He gave a small smile. "Welcome to the GCP, then. The dark era is upon us. Oh, and just so you know, you're in the city of Closias. Go ahead and get yourself ready, then your Guardian, Clark, will update you on what's going on."

He walked out, leaving the door open. I looked around again and took a glance outside the window to find myself back in my old hometown from childhood.

Two knocks came from behind. "Angie ... is that you?"

I turned around to see my dad—my real dad. My eyes widened and my legs began to shake, I felt so mesmerized at his presence. Looking at my father it was like looking at a ghost. It felt scary.

He quickly walked across the room and hugged me. "I missed you so much," he whispered.

It took him a few seconds before he stepped back and observed me. I saw tears running down his cheeks.

"My God," he said, "you've grown so much."

Saying nothing, I sat on the edge of the bed and looked up into his watery eyes, feeling such a mix of emotions surging within me. I went with the anger I felt, then asked him, "Did you know where I was going to end up after you left?"

His face reddened as he kept quiet.

"Did you know?" I said, almost shouting this time.

He gave a small nod. "Yes." He slowly backed away.

I pursed my lips and then shook my head as I eyed him. "How? How could you leave me? Do you know the abuse I went through the past seven years? You're ... You're my father! You were supposed to protect me, not push me away. All the stuff I went through and you just forgot about me like ... like I'm some trash to you. What was it? Was I bad to you? Was I not good enough?"

"No no no! Angie, it wasn't any of those." He reached for my arms.

Smacking his hands away, I glared at him. "Don't touch me!" Then my tears started to erupt. "To feel hopeless and empty like ... like the world wouldn't matter if you left or died ... to feel worthless ..." Saying that last word, memories of cutting myself came to mind.

"I had to," he said, just above a whisper. "Right after your mother died, they were looking for any family members left to take out."

I wiped my eyes and looked up at him. My father didn't have the fierce look or a strict attitude like I remembered. Life over the years looked to have taken a toll on him.

"Your mother prepared a way out for Lisa, and I knew it was best for you to go with her. I was a retired vet and it would've been easy to locate me if the two of us were to run away together. The gods ... they already knew of my identity, so it would've put you at risk. Staying in Florida seemed like the safest bet because with your mother dead, the gods had no reason to stay here. To keep you safe, Lisa never revealed her identity to you. It was so you wouldn't wonder what was going on or go looking around. It also explains the way she raised you." He frowned at this.

I shook my head, hating hearing the truth from him. "I could've stayed with you ... maybe even helped."

"You were ten. You were just too young."

I looked away. "It's ... Whatever. It's all in the past."

"But now you came back into my life ... a few days ago—when Clark entered this house with you in his arms."

My mind went to the male figure who had appeared in front of me while fighting in Billy and Lisa's home in Everglades City. "That was Clark? Wait ... how?"

"The last moment before he showed up, you must've had a little faith and that's how you can summon him. Any later and you would've been a goner, sweetheart."

As I sat there thinking about all of this, another knock came at the doorway, and then a man peeked in. "Hello, can I come in?"

I turned away, quickly wiping my face. My father looked over and nodded.

"Hello," the man said as he entered the room. "I'm Clark."

I looked at him and nodded. He had wavy chestnut-brown hair that was gelled back. He had an athletic physique and an olive skin tone, with eyes and skin that glowed a bit, just like Mandroid had told me about Guardians. I figured him to be in his early twenties.

"I saw what you went through," Clark said, stopping near the foot of the bed, "and no one in the GCP should have gone through what you experienced a few days ago. I've actually been with you since the time you came from your mother's womb because I was her Guardian too. That's how you—"

I cut him off: "Where are the gods now?" I asked, looking around.

"Gone ... for now," Clark said.

He glanced at my dad and then looked back at me, but I wouldn't make eye contact with him.

"I managed to get away with you," Clark went on. "I couldn't risk fighting if you were unconscious. Your safety is my first priority. We need to head to the headquarters. When we go downstairs, we'll teleport over there."

Still holding the black watch, I followed Clark and my father downstairs. The man with the blue suit stood in front of a TV that was broadcasting a report about what had happened in Everglades City.

"All those people ..." the man in the blue suit said, shaking his head. "Just gone. Still can't believe it." He folded his arms and looked over at Clark. "So many people died in Everglades City."

Clark frowned and nodded once. "We need to get Angie out of here, James."

The man in the blue suit said nothing but took a step toward Clark.

My dad stopped at the bottom of the stairs. "Angie, I know you've grown a lot since I last saw you. But just be careful."

Strapping on the black watch, I looked back at my dad. "I'll try." I put on a weak smile. "It was ... um, nice seeing you."

One moment I was looking at my dad and the next I stood in a dark room that had rows and rows of glass cylinders.

I followed Clark and James as they headed toward an elevator. "What is this place?" I asked.

"Communications Center." Clark pointed at glass cylinders. "And those are teleportation pods. They send you to whatever location you need to go."

We stopped in front of the elevator and Clark clicked on the button.

"Who gave you the Golden Water?" he asked.

"My ... aunt." It felt weird calling her that. "Her name was Lisa, and she gave me a ring when I started living with her. She said it was my mom's and called it 'Golden Water,' which I thought was some special name she had for it."

"Did it shine in a special way?" Clark looked back at me.

I shrugged. "Yes, but I don't know why—"

"Unbelievable," James said irritated, glancing over at Clark. "She's been a member this whole time."

Clark raised his hand. "Hold on James, this isn't the time to jump the gun." He turned back to me. "Angela, do you remember your mother saying anything odd to you right before she died? Did she say anything like you were in the GCP or you're Florida?"

I nodded a couple of times. "I remember everything that day." I looked down at the metal-tile floor. "We were playing a game, but I could tell she was nervous. She said she wanted me to be a superhero and asked if I wanted to be Florida, the hero who protected the state from evil men. Seeing it as just some game, I said yes."

Clark closed his eyes as he clenched his fists. It took him a moment until he opened his eyes. "I'm lost why would she ... Listen, I'm sorry for—"

"Don't apologize," I cut in. "Those words are just words." I stared at my reflection in the metallic doors. "No meaning or value lies in the word 'sorry.' Let's just get this over with."

A bell dinged, and the doors opened.

Getting inside the elevator, I looked over at Clark. "What exactly are we doing?"

"There's higher-ups we have to answer to. Never has the GCP allowed so many gods to be resurrected—and to lose the Golden Water at that. It's put us in a spot that means humanity's existence is uncertain. We have to know what's going on and where we stand, so I'll be attending a meeting. I need you to get caught up and familiar with the GCP, then you and I are going after the gods who took the Golden Water."

I gave a small nod, noticing that James just stood silently behind us.

Clark looked up above the elevator doors. "This is us."

The bell dinged again, and the elevator doors opened. We walked down an all-white hallway, and James opened the double doors to a crowded room. Many people and Guardians strode by us, seeming to be in a hurry. I saw holograms here and there that advertised weapons and armor—similar to the Black Beauty and the weapons in the underground base.

We stopped behind a group of people varying in skin color and age.

Everyone stood quietly, listening to one guy speaking. He seemed to be in his mid-fifties, was short, and had frizzy red hair and brown skin—and he wore a cognac-colored suit.

Clark pointed toward the man talking to the group. "That's Moses. He's currently giving a tour of the GCP for new members. Follow him and I'll be back to get you."

"Okay," I said.

Clark headed out with James. I looked over at Moses and joined the group of other new GCP members.

Moses opened his arms. "Okay, now that you know who I am and what the GCP is ... this is the official God's Chosen People headquarters of the United States. Again, I want to welcome you all. Every member—including Protectors and their Guardians—comes here to study, stock up on their inventory, or get updated on new objectives. If you follow me, we can talk in a quieter place."

As we walked along behind Moses, I looked all around. The GCP US headquarters was a huge building, with multiple screens showing live footage of GCP members from around the world fighting gods—along with commercials advertising new products. In the middle of the headquarters stood a bronze statue of a man looking down as he raised his fist in the air. The statue stood in the hub of the busy facility, with many individuals walking about or flying above the crowd. I saw a laundromat, a health center, a training center, a cafeteria, an armory, and clothing stores for members who needed new combat suits.

As we walked on, I noticed seemingly ordinary people coming and going from the main entrance of the headquarters building. I looked around in amazement at seeing so many people carrying bags from different vendors—mostly in pairs, so I assumed they were GCP members accompanied by their Guardian. Moses said something about the headquarters being a mall, but exclusively for Protectors and Guardians.

We headed outside, and I saw three other buildings connected in a circular structure. In the middle lay a walkway leading to each building.

Moses pointed to the building immediately ahead of us. "We're headed to the Guidance Department, where all meetings and conferences are held. And of course, behind you is the HQ building. As I said, inside HQ you can get news and updates. Plus, all of our inventory is there—with weapons and armor and so much more for you to purchase." Moses walked backward and pointed his left. "To your right is what we call the 'Dome' for obvious reasons. The Dome is where we conduct all training, including preparation for war. Some of you aren't Protectors, so in case there's an invasion, the Dome would be the place to seek shelter."

Now Moses stopped walking and pointed to the building on our left, the third of the connected trio. "Our last building is the Aviation Department. There we keep spaceships and war aircraft made to take out gods. This is where we test them and it's our only hangar."

We walked onward to the Guidance Department, the inside of which looked a lot like some corporate building. We entered a glass room that had a long desk up front, facing rows of chairs. Dozens of people were already seated and seemed to be patiently waiting in silence. Moses headed to the front, where a female Guardian awaited him at the desk.

"What is this?" Moses said to no one in particular, looking around at the many people already seated. "I was told I would only give an introduction to the small group with me," he said to the female Guardian. "This looks like around forty more and—Wait." He turned back quickly toward the people seated. "Nina, is that you?"

"Yes." A girl who couldn't have been more than eight stood up from her seat in the front row. Her long, kinky curls covered most of her face. "I'm Phoenix now."

"What? You're Phoenix?" Moses asked, looking at the girl and then back at the female Guardian.

I angled myself so I could see the Guardian better. She had long cornrows and wore a silver cloak. Her eyes radiated blue as she looked at Moses and said, "More GCP members died from their injuries. Washington already initiated all of them into the GCP, so they're good to go." She turned her attention to us. "The death toll is going to keep rising, and I wish the best of luck to all of you in the coming days."

The Guardian disappeared and Moses turned to those sitting down.

"Okay, my name is Moses." He looked back at us and said, "Those of you standing can take a seat."

As we did so, Moses sat on the edge of the desk in front. "The person who was supposed to show you the ropes isn't here, so I'll be taking his place. I'm head of communications for the US GCP. My department's job is to detect incoming gods and send intel to Protectors and other GCP headquarters around the world." He looked around at every one of us. Then he paused for a moment and stared at the wall to his left.

One girl sitting in the front raised her hand. "Sir, are you okay?"

"I'm fine." Moses looked back at us. "I'm sorry, um ... I only wish we were in better circumstances. I wish I could tell you that joining the GCP isn't all bad and you're in peaceful times, but I would be lying to you. So many people I've known over the years lost their lives in the past few days and now I'm seeing all these fresh new faces. Our world is hanging between extinction and survival, and we're depending on what Washington decides our next move is going to be. Our fate ties in with a meeting that's going on right now."

Moses gazed down for a moment, then stared back at us. He looked more alive to me, more energetic—his eyes brighter, his attitude exuding confidence. "In the beginning, before time could be conceived as time, our Creator named Jehovah created Creators. Jehovah is the King of the Universe and all things living. From what I was told there are many Creators, as many as the stars. Not much is told but we know that a war was waged and only a few remain at this current time. There are three Creators that we know each crafted and oversaw a part of the universe—the South, East, and West. Outside this universe, life identifies the God of Heaven and Earth as the North Creator. Here in the GCP he also goes by the North Creator or simply God, but make no mistake he's the maker of them all. Our solar system is located up north in comparison to the other universes. The South Creator made beings similar to himself. They've lived for centuries and are known as 'super gods' or 'ancients,' continuing to live in the South Universe. The West Creator crafted beings of pure light called Avians, from the Planet Avia. And then there's the East Creator, who brought about powerful beasts that are the size of planets. Each Creator also obtained powerful items."

A member raised his hand. "What does all this have to do with what we're facing now?"

Moses nodded. "A good question. What we're now facing is an evolution of gods—created by Genesis, the very first super god, and the last of them to perish in a war between North and South universes. Somehow, Genesis had obtained the power of a Creator—an abomination for a creation to obtain such power. Our Creator saw the evil in Genesis's heart and ordered him to give up such power. Genesis and his army of gods were the strongest at the time and attacked this universe. Elohim, our Creator, responded to this new threat with a new creation of his own, called Guardians. Genesis was the last standing among his super gods and continued to battle the most powerful Guardians and Angels. The fight took place in another realm. In the end, to protect his creation, Genesis put all of his power into the Red Sun, a power source that allowed the gods to exist without a Creator present. Elohim won the battle and split Genesis's body from his soul to prevent calamity. Our Creator is believed to be absent and others believe he's not. What the gods want is to return home with the Golden Water and pour it into the Red Sun which would increase its power and give life to every god in the South Universe."

Moses stood up and looked around at everyone. Our eyes met and he stared at me for a moment, then resumed glancing at the audience. "Gabriel watches over humanity and God's Chosen People—the GCP, which includes all of you here. Gabriel chose you as Protectors to watch over a collection of the most powerful items in all of the four universes. These items vary from weapons to tools that seem impossible to wrap your mind around. These items are for us to protect, not to use. You are to protect these items for the sake of Earth and the Afterworld. We protect these items to prevent the gods from resurrecting powerful enemies like Genesis. If they succeed in their agenda, it'll be the end of life in the North Universe."

Moses walked to the door. "You all can follow me now. I'll be taking you to buy your new combat suits, weapons, and vehicles."

Some of the other new members seemed eager about getting started. Not so much for me. I just wanted to get back out there and take the fight to those four gods. Everyone got up from their seats and followed Moses out of the building and back to the HQ facility. As we headed that way, I noticed that everyone else seemed to know each other and they talked amongst themselves in whispers—keeping their eyes on me.

After entering HQ, we went straight to the main hub where the bronze statue stood.

Moses turned to face us. "Okay, if you need to figure out where to go, you can always head to the elevators, where you'll find a map directory of this entire facility. There are plenty of different vendors, with some who offer more expensive weapons and outfits. We also have a cafeteria that serves international food. The Communications Center is where you can get in touch with other members from around the world—and also travel to any destination since that's where the teleportation pods are located. There's also the Mission Room, where there's a real-time list of requests from Protectors and world leaders. As you complete these, you will gain allies who can benefit you in your time of need. But seeing as how you are all new and lack fighting experience, I don't advise rushing to do missions anytime soon.

"Now, there are also other groups touring here today, as not everyone is a GCP Protector who goes into battle. There are also nurses, nursing aides, communicators, trackers, cooks, weapons experts, weapon-smiths, prison guards, clothing techs, and more. These are other positions that are available and given to certain individuals. They also live a secret life but a less dangerous one compared to some of you."

Moses reached into a nearby kiosk and then passed out a booklet that he said listed all the rules, hideouts, Protector/Guardian names, and a blueprint of the headquarters.

Since I was in the back of the group, I was the last to get a book. When Moses handed it to me, he said, "So you're Angela, eh?"

All the other recruits turned to face me, which I hated.

Moses extended his hand to me. "It's an honor. I saw your fight and you're one brave soul."

"Thanks," I said, barely above a whisper, as I shook his hand.

"Everyone has been expecting you," Moses said. "We were cheering for you. I just want to say I looked up to your mother. I grew up in the GCP watching her defeat a lot of the notorious gods that are written down in history."

I nodded, acknowledging his praise. "Thanks," I said again. "So you saw everything, huh?"

Moses frowned. "Yes, at the time we were ordered to leave and so we couldn't rescue anyone. Cade was supposed to get to you before the gods could ... Anyway, I'm already saying too much. You'll know all you need to in due time, I guess." He smiled, then turned his attention back to the recruits. "Now if you all would open your *GCP Handbook,* you'll find the ten rules to the GCP. Take a moment and read them all to yourselves right now."

I looked down and read the list:

1. Your identity as a GCP member must be kept a secret from the public's eye.
2. Never commence a battle where innocent lives are at stake.
3. Never use your given power for your agenda; only for the protection of your given item.
4. Under no circumstance should you or your actions result in human casualty. If so, you'll be terminated and scheduled to the GCP Court for your actions.
5. Under no circumstance should you murder a god to the point of nonexistence.
6. Never use the given item you were chosen to protect.
7. Your Guardian can only assist you in battle; he/she cannot kill your opponent for you.
8. A Guardian can never fight his or her Protector.
9. A Guardian is only permitted to assist his/her Protector only if asked to or called on.
10. Never hand over the item you were given to protect even if it means your life or a Guardian's life.

"Okay," Moses said, glancing down at an open book in his hands. "Anyone who breaks these rules will be suspended from the GCP and will be held at GCP Court to weigh your crime and decide on a suitable punishment depending on what rule or rules you broke. If anyone betrays the GCP or goes rogue, your Guardian has the right to kill you—and they will ... without hesitation." He closed his book. "Oh, and I forgot to mention that you do get paid a hefty amount of financial compensation for every mission you partake in, but only if you complete it. You can also get upwards of millions of dollars if you participate in a special mission or you're involved in a war. These rewards help you pay for new weapons and armor we have to offer."

Then he turned and said, "Alright, everyone, follow me. I'll show you certain stores for your basic needs."

We all followed as Moses continued, "Okay, so this store is where new arrivals usually come since the price is much cheaper here."

We walked into a weapons store, where every piece looked unique—made from materials that couldn't be found on Earth.

Moses waved a hand toward the man behind the counter. "This store is owned by Al, a former GCP Protector. Now he's one of our weaponsmiths for the GCP." He leaned against the counter and shook Al's hand.

"Welcome to the GCP, newcomers," Al said. Then he bent down and lifted a box from behind the counter. He walked out and gently placed it onto a table. "Everybody take one. Made from Guardian material. It's a welcoming gift—and the only thing you're gonna get from me that's free. And if ya tools eva need fixin', don't be afraid to holler."

I waited as everyone else dug into the box, then I went up and took one of the weapons—a simple dagger that had a blue shine to it. But I knew it had to be more than it looked, since Al said it was made of Guardian material, like my combat suits.

Moses stood up straight from leaning against the counter. "Everyone follow me. Onto the next one."

We followed him into a room labeled *"Guardian Outlet."* Moses explained that this was where new Protectors would be assigned their Guardian. He handed each of us a touch-screen tablet that listed all currently available Guardians. It showed their attributes, powers, and previous Protectors they trained and/or partnered with. When he handed me a tablet, Moses gave a little nod and winked at me.

As other new Protectors decided on who they wanted as their desired Guardian, that individual appeared by their side.

I stood and watched as the other recruits continued to pick the Guardians they wanted from their tablet.

"There will be instances where you'll be the only survivor in a battle and your Guardian is KIA," Moses said. "If that happens, you come here to find a new Guardian."

As the others continued to pick their Guardian, I looked around the outlet and focused on one of the many big screens high on the walls. One was showing a promo video of Clark battling some gods.

Next to me, a female recruit raised her hand. "Excuse me, sir, but I'm searching the database for that one." She pointed at the video. "Clark—but I can't find him."

Moses shook his head. "Clark has already received permission from the leaders of the GCP to specifically work with Angela. The future of this universe depends on it."

The female recruit just looked at me, then shrugged and went back to looking at her tablet.

"Alright, people, let me have your attention." Moses snapped his fingers above his head. "Downstairs is an elevator that leads to another elevator that'll take you close to Earth's core within a few minutes. There you'll see every god and goddess that has been captured by the US GCP. That is where we hold all of our gods after we defeat them since having them sent back to their planet of origin is a risk. It would be an ongoing threat. We can't have—"

Moses stopped talking when everyone looked toward the entryway and started chattering.

I looked that way and saw Clark entering. Now whispers started as he approached me.

"We need to go," Clark said to me.

I saw the seriousness in his eyes. "What's up?" I asked.

Clark got closer and spoke low. "The world could be ending in less than forty-eight hours. There are things you need to know." He straightened up and looked over at Moses. "You're needed at the meeting."

Moses nodded, then said, "Okay, everyone, finish up, and then I need to get you to someone who can continue your tour."

I kept my focus on Clark.

He pointed at my black watch. "Suit up."

8

∿

Plan To Save The World - Angela

Clark led me down many hallways and through several doors until we stopped by a glass-enclosed room filled with people sitting around a brown oval table, clearly arguing.

Hand on the doorknob, Clark turned toward me and said, "Your mom signed off on you becoming a GCP Protector—more importantly, a captain at that. Your code name is 'Florida' from here on out. Listen and only speak when told. You'll be sitting in there with other Protectors to figure out what we need to do—and those are their Guardians standing behind them along the wall."

I nodded.

Clark opened the door and we entered. The room fell quiet as Clark and I made our way to an empty chair.

"Sit here," Clark said as he eyed the chair. Then he stood against the wall with the rest of the Guardians, all of whom had the telltale eyes and skin that glowed.

Men and women of different ages and skin color sat at the table, all eyeing me. One Protector leaned back against his chair and said, "All respect to you, Clark, but we captains don't need a newbie teen recruit right now."

Clark stepped forward to stand by my side. "She isn't just some recruit. This is the new Florida, granddaughter of Elizabeth Proctor and daughter of Marie Proctor—a captain just like the rest of you here."

The Protector straightened himself and then looked around at the rest of the group, all of whom couldn't hide the shock on their faces.

A single knock on the surface of the table caught everyone's attention, and we all turned toward the end of the table.

"Ladies and gentlemen," said a Protector who had striking purple eyes and gray hair styled into a Caesar haircut. "Would someone care to explain exactly what took place in the last couple of days? I've been hearing bickering from you captains for the last ten minutes and no one has made it clear what is going on. As a leader, I want us to get some focus now that I'm back." He folded his arms on the table and leaned forward. "Is there anyone here who can explain what happened and why someone put this city underground without my permission?"

A teenage boy raised his hand; he looked no older than me. His long black hair covered part of his face. "Washington, sir, I can give you an answer."

A huge smile appeared on Washington's face. "Colvin—yes, the recently appointed New York. So far you have impressed me with your maturity and wisdom. Please fill me in on what's been going on in light of the previous New York perishing in these attacks and your brother getting captured—and Closias going underground." He quickly raised his finger. "And please don't leave out any minor details."

As I sat there looking at him, I realized that New York's face looked familiar to me. *Colvin ...* I thought. *Even his name seems familiar.*

New York slowly closed his eyes, then reopened them. "I was on a date with Amelia Rose codename England. She got a call saying multiple gods strangely awoke out of nowhere in the prison that held Vera. Before the call I gave warnings to her and all of the United Kingdom about heavy movement from outer space that could make its way to one of their headquarters." he said, looking at me, "I had a feeling they were aiming to awaken Vera. Once England sent word on how bad things were, I called in most of our Protectors to give aid ..." He looked at Washington. "after receiving permission from you. A man by the name of Malachi Walker had infiltrated and somehow managed to resurrect the thousands of gods that had been turned to stone."

"Hold on!" Washington said, almost glaring at New York. "You're skipping the part when he took the Golden Water. How is it that this nobody shows up out of nowhere and gets his hands on the Golden Water, then—"

"That's the thing, sir," New York cut in. "He never used the Golden Water. Malachi and I share the same last name, and he worships Zaygaian gods like the rest of my ancestors. I know all about those gods. They will kill any human to feed on an individual's life force. They can either keep it for themselves to get stronger or transfer it to another being. My guess is he consumed enough energy from people—probably millions—and resurrected the gods." New York shook his head and got up from his seat. "We fought thousands of gods and we were still close to winning. But then ... then he revived Vera—the goddess of wisdom and death. At that moment gods and goddesses from all over the UK and neighboring nations were resurrected and caught the GCP members there by surprise. We started out fighting thousands of gods, then it turned into millions—and that's when the tables turned."

He stood there and stared off into space, his eyes reflecting vengeance. He clenched his fist and his eyes became dark.

"It's okay, son," Washington said in a quiet voice. "Tell me what happened."

New York nodded, then went on, "George Proctor was killed in the act of trying to transport the Golden Water he had to the US. So, Vera sent gods to Closias in hope of capturing the rest of the Golden Water and to find out information on the soul of Genesis, even coming here herself. Moses has since told me that when the gods and Vera showed up here, my brother Cade decided to put this city underground. Vera ceased the attack the moment she had my brother in captivity. So those of us who survived the fight in the UK immediately returned here."

He sat back down, and the room was silent for a moment.

Washington stared at the glossy wooden table and seemed to be thinking for a bit. Finally, he said, "You're only assuming, of course. I mean, it seems most logical to you. For Malachi Walker to resurrect thousands of gods without the Golden Water means he would have to take the life force equivalent to those he revived. But Gabriel would have contacted us if thousands of humans were suddenly and randomly dying. The fact is, Vera was resurrected and knew where to aim and led an army with success. She's the target, not Malachi. Speaking of a target, did you capture Malachi?"

New York shifted in his chair. "No ... I killed him. He couldn't be taken down for questioning. Anyone close to him ... he just killed. So I engaged with the intent to kill. If it wasn't Malachi's doing then it had to do something with the large energy force I sensed in space."

Yes, regarding your concerns on what lies outside Earth." Washington looked at everyone at the table. "I went out to Planet Elyza and spoke to the Elyzians, Angel Gabriel, and the Habaranians who're responsible for guarding this universe. None detected any life force." He turned his eyes to New York. "Your suspensions came up false. Which means there isn't a real explanation of how this happened. We searched the entire North Universe for gods while you all were engaged in battle." He frowned as he breathed heavily through his nostrils. "Tell everyone what we are dealing with, Colvin, since some are new or relatively new."

"What is he talking about?" I turned back to Clark. "what're Elyzians and Habaranians?"

"Other kinds of Guardians, I'll explain later." Clark kept his attention on New York.

"In the South Universe, Vera is a royal goddess—a renowned general who has never lost a single battle. Something tells me this wasn't a coincidence. Humanity would have been lost today if we didn't still have Alice Lombardo. She has what they want, and that's the soul of Genesis within her. But Vera took Cade, and the fact that they didn't kill him on the spot means she's squeezing out every bit of information he has on the GCP. Our best estimate is that Vera has about a million gods at her disposal and now the knowledge of a GCP member who knows practically everything vital to our operations. I'm betting my top dollar her next move against humanity will be her last. We need to act now."

"I agree, so it's settled then," Washington said. He looked around at everyone. "We locate Cade and go to war—with Gabriel's permission. Until we get confirmation from him, we need to exterminate every god we are holding anywhere in the US. We keep this contained and try not to get any other country involved, understood?"

Everyone nodded in agreement with Washington's command.

Colvin switched his eyes to the Guardian behind him, then turned to Washington. "Sir, I have a favor to ask."

"Speak it so can I deem it worthy or not."

"With your permission, I need access to land on foreign soil again. I studied Vera, the way she thinks, how she fights, and her reasoning. Considering that she didn't go after all the holy items in England. She took the Golden Water and just left. Unlike the other gods and goddesses, she's looking to take out this world, not rule it. I need access to go anywhere on this planet to track Vera."

"She'll kill you if you go alone." Washington stared at Colvin. "Your father didn't take her lightly."

"I've been killing gods since I was ten. Never have I failed a mission or lost a fight. Let me kill her to prevent Earth's end."

"Don't return here without her head." Washington looked at everyone. "No one will utter a word that was spoken here. We made the mistake of not letting Gage kill Vera. He was probably the only one capable of accomplishing such a feat. Vera plans on eventually resurrecting her father, and if he rises, no one will be able to stop him." He turned to Colvin again. "Leave no remains of this goddess. I permit you to do so. You'll do this alone, and if your crime is brought before Jerusalem, I will see to it that it's pardoned. You can start immediately"

Colvin's face held no expression. "I won't fail humanity."

Just then a young woman about my age barged in, gasping for air. For some reason, she also seemed familiar to me. I saw her look directly at New York as he stood up.

"We got Cade," she said. "He's alive and okay. He's got a lot of intel on what's going on."

Washington turned to look behind him at his Guardian. "Contact

Gabriel. A meeting needs to take place." Then he turned back to everyone sitting at the table. "Everything I just said is on hold until we meet with Gabriel. This meeting is adjourned. You're all dismissed."

Everyone else got up and headed to the door as the young woman drew closer to the table. I sat there, not knowing what to do and waiting for Clark to advise me—and still wondering why the woman seemed familiar to me.

Then I saw the Guardian behind New York approach the young woman. The Guardian had glowing bronze skin and was tall with a clean shaved head. "Where's Cade's current location?" he asked.

"In the Health Center with Dr. Cullinghan. I haven't gotten the chance to see—" She froze when her eyes happened to catch me sitting there. "Angela!"

She dashed over to me as I got up from my seat, and before I could say anything, she hugged me. "It's me—Alice. Remember, we were best friends before you disappeared?" She released me from her hug, then examined me from head to toe. "You've gotten so beautiful. Oh my gosh! The transformation is surreal."

It all clicked into place and old memories unlocked in my mind—no doubt buried over the past seven years of my life.

I smiled back at her. "Of course, I remember you, Alice. We used to tell each other everything. It was you, me, and Colvin. Sorry, I left without saying good-bye."

"No need to apologize. I know why you left." Alice grabbed hold of my hands. "It's been so long! Listen, we should hang out sometime. At my place, maybe—we still live in the same house too. My mom would be psyched to see you. And we have a lot of catching up to do."

"Angela Lopez?" New York said from behind me. "I'm Colvin ... you remember—"

"I remember," I said, nodding. "You looked familiar across the table."

"Wow, you've grown up and changed," New York said. "So sorry about your loss. I do believe we can fix all this before things get out of hand. I gotta get going to see my brother. Oh, and we'll be holding a funeral service for your great-uncle and your aunt. Have you been to the Communications Center?"

I nodded again.

"You can use a pod there to teleport to the burial site. Enter a pod and it'll ask where you want to go, so just say 'Proctor Graveyard in England.'"

"Colvin," came a voice from near the door.

The three of us turned to see New York's Guardian looking at us.

"It's time, Colvin," the Guardian said. "We need to know what happened to your brother and what Vera plans on doing."

"I know, I'm coming." Colvin turned to me. "Going to see Cade with Alice and then we can talk later."

Alice grabbed my hands again. "It was so nice seeing you again! Come see me when you get the chance, okay? I live in the same address, if you don't remember just ask Clark to transport you to my house. Bye!"

I smiled and said, "Bye."

Alice followed behind Colvin and his Guardian as they headed out.

My smile disappeared as the door closed behind them. I turned around to look at Clark, and the thought of Lisa and my mother came to mind again. I could feel the tears welling.

They didn't deserve to die, I thought.

"I can feel your pain from across the room," Clark said.

I looked over at him and saw a concerned expression on his face.

"What's your next move?" he asked.

"Headed to the funeral for my great-uncle and my aunt ... by myself. I don't want you or anyone else around me right now. Just find the gods who killed Lisa and then find me."

I headed out the door, and once I was alone in the hallway, I let my tears come.

9

Evaluation - Cade

I'd almost died.

This kept playing over and over in my head as Dr. Cullinghan checked me for signs of injury and trauma. Everything had happened so fast back on the field. It was as if they knew my every move. I could've—should've—maneuvered differently, but I figured they would have adjusted to any attack I launched against them.

I frowned as I sat on the edge of an exam table while Dr. Cullinghan now checked for any curses the gods had likely left in some part of my body.

The doctor pointed a flashlight at my pupils. "You feel different or see images you've never seen before?"

"No, Doc. The only thing that clouds my mind is me almost dying."

He nodded. "That's normal. You've been through a traumatic experience. If this continues to bother you over the next several weeks, you have to let me know." The doctor stood straight and removed his latex gloves, then held on to my forearm. "Everything about your body seems normal. By the way, you teleporting everyone out of here was a brilliant idea." He stood back and smiled in obvious amazement.

"Thanks," I said in a quiet voice.

The door opened and I looked that way to see my brother.

Colvin stopped next to Dr. Cullinghan, not looking at me. "How is he?"

Raising my hand, I caught Colvin's attention. "I'm fine, bro. Nothing I couldn't manage. Listen, we need to head to Florida. The gods are going to—"

Colvin cut me off with a wave of his hand and then looked at Dr. Cullinghan.

The doctor nodded, then left, closing the door behind him.

When Colvin looked back to me, I could see irritation written on his face. "What were you thinking? You could've died."

"I made a move that benefited the GCP."

"No, you took a risk that put yourself and the entire GCP in danger. Why didn't you call me if the gods were heading for Closias?"

He placed his hands on his waist. I knew this stance. This was him trying to lecture me as if I was a child.

I got up from the exam table. "Who knows how long it would've taken you to get back? The moment the gods had intel on where the Golden Water was located, I knew something must've gone wrong on your end and Florida was in danger."

He stepped closer, looking deep into my eyes. "Florida is fine for the moment. Forget about that right now. As acting captain, you didn't have the authority to put this city underground—or the thousands of people in this city to sleep. You aren't even a Protector, so for you to go out and even fight the gods wasn't something you had to do ... or should've done. If you died, they would have used you as a soldier, stolen your holy items, tried to get to me, and—"

"I knew the risks." I sat back down, slouching against the wall.

"You clearly don't. You aren't ready ... not yet."

"Right ... because my turn will only come after you're done being New York now that you've risen to captain. When's that? Twenty, thirty, forty years from now?

"No, when you learn that putting your life in death's hand isn't a brave or wise move. If every encounter you have with a god ends with someone losing their life, then you aren't ready. When you devise a plan that results in you and those around you in a positive outcome, then you'll be ready to go out in the field as a Protector. But with this event, you showed you didn't plan correctly and you put others in danger. You'll never be ready with your current mindset. Why our father never got touched ... why I've never lost a fight ... is because we followed orders and listened."

I opened my mouth to reply, but just then the doors opened. In walked many GCP leaders from different countries around the world. All of them filled into the room. The last to enter was the Guardian Adumay, my caretaker. After our father's death, he had taken the role of becoming a father figure to me while also serving as Colvin's Guardian.

A moment later two individuals stepped forward through the crowd. First, I saw Washington, our leader. And then came Jerusalem, supreme leader of the GCP. Both stood in front of me. Jerusalem hadn't aged a bit since I'd last seen him many years ago. He still maintained his youthful looks. His dark brown beard was neatly trimmed—enough to see his strong jaw—and his hair was cut short. I could always see myself in him for some reason. He had worked hard to reach his current place, and he'd lost a lot of loved ones along the way.

Then I noticed that Jerusalem also held a Karui necklace. The two of us were the only members to hold and control such power.

Jerusalem folded his arms. "Tell us what we need to know."

"Vera is in control of what's been going on. She knows where the three kings lay and who holds Genesis's soul. She found out by taking a piece of my life force. She seems so sure—"

"How does a kid who's only sixteen years of age—and not even a Protector—know confidential secrets that only leaders should know?" Jerusalem asked, turning to Washington. "Secrets are something that need to be kept in times like these."

Washington stepped closer to me, ignoring Jerusalem's words. "War is inevitable, Cade. We've been training you since you were a child. Now is the time. Be the savior the world needs you to be."

I looked into his eyes, wanting to be what he needed me to be, but I lacked the strength to do so and something inside me knew it.

Jerusalem faced the other leaders behind him. "All gods in confinement are subject to death, effective immediately. Not a statue standing, then prepare for war." He walked through them to leave the room, and they all followed behind.

I sat there watching as they all left until only Adumay and I was alone. The image of Alice came to mind again. The thought of her and the gods going after her ... and then me almost dying and not keeping my promise to my dad. I squeezed the paper sheets on the exam table and began to cry at the thought of my family.

"Why are you crying?" Adumay asked. "You're alive. You should be rejoicing."

"I came so close ... to death. I almost lost my life in that fight. It was horrible. It's like everything I trained for went out the window. They were better than me ... those gods. I didn't even stand a chance." I looked at the floor and let my shoulders slump. "I can't be like my brother."

"Cade, you're strong. Don't ever forget that."

Adumay got closer and lifted my chin until we were face-to-face. "You understand me?" he said. "You didn't lose; you survived on your own. Surviving is only the beginning. You'll only get stronger."

"How long will that take? Colvin has gotten stronger so fast."

Adumay took a step back, heavily exhaling. "Will you stop comparing yourself to him?"

"Do we not share the same blood?" I shouted as I sprang to my feet. "Why is he just like my father and I'm not?" I turned around, looking at the floor again. "I'm half Avian. I should naturally have enough power to be stronger than anyone in this building without a suit. I'm so weak."

"You want to get stronger? You want to stop feeling sorry for yourself? Then you have to release yourself from earthly desires. Only then will you open a greater you. Then you can save everyone." He placed his hands on my shoulders. "You have to let her go for good. Kill those feelings you have for that girl and do what's best for you."

I met Adumay's eyes. "I'm not leaving Alice. She's ... pregnant. I can't just leave now."

He backed away and watched the tears continue to fall down my face. "Cade Walker, you or Alice or both of you will die if you continue down this path. Abandon whatever you have with her and you'll have power beyond the gods or any creation. You'll unlock enough Avian power to protect this universe like your father requested from you. There's a reason Gage ordered me to be a father to only you and to guide you."

The image of Alice smiling flashed in my head as I sat back down. "I know I'm wrong for falling for her, but if falling in love is wrong, then I'll continue to be in love fulfilling what my dad wished and I'll save this universe at the same time."

Adumay wiped at his face, revealing the tiredness that he tried to hide. I could tell he was done trying to convince me. "Such ideals are childlike and unrealistic ... You'll find yourself dead because you were too weak, or you'll change your destined path because you fell for a girl you weren't meant to be with. She's a counterfeit and you're deviating from your destined path." He waited for a response but I had nothing to say.

"Cade Walker, Avians are powerful and gain their power from meditation and consecration. You're called to sanctification. Separating from the world and becoming pure. In that, you tap into the power of the West Creator. But when you begin to form soul ties with someone who's going through their own issues, someone who's not called to be your wife, out of the will of your creator you leave room for attacks spiritually. That's dangerous, you open doors in the spirit. Premature death is real."

"She never did anything wrong to me. She's going through issues because of her mom who's depressed. I'm not just leaving her."

"You can't be her savior."

"I know but I can put her in a better environment. After I'm done doing what my father left me to do, I'm bringing Alice with me to my home planet."

"It's not that simple. She's dragging you down. You started drinking, you barely meditated, you smoked with her, your body is your temple. You're taking on her characteristics. You're not in the will of God."

"If God loves me, he'll honor it."

"He won't submit or honor what's corrupt. Can't bless what's not pure. When did God serve his creation?"

A knock came from the door, and Alice peeked inside, seeing my wet eyes. "Are you okay?" she asked.

Adumay looked at us both, and by reading his energy, I could tell he had unconditional love for us. He shook his head and left.

"Yeah," I whispered. I wiped my face dry and looked down at her stomach. "How about you? You said you were pregnant. Are you?"

"Yeah. I kept vomiting everything I ate. Took the test twice. I even took different brands. I cried in the bathroom when the result came out positive."

"Why didn't you tell me sooner?"

Alice shrugged and sat next to me. "I didn't think we would get back together. But ... are you going to stay for the abortion at least?"

I snapped my head toward her. "What?" I saw her red eyes. She must've been crying a lot since I disappeared. "You're not having an abortion."

"I told you I'm not going to be like my mother. I'm not going to raise a child by myself. I refuse to live like that. I want you with me every step of the way, but it's not possible if you're so glued to the GCP."

"Do you know what's at risk?" I squeezed the edge of the exam table. "From here on out things are going to go bad. I can feel it in my bones. I can't just leave the—"

"Everyone's been informed, Cade. You don't have to fight anymore."

"Vera knows who you are ... how you look ... your name. You're not safe, so running away with me and hiding won't solve anything. Why don't you see the bigger picture?"

"If the world was going to come to an end, I would've had a dream of it. In the end, Gabriel is going to finish all of it."

I shook my head. "This is bigger than even him. Vera is going to wipe out Earth and every soul in the Afterlife. She already has almost all the Golden Water. She's going to kill Angela and capture you. She spared me because she already knows she won. When she spoke to me, it wasn't confidence. She was speaking the truth." I paused, then said, "I'm going to kill her and every god to prevent the First Resurrection from happening."

She started crying again. "I won't stick around, Cade. I can't have this baby ... not like this. I still want to go to college."

"Then take online classes. I'm a billionaire, I can pay to have professors visit you. Whatever the costs are I can cover it."

"It's not that simple."

"Then let me take care of it. You don't have to be there for the baby."

"Maybe if I was twenty-six, I would keep it. But I have a lot going on and every god wants me dead. They can even kill this child a year from now when I'm off or—"

"Don't worry about the baby. I can take care of it or even put it up for adoption."

"I'm not having someone else take care of my child."

"Then what are you going to do? I'm putting my foot down on this one. We're not killing it."

"So ... what—I don't have a say? Very mature of you but you're not my dad."

"You know what? You want to kill it, then you pay for the abortion and go there yourself."

Alice stared at me, and I knew a million things had to be going through her head. I knew she didn't have the money or the insurance to pay for the abortion. I also knew she didn't want to go through it alone.

I got up. "I can't live with myself knowing I killed a child. It goes against everything I believe in. I refuse to kill an innocent life ... I'm sorry."

Alice got up and I could see she was about to cry again. "If you had the decency to show me that you still love me by leaving the GCP, then maybe I could consider keeping the baby. But you have to put yourself in my shoes. I have a lot more to lose." She headed for the door and left.

My father had entrusted me to do what he was supposed to do. As a father, he fought to protect me and humankind. He returned to fight those who had murdered his family, and in the end he stopped fighting the moment he saw I was alive. Instead of trading his life for mine, he entrusted me with his duty and then disappeared.

I have to kill Vera and every god on this planet if I want to save Alice and our baby. I took a deep breath. *I'm going to save everyone, Dad—that I promise.*

First, I needed to head back to Death's Temple and retrieve the Golden Water to prevent the First Resurrection—and take out the ones who were seeking it.

Then Vera ... I manage to take her out and I'll save millions of members from entering a war.

"I need to get Angela Proctor," I whispered to myself.

10

〜

The Proctor Family - Angela

After finding a clothing store in the HQ and buying some appropriate funeral attire, I changed and headed down to the Communications Center, where rows of white pods all stood. I entered a teleportation pod and shut the glass door behind me. Then I leaned back against the soft fabric and stared ahead at the glass, which now showed a globe of the world.

A speaker above my head chimed and then an automated voice spoke: "Please name your destination."

Remembering what Colvin said, I said, "Take me to the Proctor Graveyard in England."

A light flashed, and the next thing I knew, I had been teleported to a courtyard. Ahead of me, I saw a lady wearing black as she stood and handed out pamphlets to a streaming line of people who walked toward a cemetery. I looked around and found myself surrounded by men and women covered in bandages and others who weren't hurt, with many of them speaking to each other in a foreign language. I knew they had to be GCP members, as more spontaneously appeared and started walking down the cemented walkway that led to the graveyard. I followed the crowd but looked back at one point, seeing a castle on a hill in the distance. The sounds of low cries, whispers, and clicks from high heels filled the air. Everyone varied in age, skin color, height, and weight but we all shared something in common: we had all lost someone precious to us.

As I walked into the cemetery, I saw that every name on the nearby headstones had the same last name: *Proctor*. I continued to walk with the crowd until I found my way to the front amongst dozens of people, just in time to see the coffins for George Proctor and Lisa-Anne Proctor being slowly lowered into the ground. I swallowed hard, thinking back to how Lisa had tried to help me there at the end. And then I thought of my mother, fighting back the tears that wanted to flow.

A hand from behind touched my shoulder. I turned to see Colvin as he said, "Sorry for your loss. I fought as hard as I could to get to George." He had on a wool coat, and he stepped forward to my side. "A lot of calamities happened that day."

I shook my head. "Don't blame yourself." I stared into his eyes, which were completely black. "I'm fine."

"I know how it feels to lose someone close to you. To lose a mother and then someone who took you in ... it's all too similar." He looked down as a few Guardians now began covering the coffins in dirt.

I continued to stare at him, feeling a stab of anger in my heart. "Do you really know how it feels? 'Cause my pain doesn't stop."

Still looking down into the grave, he said, "My mother ... She despised me because of my father. He awakened a part of her that she didn't think existed. He made her feel alive. How she grew up ... she was in an abusive home with parents that were drug addicts. At that time, she hated everyone ... until she met Gage Walker—a boy who didn't even get to experience a real childhood ... someone who was supposed to be sacrificed to Ominous, the Zaygaian king until he was saved by Elizabeth Proctor." Now Colvin turned his head my way. "Your grandmother led the GCP into massacring the Walkers and anyone else in Death's Temple. Saving Gage though, she took him in as her own son. Lisa and your mother saw him as their brother. So when Eve, my mother, eventually got to know him, he became the missing puzzle to her broken heart. By the time she found out she was pregnant with me, he'd been kidnapped by the gods and thought to be dead. My mother went mad and wanted Colvin Walker to be Gage Walker. I wasn't her son anymore in her mind; I was just a tool to keep her sane."

He paused and frowned. "So I lived the life that Gage had lived.

Abuse and neglect became my childhood. Years later, Gage escaped from Planet Genesis where the gods had held him captive. He found himself on Planet Avia, in the West Universe. There, he fell in love with the queen of that planet, and she awoke the light within him. She had three kids with him. When he returned back to Earth with his new family, he walked in on the Second Great War, where Elizabeth Proctor died at the hands of Amentous. Gage Walker saved humanity by winning that war. He became the leader of the GCP of the US and then the supreme leader of the GCP. He had no interest in Eve or me."

Colvin stopped again, this time rubbing the platinum rings on each of his fingers. "This birthed a new hate within my mother, and it made her crazy. She turned me into a weapon rather than a tool to keep herself sane. Her world became dark again and she couldn't take it. She sacrificed herself to Ominous to give me the power to kill Gage. It wasn't long 'til Gage learned what I'd become. He wasted no time and found me at my home, then took my life from me ... Yeah, I died." Tears began to form at the rims of Colvin's eyes. "I died that day ... Can you believe it? Hailed and prophesied hero Gage Walker killed his own son." Now his eyes turned from black to red, which took me by surprise. "I was a monster to him, even though I was half-Zaygaian." Colvin took hold of my hand and placed it against his chest. "What do you feel?"

I shook my head. "Nothing." I looked around while people began to leave, even as it started to rain. "What are you doing?"

Colvin pressed my hand harder against his chest. "Focus and tell me what you feel."

I stared at my hand on the left side of his chest. "I don't feel anything." I looked at his face and waited for a moment. "There's no heartbeat."

He backed away and watched as the Guardians finished smoothing the dirt over the newest Proctor graves. "The human part of me died in that living room years ago as I breathed my last breath. This Colvin that you see is a killing machine who can take any life force at will. No matter how I try to run away from Gage, I still see myself in him."

"How are you alive then?"

"Because of Gabriel. He saw perfection in me once I was in the After-world and declared me as his only son. Giving me a second chance at life, your mother Marie took me in and—"

"And that's how we met." I nodded. "You were a shy kid growing up with me and Alice ... and now I know why."

"Right ..." Colvin blinked a few times to clear his eyes. "In the end, Gage and I both lost our families."

"And Cade ... he's your half-brother? One of the kids from Planet Avia, from what you said."

Colvin nodded. "The only survivor. Ominous killed Gage's wife and their two other children. So I know how it feels to lose two mother figures. I lost Eve, then I lost Marie. I do know your pain." Colvin reached out and squeezed my hand.

I turned around to head out of the cemetery, with Colvin walking next to me. "Have you ever thought about seeking revenge against Ominous for what he did?" I asked.

Colvin put his hands inside his coat, then shrugged. "There's no satisfaction in revenge. Anyone who has killed for revenge can tell you that. All you're going to have is the same hatred in your heart. Nothing changes."

I stopped walking just outside the cemetery and turned to face him. "Who is Amentous anyway?"

He came to a halt and looked at me. "Why?"

I slit my eyes at him. "Did he kill my mother ... or was it your father?" I watched his face, looking for the slightest hesitation.

He pursed his lips, then said, "Amentous killed your mother. Gage did battle your mother because of her ideals. In the end, Gage killed Amentous for taking Marie's life." Colvin stepped back a little. "Amentous was revived ... but you leave him to me. The GCP needs you to focus on the real enemy—Vera. She plans on heading home with the Golden Water. If she accomplishes this, she'll resurrect every god in the South Universe. Their power will be replenished and Earth will have to deal with trillions of gods invading. It sounds like you know some of what's going on, so how are you preparing for all this?"

I looked at the ground, thinking of what would happen when I encountered the gods again. "I have Clark searching for the gods who killed Lisa and stole the Golden Water from me. They won't get far with what my mom fought to protect."

"Then I suggest you get well acquainted with the GCP. Know what you have access to and use it to your advantage. You can't save this universe without knowing everything that's going on."

I nodded, and Colvin turned to see a group of male Protectors approaching. They all wore black suits and shades, preventing anyone from seeing their eyes. Leading the group was a man with African tribal marks on his face: three lines resembling scars imprinted under each eye. He raised his hand and the other men stopped walking even as the leader continued to walk.

Colvin faced the leader and nodded. "Benin, what do I owe the pleasure to?"

Benin stood in front of Colvin and removed his shades. He stared into Colvin's eyes for a moment, then broke a smirk. "My brotha, how are you?"

"I'm okay. It's nice seeing you." Colvin reached for a hug, ignoring the hand Benin offered.

Benin welcomed the hug, giving a tight squeeze for a moment before he took a step back. "Hearing news that they're still counting up the numbers of dead members. We've been exposed and this battle proves we've been sleeping for far too long."

Colvin put his hands into his coat pockets, then looked at the ground. "This isn't a battle to them. They're trying to wipe out this entire planet. I can sense Earth crying out for help. I'm going to say what I told every captain: the gods' next move will be their last and that's what scares me."

Benin's face changed to a serious stare. "That's why I'm here."

Colvin looked up. "What do you mean?"

"They captured your brother and now they know all our secrets. They know what we have stored and they're at our doorstep. That will be their next move." Benin stopped and shot a glare at me, then looked at Colvin again.

Colvin glanced over at me, then nodded to Benin. "She's okay. This is Angela, a good friend of mine. She's also the daughter of Marie Proctor."

Benin's eyes widened at that, then he scanned me over. "Your resemblance to your mother is shocking. My advice to you: find your loved ones and stay close to them. Tonight could possibly be the end." He turned to Colvin. "My Protectors are protecting the body of Ominous from the gods. A different army of gods is also attacking us. They plan to surround us. You entered the war in England on the front line and you managed to stay alive with the most kills. We need you. All of Africa has united as one. The gods are here and war is commencing. Gabriel has left the Afterworld for this cause and will be aiding us. Heroes from around the world are waiting for my command. Will you—"

"Yes, of course," Colvin said. "Let's move. Have you located Vera yet?"

"Not yet. We're trying to identify who's leading this new army of gods. Addis will protect Ominous and we'll fight this new army." Benin turned toward his men. "Moving out!"

Colvin looked my way. "Until we meet again."

I gave a little nod and then he was off. Seeing Colvin taking his leave, I realized how little he had changed. Except for his height, he still hid behind the long hair that covered his face. I believed there was more to him than the simple, straightforward act he projected to the world.

I looked around and just watched as everyone continued to mourn at the entrance of the cemetery. Then I saw someone walking toward me, wearing an all-white suit. People who were crying instantly changed their focus to this guy. He was surrounded as people approached him from every direction wanting him to perform healing miracles. He lifted his hand, sent a wave of light and everyone around him stopped and they were in shock and others were happy as they began saying they were healed. Some who had crutches from the battle with my great uncle walked as if they were never injured. Catching my eye, he smiled and waved at me and then continued walking my way.

"So sorry about your loss. I'm Cade," he said as he stopped in front of me. "The Proctor household made the GCP what it is today in England and in the US."

I really had no interest in talking about it anymore. "Thanks. Never knew my great uncle George though. I need to go. Nice talking to you." I turned and glanced down at my black watch, preparing to visualize myself in my Black Beauty combat suit.

But I stopped when Cade said, "I heard from the higher-ups that you lost the Golden Water."

I turned toward him. "And?"

"I'm being blamed for making the wrong decision in Closias when the gods attacked. And now you got thrown into this and had something bad happen. Maybe we can help each other. I know where we can find the Golden Water."

I eyed him. "And you want to help me because?"

"Where we find the Golden Water, we'll also find Vera. She started all this and she plans on reviving an entire universe with the Golden Water. Vera is bad news. I want her gone for good and you want the Golden Water back. Plus, our parents knew each other."

"So I've heard."

"Then let's work together and save humanity before we're faced with extinction."

"I already have Clark working on finding the three gods who stole the Golden Water."

"That's good, but we need to do more. Alice has the ability to see into the future. She saw the end, including her death and the end of this universe." Cade leaned in closer to me. "There's no North Creator—the Creator of this universe. He's gone. We don't know where he is or if he's even alive. All we have left is Gabriel, and he's depending on me, my brother, Alice, and you. If we're going to end this, then we need to work together. You want revenge ... you want justice? Then let's take them out before they make their move."

"Fine. When do we get started?"

"Now."

I watched as Cade reached into his pocket and then put on a necklace. The link to the necklace carried a strange symbol. He closed his eyes and his body began to shine. His white suit changed to all-white armor. The one-piece combat suit featured an emblem of a snow-white owl on his chest. His outfit, though, looked different from mine. He also had extra protection on his forearms, knees, and elbows. And he had a long white cape that glistened with its own light.

"We're going to teleport to Death's Temple," Cade said. "Vera may be there. If she is, then we take her out and retrieve the Golden Water, preventing a war from happening."

"Let's do it." My clothing transformed into the Black Beauty.

Cade laid his hand on my shoulder and we disappeared.

11

Africa Fights - Colvin

Being transported to the Headquarters of Ethiopia, I looked around at their teleportation center. All their pods to send individuals around the world were off.

"War time," I told myself then shifted to Benin. "I've been around here plenty of times I'll go check out things."

Benin nodded his head and went his separate way.

Taking the elevator to the lobby, the doors slid open to everyone striding in different directions giving orders out loud. Walking to their main station where Heaven's Eye was located, I looked at their Head Communicator who wore a traditional green dashiki.

"Dios Mapago," seeing him turn to me I smiled. "How are you?"

He opened his arms and I embraced his hug. "Colvin, what are you doing here?" He pulled back and got a look at my face. "Don't tell me they requested you?"

"Both kinda," I looked around remembering my time here training with his sons. "Vera was England's problem and now it's spilling over. I'm here to kill her and prevent the Third Great War."

Dios turned back to the screen. "War is about to start. Addis will be leading this one instead of protecting the body of Ominous."

I walked closer to the screen and watched every Protector of South Africa and Africa stand shoulder to shoulder in columns and rows waiting for Addis's move.

"I don't have time to waste, I'm heading to the battlefield." I looked at the armies of skeletal beings standing on the field. These were fiends that were eight feet with solid strong bones that were very thick. Leading them was Vera, who was sitting on the ground facing Addis.

Dios kept his eyes on the screen. "Be safe out there. All my sons are there if you need help."

"This will be an easy fight." I looked away from the screen and teleported to the large barren field where war was soon to take place.

I made my way past the Protectors who all stood still in columns. Walking to the front line, I saw Vera sitting on the floor with her legs folded and her army of fiends behind her standing still. They wore silver plated armor and red capes.

I looked at Addis, supreme leader over all of Africa as she strode back and forth shaking her arms vigorously. Her bright brown skin shone as she barely wore any armor, being half goddess, she didn't need protection. Her armor consisted of just black spandex pants that stopped at her mid-thigh and a black sports bra woven by Guardian material. She removed her headscarf revealing her long black jumbo twist, each twist had gold cuffs and her twists were tied behind her back. She also wore gold plated armbands on each arm and a gold headband made to contain her power. Seeing her vigorously moving her arms, she began shouting as she strode back and forth in front of the entire GCP.

"Father God, we pray for your divine presence. We pray for your presence father God. We call upon your name because we face a challenge Lord God that requires your attention. We demand you here."

At those words, everyone around me began yelling out and praying. Adumay teleported to my side checking the scene out.

Addis faced us and shouted. "Yes, lift up your voice and cry out to him. We will not compromise with evil. For he says many are called but few are chosen. We are the GCP, God's Chosen People who'll lift up his kingdom!"

The presence in the air shifted and I began to form goosebumps. Some Protectors fell to the ground and screamed out in prayer.

"No weapon formed against you shall prosper and every tongue which rises against you in judgment you shall condemn." Squeezing her eyes shut, she looked up. "Yes! If God is for us, who can be against us. God, we call out to you for your strength, your power, and your glory. But he said to me, My grace is sufficient for you, for my power is made perfect in weakness. Therefore, I will boast all the more gladly about my weaknesses, so that Christ's power may rest on me." She began beating her chest with her fist. "We need you father, pour down your heavenly fire!"

Everyone cheered and shouted Amen. "This is different, she's calling on God, I thought he was absent?" Confused, I turned to Adumay.

"The mistake the United Kingdom made was calling upon an Angel to do God's work. This time, it'll be different. This time, our father will intervene and save humanity because we've cried out to him." Adumay set his eyes forward. "Be strong in the Lord and in his mighty power. Put on the full armor of God, so that you can take your stand against the devil's schemes."

I looked into the eyes of Vera and saw pure evil. "No, we're not fighting against the devil. The gods went to hell and killed the fallen angels and made it known. We are up against a stronger foe and God isn't here. I rely on my own strength and on Gabriel, the angel that saved me."

"Do not put your trust in Angels, kings, humans, who cannot save. When their spirit departs, they return to the ground; on that very day, their plans come to nothing. Blessed are those whose help is the God of Heaven, whose hope is in the Lord their God. The king of the universe."

Addis turned to Vera and pointed to the ground and fire shot forth from her fingertips and she drew a horizontal line between Vera and herself.

Vera stood up and her eyes shone. "Kill them."

Her army lifted their heads and their eyes shone red and they ran forward. Clenching her fist and pushing her chest up, Addis looked at the oncoming army of skeletal beings. "Keep the faith!" She yelled out and threw her fist forward and rolls of thunder continuously fell down from the sky into the ground destroying Vera's army. None were able to pass the line. Loud thunderous noise filled the air and I could feel the anger of Heaven through the thunder. Addis fell to her knees and began to cry out and I could sense a mixture of fear and faith. On her knees, she bowed touching the dirt with her forehead, and began to pray.

Through the strikes of thunder and the dust that lifted into the air came Vera with her arms lifted up as she walked forth smiling. Large black portals in the air opened to thousands of gods. Looking behind me, I could see everyone's jaw dropped as they looked up. The gods covered the sky and immediately shot down.

"Addis!" Looking at her as she continued to pray. "Addis Ababa look up!"

Seeing the gods getting closer I opened my hand to my scythe and concentrated on what was to come. "Adumay how many are coming at us?"

Adumay's body shoned to his armor. "Fifty thousand and counting." and he shot up into the sky.

Addis finally lifted her head and screamed as Vera approached. A swarm of Guardians flew up from the ground spiritually and their bodies became normal as they crashed into the gods. The impact caused a wave of air pushing us all back.

Addis' body exploded in fire and her eyes shone blue and she dashed to Vera colliding fists with her. The collision sent Vera back into her army. Addis moved in and I watched the gods on the field and every fiend nearby shoot out energy blasts to Addis. None penetrated through the coat of fire protecting her body. All of Africa yelled and ran forward and crashed into the skeletal beings. Running forward into the collision of bodies, my senses alerted me to look up. Focusing on my surroundings, I jumped back to see a body crashed into the ground.

It was a goddess, she quickly got up and I moved in not giving her time to assess the situation. Grabbing her face with one hand and her throat with the other, I released an arrow through my palms decapitating her head and she was turned to stone. Seeing armies of fiends and gods coming for me on my right and left, I threw the head to my left onto the approaching fiends. Standing still, I extended my arm towards them and opened my hand and shot out an astral arrow to the stoned head. It exploded killing the skeletal beings. I threw the headless body to the oncoming gods to my right and ran forward shooting out arrows from my hand that also exploded. Summoning my scythe, I began swinging through the debris that filled the air and sliced the necks of any god I sensed inches from me.

I could hear a million voices in my head at once telling me to move as gods from all directions swarmed in. Flying up to distance myself, a bright light appeared in front of me. From the light came Amentous in his gold armor. Striking me to the head, I crashed to the ground. Seeing the gods coming from all around, I created a force field as they began shooting energy blasts at me. Closing my eyes, I concentrated on Addis's location. Within a few seconds I sensed her."

Seeing Amentous flying down with his spear, I inhaled and exhaled. "Here goes nothing. One, two, three."

I removed the force field and allowed Amentous to drive his spear into my stomach. Screaming out in pain I grabbed his forearms and shifted the power of the Kurai to the power of planet Zayga. Forming goosebumps, I activated Ominous power and began consuming all life around me, instantly killing all gods and weakening Amentous. Being healed, I sensed Clark heading my direction; I shifted to being human again and used the strength of my suit to kick Amentous back into the air. Clark flew down from the sky and shot out a white light that killed Amentous. The explosion from the light slowly disappeared revealing a human corpse.

"It was a clone... the real Amentous, my father Gage actually took out," I said to myself. I looked to Clark who had a serious face and was covered in blood. "Amentous had to use Lucius' abilities to make a clone to retrieve the Golden Water if he was ever put to sleep."

"What a shame." Clark looked up, shot up into the sky continuing the battle.

Still sensing Addis, I teleported over to see her deliver blows of punches to Vera sending her into the air.

"This war is over, it's time to end this." Addis looked up at the sky. "I thought she'd be stronger."

"Finish her then, I'll take care of the rest." I watch the ongoing battle. "We just prevented the Third Great War."

We both exchanged smiles and continued fighting.

12

Death Temple - Angela

An instant later, I found myself facing a black building on top of a hill in what seemed to be the middle of nowhere. Turning, I looked up to see a full moon casting light down on a big city in the distance. Out of the corner of my eye, I saw a bright light shine and I turned back around to see Cade summoning a beautifully carved bow that sparkled white.

"We're just gonna talk, but you never know," Cade said. "Pray for the best and prepare for the worst."

"So this is it?"

"Yes ... Death's Temple, not far from London, England—the original sleeping place of Ominous, the second son of Genesis. Follow my lead."

I nodded, and Cade proceeded to walk up to the building and kick open the metal doors.

"Alright alright!" Cade called out. "I want answers right away and we'll be out of your stankin' hair." I saw seven dark-skinned male gods with blond hair, sitting around a table playing cards. They all stood at our presence, except one. The look on their faces was not welcoming. As my eyes adjusted to the lighting, I noticed they all had the same tribal marks on their faces: three blue lines going down beneath their eyes—which made me think of Benin. The only clothing each of them wore was a long drape around the waist and a large gold belt holding it up.

Cade looked at me and gave a small nod.

So I went ahead and asked the obvious: "Where are Amentous and his three followers?"

The one god who had remained seated now stood up and started walking my way. He looked a lot like the rest of the gods, but he wore a blue head wrap and matching armbands.

"Now why would I betray my own kind for scum like you?" he said to me. "You want him, then you're going to have to force it out of me."

He drew closer to me until Cade blocked his way.

"Yeah, but we don't have the time, so why don't you just tell us, okay?" Cade said, eyeing the god. "I'm not here to play games, Gonhuru. You tell me where the Golden Water is, along with Vera's location, and I won't kill you."

"Oh, excuse me." Gonhuru smiled and took a few steps back. "I see you know my name. You should be asking what I know." He looked my way. "Like when will Alice die? How or when your so-called father, John, will burn up screaming for your help as a child. Tell me, is he still going crazy as you remembered him?"

He laughed and the rest of the gods laughed with him.

Cade's eyes shone white. "Watch how you speak of those names."

Gonhuru continued laughing along with the rest of the gods. "Kid has grown up!" He looked past Cade toward the door. "Where's New York? Is he waiting outside?"

"No, I came along with my friend here. If you even think about trying something, I promise you won't win."

"Such small words, child. You only confirmed your death coming here. Leave while I still provide you with that option."

I moved to stand side by side with Cade. "Start talking," I demanded.

Gonhuru looked down at me, smiling. "What makes you think I would know where the Golden Water is now?" He turned his attention to Cade. "Or where Vera is located? You humans are worried about her presence and your precious items. You should focus on how you're going to survive when we make our move. But if you're so anxious to find Amentous, he'll be in the city of Closias, so you could just wait there." He stared at each of us in turn. "You should lead your kind to another planet. We're growing more numerous and more powerful by the second."

Gonhuru turned his back on us and walked away. "You should be thankful for my warning. But then again, I shouldn't be worried about an amateur who hasn't trained a day in her life and a wannabe Protector who never beat a god before. Just two teenage fools thinking they can capture a legendary super god."

"No," I said, moving forward to follow him. "I'm not looking to take Amentous in. I'm going to kill him 'til there's nothing left of him but dust."

Gonhuru turned around to face me again. "Always new energy coming to the GCP." He shook his head. "That line never gets old. Hear it all the time. Tell me, you think it was all Amentous's doing? You want to avenge your mother's death? Those three gods you're ignoring also joined in on the killing spree of your relatives. That's how your father knows them, and he couldn't do anything. Typical humans—hopeless, always relying on a superior being or on one another. He let his whore of a wife just die."

Right then and there, I felt something snap inside.

I charged toward Gonhuru even while seeing Cade reaching for me from behind.

"Florida, no!" Cade yelled.

But he was too late. I threw the first punch to Gonhuru's face with all the speed and strength I had. He caught my fist and squeezed. Ignoring the pain, I threw my leg to the side of his head, only for him to grab hold of my knee and throw me across the room.

Just before I slammed into the rows of chairs, Cade teleported to me and caught me. "I got you!" he said. "We should—"

"Get off me!" I shoved him away.

This time, though, I didn't go to Gonhuru. Instead, I charged straight for the crowd of gods, but then I sensed someone from my right coming toward me—Gonhuru. I turn in that direction and moved at super speed to slow down time. Gonhuru's speed matched mine, and our fists collided with each other, causing a wave of energy to blast the rows of chairs into the air and send some of them crashing through the boarded-up windows. Surprised by this, I didn't have time to react when he punched straight at my sternum. As his fist struck, time resumed to normal and I crashed to the floor. I held on to my chest, groaning and slowly trying to get up while heaving for air. Gonhuru stepped forward and grabbed my right arm. Three gods teleported to my left, and the other trio appeared near Cade. Two of the gods by me held my left arm, and the other one stood over me while Gonhuru continued to hold my right arm.

Gonhuru looked up at the god standing over me. "Finish her!"

The god said nothing but jumped into the air. I tried to use every bit of my muscle power to break free, but my super strength probably seemed normal to them. I watched as the god descended toward me and drew his fist back for a finishing blow. But then a deep humming noise came from behind him. I saw a bright arrow pierce halfway through the god's body, pushing him forward and past me. I followed his path with my eyes and watched as the arrow exploded into glisters of light and that part of his skin turned to ashes. The remainder of his body turned to stone.

That shot caught everyone's attention. The two gods on my left leaped forward to catch the body before it crashed to the floor. All eyes darted to Cade.

"Yeah," he said, "I'm a little crazy today, so step away from her or I start making my arrows fly and maybe I'll just turn you into a garden statue or a historical sight if you don't piss me off."

Gonhuru released me, glaring and stepping away.

With all eyes on Cade, I staggered to my feet and saw that the other three gods surrounded Cade but were maintaining their distance. He must have held them off long enough to get that shot off to save me.

"I see you weren't bluffing," said one of the two gods who caught the stone body of their comrade.

This god looked similar to Gonhuru but had blue-colored tribal marks that looked like claws beneath his right eye.

He walked past me toward Cade. "You couldn't kill me even if you try. And you won't be breathing the moment you pull that string."

"Okay, Gonmu shut up," Cade said.

He pulled the silver bowstring, and the sound of a deep hum came again. A bright arrow appeared, ready to fire. The arrow wasn't made out of wood or anything I'd recognize from the periodic table. It was bright white with glitters of light falling from it. Each sparkle of light that fell burned through the floor.

As Cade pulled the bowstring back farther, four arrows appeared instead of one. He moved the bow back and forth, driving the other three gods away from him and closer to the ones near me. I took the moment to step away from them, still feeling the pain from Gonhuru's blow but also able to tell that the injury was healing quickly.

"One down and six to go, and I can shoot four of these all at once, Gonmu," Cade said. "You want to be one of the four for running your mouth?"

"Big mistake coming here," Gonmu said as he ran straight for Cade.

The four arrows launched at Gonmu and three of the other gods, but I saw Gonhuru extend his hand in Cade's direction. A portal opened right in front of the four arrows, causing them to disappear. Before Cade could draw another arrow, Gonmu grabbed Cade by the throat, lifting him into the air. Cade kicked the side of Gonmu's face, again and again, trying to break free, but it was useless.

I knew Cade was in way over his head fighting them head-on, but I still felt too weak to make a move.

Gonmu flew up in the air, still holding Cade's throat. "What was it you said you were going to do? Turn me into some kind of home décor?"

Then he hurled Cade to the floor. As Cade's shoulder struck the wooden floorboards, I heard a loud snap. Hearing the pain in the scream that followed, I decided I'd healed enough. I flew up toward Gonmu, but the two nearest gods each grabbed hold of one of my legs and slammed me back down. As I pushed myself up to my hands and knees, I saw Gonmu fly down and land on top of Cade. He began punching him in the face, and I could hear the blows and grunts as Cade lay there, unable to defend himself.

I got up and pulled out the dagger I'd gotten at HQ, which I'd hidden in my belt. One of the gods closest to me noticed my movement and threw a punch at my face. I dodged and planted my knife into his shoulder. Sensing something behind, I whirled around, only to be greeted by an elbow to my nose. I groaned at the pain, then staggered back. Before I could even clear my head, I felt a hard punch to my jaw. I crashed to the floor.

Lying there, I heard Cade shout something, then somehow he teleported to my side. I looked up at him as he twisted around to smash his bow into the nearest god's head, sending him crashing into the wall.

I could feel my body healing, but the injuries still hurt—a lot. As Cade stood over me, I managed to get up to try to help him, standing side by side with him. That's when Gonhuru walked forward. The tribal mark below his left eye glowed blue.

"Freeze!" he said as he drew closer to us.

I froze in place, every part of me except that I could still breathe, and my eyes also could move, so I looked to my left and saw that Cade was also frozen in place. I figured that Gonhuru had some kind of ability similar to Aerozayle.

"Time has stopped for everyone but me, and I have full control of you and every object here," Gonhuru said as he looked over at the other gods, all of whom seemed to have freedom of movement. Gonhuru shook his head at them and said, "We're gods who have fought for centuries, and you can't handle one girl with barely any training and a boy who's not of age to even have hair on his chest." Gonhuru stepped forward and pulled my knife from the wounded god's shoulder and then turned to stand in front of Cade and me. "It was a mistake coming here," he said. "For both of you." He looked directly at me. "We need to go home—back to our planet. Tell me where the last of the Golden Water is, or I will kill your friend right where he stands."

I felt my mouth release, so I said, "Do whatever you want. I have no friends."

"You dare challenge me?" he said.

I watched as he tightened his grip on my knife—and then drove it into Cade's stomach.

"Fool!" Gonmu shouted. "You actually pierced the kid." He pushed Gonhuru aside. "We need to kill him quickly before New York gets here!"

Gonhuru extended his hand and I felt control return to my body, collapsing to the floor. Cade fell next to me, and I watched the shocked expression on his face as he realized he had a blade stuck in his gut. He looked so innocent, almost like a baby.

"Brother!" Cade cried. "Colvin!"

I could hear the pain and desperation in his cry. Cade didn't seem tough or threatening anymore. His eyes looked red, brimming with tears ready to trickle down his face.

Meanwhile one of the other gods had drawn his sword and now stood over Cade. I tried to move as Cade continued to cry out for his brother. The god swung his sword downward. It was inches from decapitating Cade's head when a loud explosion wrecked the front doors. A dark figure of a man dashed in front of Cade to stop the blade before it found its mark, then threw a blow so powerful that it reminded me of the fight in Florida. The figure punched the god so hard that the blow caused the god to slam against the wall and turn into stone.

Even though I could barely see his face because of the hair, I knew our rescuer had to be Colvin. He wore an outfit exactly like Cade, but it was all black. The remaining gods moved to surround Colvin. I'd already met Colvin, but seeing him here like this terrified the hell out of me. Colvin glanced down at his brother, and I could see the outrage on his face as he saw Cade's wound. Gonhuru hung back as Gonmu and the other three gods charged at Colvin.

I could only stand there and watch as Colvin went berserk, seeming to have no trouble fighting four gods at the same time. Fists flew back and forth as the gods attempted to land a single blow against Colvin, but he dodged every fist that came his way.

The movement of Colvin and the four gods became so fast that I couldn't keep up. Then Colvin shouted, causing some kind of an invisible wave that pushed the four gods back. As Colvin ran to them, the god in front threw a dagger at him. Colvin ducked to avoid it and then caught it after it passed over his head. Allowing his momentum to carry him forward, Colvin slid under the god and sliced his knee with the dagger, bringing him down. He went straight at the next god, stabbed him in the stomach, and then he rolled over the god's back, grabbing his head in the process and cracking it against the floor. Another one turned to stone.

I thought about going to the two other gods who were getting ready to attack Colvin, but then Colvin turned away from them and faced the one he'd wounded in the knee. Colvin pulled out a glistening black bow and launched an arrow that multiplied into three, with all of them going straight through the god's chest. Another one stone. That left Gonhuru, Gonmu, and one other god.

Colvin raised both his arms, and a moment later twelve black skeletons appeared, each holding out swords, axes, and knives for Colvin to use. Gonhuru and Gonmu motioned for the other god to attack. He nodded and ran at Colvin, holding a sword. But Colvin hurled a metallic disc that exploded as it hit the floor in front of the god, becoming a smoky gas. The gas had some kind of gravitational effect that pulled the god inward on himself. He exploded and turned to stone.

Colvin finally stopped fighting and spoke with a broken voice: "They should have known better than to send any gods after my brother."

He got on a knee and covered Cade's stomach wound with his hand, and it was instantly gone.

I gasped.

Colvin looked up at me. "I'm glad you're alive. I'll take care of this."

I gave a little nod, then turned my attention back to the last two gods.

The eyes of both Gonhuru and Gonmu showed the terror they felt.

Colvin rose and stared at the two gods. "Which idiot touched my little brother?" His voice sounded low and cruel.

"I did." Gonhuru walked forward, and I could see the sweat running down his face.

"Then you're last," Colvin said.

Gonmu grabbed Gonhuru's arm and stepped in front of him. Gonhuru nodded and stood with his arms crossed near the entryway. Both Gonmu and Colvin took a fighting stance across the room from each other. With Cade kneeling on one knee next to me, and the black skeletons standing in a near circle against the walls, I watched as Colvin and Gonmu just stood there facing off for a moment. Then, without warning, they charged forward. Their speed caused the entire room to vibrate, and then the whole building shook when their fists found their mark. Gonmu jumped back and extended his arm to release a powerful energy blast. Colvin dove forward to duck under the blue blast, hitting the floor and rolling straight ahead before coming up to use both feet to kick Gonmu back. The force of the blow sent Gonmu flying into the air.

Colvin teleported behind Gonmu to kick him down to the floor while he was still in the air. Teleporting to the ground, Colvin set his eyes on Gonmu as he got up and charged forward. The angry god threw punches and kicks, but every attempt failed, as Colvin either blocked or dodged each strike. He blocked Gonmu's next punch but this time held on to the god's arm and then gave a hard kick to Gonmu's front knee. Gonmu grunted and tilted toward the floor, but Colvin didn't let go of his arm. He elbowed Gonmu to the chin, then kneed his head, and finally twisted him around. Colvin held him there, and Gonmu looked like he didn't have the strength to fight back. Colvin extended a hand toward the nearest skeletons, and one of them threw him a sword. My breath caught as Colvin drove the sword through Gonmu's back, so far that the tip of the blade protruded from his chest. Then he took the remaining weapons from the skeletons and sank each bladed weapon into Gonmu's shaking body.

After plunging the last knife into Gonmu, Colvin grabbed the god and pulled him up close to his face. "You're done in this life," Colvin said.

He threw an icy glance at Gonhuru, who just stood there with his arms crossed, but I could see the fear in his eyes.

Colvin dropped Gonmu to the floor, then took his bow and drew the string back. An arrow appeared, then shot forward and went straight through Gonmu's head, turning him into stone.

As Gonmu's skin turned into stone, I saw Gonhuru uncross his arms. Then he launched himself ahead, no doubt intending to end this. But Colvin was ready. He leaped forward and performed a front flip over

Gonhuru's head. As he passed over Gonhuru, Colvin grabbed a hold of the god's hair. As soon as Colvin's feet hit the floor, he used his momentum to throw Gonhuru across the room by his hair. By the time Gonhuru landed in a heap on the floor, Colvin had teleported ahead and began stomping on the god's face. Each stomp came with a loud grunt, and slowly the god stopped his struggle to get up.

"No one lays a finger on him!" Colvin shouted.

His eyes became red like Vera's—and so did Gonhuru's. The god started to scream and then shake uncontrollably as Colvin stared down at him.

I turned my body toward Cade but kept my eyes on the fight. "What is going on?"

Cade got up and nodded toward Colvin. "My brother's eyes are death. That god is experiencing Hell's wrath. That's what you're going through when you look into his eyes."

Colvin lifted Gonhuru by his hair. "Open!" Colvin shouted.

I saw a red portal open up to Colvin's right. It must've been the Underworld 'cause I could smell smoke and hear the sound of thunder. Colvin tossed Gonhuru into the portal, and then it disappeared, along with the black skeletons.

"Brotha, you came to save me!" Cade ran forward and fell heavily into his brother's arms. "If it wasn't for you, I'd be—"

"Dead ... yes," Colvin said. He held on to both of Cade's arms and scanned over him, probably to see if he still had any injuries. Then Colvin shook his head and said, "You're not the GCP of New York—I am. I'm out helping other GCP members and you're causing trouble!" He glanced in my direction and froze. "Angie?" He let go of Cade and slowly came my way. "Were you not contacted?"

"By who?" I looked closer to see that Colvin's armor was covered in dried blood.

Cade came up next to his brother and also noticed the blood on Colvin's armor. "Where's all that blood from?"

Colvin turned to face Cade. "The war has already started." Colvin looked at me again. "The GCP is evacuating everyone from this planet. You both need to leave now to help."

"What? Wait, hold on!" Cade said as he got between us. "That's never been done before. We're supposed to do that only if we're facing total defeat."

Colvin closed his eyes as he raised a hand. "Cade, please!" he opened his eyes and fixed them on me. "You ordered Clark to find Amentous—well, he did and it was a fake. Vera is at war with Benin, and all of Africa is headed to support him. Right now, there's an estimate of half a million gods who have been revived. The GCP is outnumbered, and humanity is going to be wiped out if we don't transport everyone from Earth. In a matter of minutes—or maybe hours if we're lucky—Earth is going to be a wasteland."

"Uhhh ... are you serious?" I said. It was hard for me to wrap my head around what was going on.

Colvin nodded and said, "You need to get to your home state and start helping with the evacuation."

I just stared at him, then said, "How am I going to transport—"

"Our spaceships are headed to your GCP base in the swamp. Miami and Orlando should be there already. Fort Lauderdale is definitely already there, sending the populations from each city, and he'll determine how many spaceships the state needs. So like I said, I need you to head to Florida and go to your base at the safe house. There you'll meet the other Protectors from your state. You have to lead them and the state's population to Planet Peace as soon as possible. After the gods are done in Africa, they're heading here and then the entire US. I'm heading back to take out Vera."

"Today is my first day. I don't know the procedure in transporting millions of civilians in Florida to another planet. My plan stays the same I'm not leaving until Galoriah, Aerozayle, and Lucius are dead. Whoever has been leading Florida before can continue that."

"There won't be a planet to stay on to even fight."

"The people of Florida aren't my responsibility. I'm here for the three that came after my mother and aunt."

We both exchanged looks and he understood how much it meant for me to avenge my family. Colvin shook his head giving up. "They're in this state looking for you. Sooner or later they'll be after Alice and you. When they appear before you, I hope you're ready. It's tense back in Africa. Do what needs to be done this planet could explode."

"Right ..." I looked around. "First ... I-I gotta get my dad to safety."

13

Reminisce - Angela

After teleporting back to the city of Closias, I headed to my old home. Opening the door, I was greeted by Miss Lombardo—Alice's mom—who didn't hesitate to hug me. "Your dad's upstairs resting. We came to visit and waited for you to come back. I'm sorry to hear what happened." She pulled back to get a full view of me. "Don't ever feel like you're alone in this."

I nodded but could only think, *How am I not alone?* No one shed the tears I shed. No one walked the path I had so far. No one had been in my shoes.

"Your mother was brave," Miss Lombardo said. "Even with losing the people she held close, she continued to fight. I couldn't continue in the GCP knowing I would be losing loved ones. Your mother was the stronger one after I lost Alice's father. I fell short of what was needed of me."

I walked into the living room, taking a seat on the couch next to Alice, who was sipping tea quietly. "You were in the GCP?" I asked, looking at Miss Lombardo.

"Of course," she said. "I was a Protector. I was West Orange at the time—a city in New Jersey."

Then I saw Alice's mother turn and glance at a man who stood in the corner of the living room. His irises were light blue, shining just like Clark's and his presence was exactly like a Guardian. "Your mother was like my sister, and your aunt was my best friend. I retired because I didn't want to risk my child's life, as well as any of my loved ones. Your mother had no choice whether she quit or not. The gods wanted her dead, and your mother was never a quitter. 'Til this day I believe your mother could've killed Aerozayle and her friends. But she reserved their death for you. She wanted you to kill them. So do me a favor."

She looked into my eyes, and in her eyes, I saw hurt, loneliness, and wisdom.

"Kill the four of them," she said, "and most importantly protect the ones you love because that's all you have in this world."

"That's the goal," I said.

Then I turned to some framed pictures near the fireplace, showing a group of teens with my mother, along with Lisa. The teens all looked around my current age. I stood and walked to the fireplace and lightly touched the picture frame that hung on the wall. "My mom and my aunt ... How old were they in this picture?"

Miss Lombardo walked up to the picture, sipping her tea. "About sixteen or seventeen. Lisa was a freshman and was shy." She pointed to one of the guys, who had long black hair. "That, as you might have guessed, is Gage Walker. Next to him is Michael Alpuna—Alice's father. He was New Jersey at the time and had New Jersey under his supervision. That was the best and worst year for us." She walked to the couch and sat down, picking up a photo album from the coffee table. "It was around that time Gage disappeared and when your mother first gave birth. She was so scared, it being her first time. We all knew the reaction your grandmother would give. Marie left and went to Florida, where she stayed until she gave birth to her first baby."

I turned back to Alice's mom. "First baby? I'm my mother's only child."

"No, sweetheart," she said. "Her first child was a boy. Then you came a year or two later." She started flipping through the book, then patted the seat next to her.

I walked over and sat, seeing a picture of my mother holding a baby boy with dark blue eyes. "I had an older brother?"

"Yes." She raised a finger. "But a different father. I don't know who the father was to that baby. Your mother never told me, and we told each other everything. All I knew was Marie was going to stay in Florida with whoever the father was for that baby. She talked about him before the pregnancy like he completed her. She was madly in love."

I continued to stare at the picture. "What happened?"

Miss Lombardo exhaled through her nose. "The child came out of the womb sickly. Months later he died, and that's when the boy's father left. Marie took a plane ticket back to New York and tried to move on with her life. She was happy again when she had you."

"What was the boy's name?"

Miss Lombardo smiled, then closed the photo album. "His name was La-Naious. I asked her why, and she said it meant 'true deliverer.'"

Alice stood up. "Okay, Mom, this is me and Angela's time alone."

Her mother raised her hands in the air. "Yes, of course. Sorry, I think I spent too much time running my mouth." She smiled, looking at me. "Keep in touch, okay, Angela? And if you need anything, you just let me know."

I nodded. "It was nice seeing you again, Miss Lombardo." I returned a smile and then headed upstairs to my room with Alice following behind.

I opened the door to a much different room then I remembered. Stickers of stars were stuck on the ceiling, pushpins held pictures of myself and Alice in place on the walls, and multiple pillows lay stacked on my bed.

"You still had these pictures of us after all this time?" I said, walking around observing each picture.

"Why not? We're practically sisters." Alice sat in the middle of my bed and folded her legs in front of her. "What's been going on with you all these years?"

I sat down on the edge of the bed and shrugged as I looked down at the comforter. I couldn't put on a fake smile or lie. "I don't know ..."

Alice put on a smile and looked at me, trying to get my attention. "You don't know how you have been for the past, what ... seven years?"

I shook my head, thinking of my time in Florida. "I hate my life."

The room was silent. No one could want to hear that. It could bring people to an awkward place. They would start to look at you differently, or they'd feel sorry for you, then slowly distance themselves.

"Angela." Alice lowered her head to catch my attention. "What did you go through?"

"It doesn't matter," I said, finally looking up and meeting her eyes. "It's all in the past." But memories of enduring the challenges of living in that prison brought tears to my eyes.

"No ... no, it's not," she said. "It's affecting you. You're depressed ... You have to talk to somebody. You can't hold these negative things inside."

"I already found an outlet ... I'm going to kill the gods and make everything right."

"You think killing the gods will make you feel better? It won't."

"It will." I glared at her.

Alice looked away and softened her voice: "They killed the god that took my father's life and it didn't make my mom any happier. Whatever you're keeping inside or ignoring, it's going to continue to build up inside. Before you know it, you'll feel overwhelmed. Then you might even take your own life."

I frowned. "I don't know what's going to happen in the future—and it scares me. I don't even know if I can protect my father. How can I be happy if death is constantly at my doorstep or threatening the people I love?"

"Nobody knows the future. And nothing is constant. Nothing lasts forever—not love or pain. So that's why we enjoy the present ... enjoy what you have now. If you keep focusing on the future all the time, then before you know it, you're old and you missed your youth and you'll be filled with regrets. I will always care for you, but I'm also your friend and I can't see you hurting so much ... I think you just need some sleep."

"No. Sleep is the enemy. Every time I close my eyes, I see visions of people—people I know or don't know—and they're dying, screaming for help. I ... I'm useless."

Alice slid over and hugged me. It took me a moment to wrap my arms around her.

"It gets better," she said. "You'll see, and when it does, I'll be there to say I told ya so." Alice unwrapped her arms and looked at me. "Just start hanging around me from now on—like old times."

I put on a smile. "Yeah, that sounds good." I repositioned myself on the bed, crossing my legs and facing Alice. "Well, how's everything going for you?"

"Right now it's complicated ... Is it wrong to be pregnant and not want the baby?"

"I don't know ... guess it depends on the circumstances and your morals. Why do you ask?"

"Been in this on-and-off relationship with Cade. You might have met him—Colvin's half-brother."

"Yeah, I know him. We met earlier today."

"I'm pregnant with his child. I knew it that night, but two weeks ago I took the test and it came out positive. It wasn't supposed to be like this. We were never officially together. I always pictured myself head over heels being pregnant with the guy I love. Am I wrong for not wanting this baby?"

"This isn't really my forte, but why don't you just spend more time with him? You'll eventually get closer to him, then raise the baby together. The Walkers are loaded, so there shouldn't be much stress when it comes to money."

Alice shrugged. "He's the future of the GCP, and Adumay doesn't want him being distracted. Part of me deep down inside feels like maybe we were just meant to cross paths in our lives ... that maybe what we had was meant to be temporary. Who knows what the GCP will do with my baby or to Cade when we're confronted? But then again, I am their prize possession."

I shook my head. "You're the GCP's prize possession?"

"Yeah, I hold the soul of Genesis within me. I'm what the gods are looking for. If they get a hold of his soul, it'll be the end of this universe—and the second coming of every god and goddess that ever died."

A knock sounded at the door, and then Miss Lombardo peeked in. "Sorry to crash the girl talk, ladies." She looked at Alice. "We gotta go. It's late."

"Aw ... okay." Alice got off the bed and looked at me. "Feel like we should spend more time like we used to."

"Right." I gave another fake smile. "Love what you did with the room. Brings back memories."

"I knew you would love it. Wanted you to feel like you from ten years ago."

I looked around. "Yeah, you did a great job. Feels like home already. It was nice of you to visit. Thank you."

"Anytime love." Alice smiled, then headed out of the room with her mom.

I fell back on the bed in exhaustion. Although Alice was a true friend, I didn't want to put her in harm's way. And my life just wasn't the same anymore. I couldn't simply just be happy and pretend everything was alright now. I lay in bed thinking everything over in my head until I heard the laughter of a little girl upstairs, then the voice of my mom calling my name. I jumped out of my bed and ran upstairs to see if it was really her or another message. I barged in on my dad sitting on the end of his bed, gazing at the TV while watching old videotapes of me and Mom. He seemed so fascinated by the sight of my mom and me, that he didn't notice I was in the room.

"Dad?" I walked in slowly and sat next to him.

"Oh, sorry ... didn't notice you come in." He gave me a weak smile. "Did you find what you were looking for?"

"Ehhhh ..." I shrugged.

We both fell silent for minutes while watching old videos of Mom celebrating my birthday. We gazed at the TV, taking in every second of the video, trying to relive one of the most precious moments of our lives.

Looking over at me, Dad finally broke the silence: "Your mother was a strong, independent woman. She was just unbelievable. She was a lot like you—young and eager for the next challenge ... I miss her a lot." He looked away and continued to watch the video of Mom.

After a moment I turned toward Dad. "I didn't know what was coming my way. When Mom died, I was there. I thought after the funeral I would get over it or move on with time, but it stayed. I wasn't prepared for any of it—the emotional, physical, and mental chaos. There were days I ran forever, hoping to kill myself from exhaustion. Other days I would immerse myself in the dark, shut myself off from the world, or not eat anything. There would be nightmares and I started talking to myself ... It's hard to remember Mom without seeing how she was that day she died."

I knew it was weird—and sad—that I couldn't remember my own mother ... except for some memories of the day she died. It had all happened so fast. I couldn't even recall how I—or Mom's body—had made it home from the safe house in the swamp. Maybe Clark got us home. But I could remember my dad running to me. I knew I would always remember that look—that terrified look on his face. He was sweating and shaking, and I felt so confused at the time. Dad hurried to buckle me in the back seat and then we sped off to the hospital. I kept calling his name. I asked him where they were taking Mom, and he finally just lost it. He started breathing heavy, and with the way he was acting, I knew my mom wasn't alright. I started crying, yelling at him to ask if Mom was dead. I cried the whole way to the hospital, and nothing my dad said calmed me down. By the time we reached the hospital, I felt so numb that my dad had to carry me into the emergency room, where he immediately started shouting to see his wife. A nurse led us to her room, and Dad prayed out loud that she was still alive. When we reached her bedside, I saw Mom lying there, motionless ... dead. At that point I experienced a pain I never knew existed—a pain that only came when you lost the person you love most ... a person whom you thought would never leave this Earth so soon.

My dad had always been the strong one. He was old-fashioned that way, plus he'd been in the military for many years. We sometimes might think our dads can be arrogant or tough, but my dad was the real deal. Rock solid, well built, he came from a family of ten and grew up on a farm. He was the type of guy who would rather die than accept failure. I'd seen my dad angry and loving, but never scared or sad. When he'd visit the city as a teen, he'd get into street fights and even did some bare-knuckle boxing. Eventually, he joined the army. Much bigger guys would back down from my dad in confrontations. Just looking at him would make someone think twice. He was what I called a stone-cold killer. Some people even said he was as cold as a dead person ... but looking at his dead wife, he lost it and sobbed for the first time. He held me close and we both cried on each other's shoulders. After that, everything went downhill. That day left a deep wound in my heart that could never be healed—and the love of friends and family couldn't fill that hole of pain. I kept asking myself why someone would kill my mother. It felt like I never really knew my mom at that moment. The longer I lived, the worse my life got. It was like my mother had been the key to my happiness.

"Dad, what was Mom like, besides being eager?" I asked.

"Well, by now you know that your mother lived a double life. She had it hard in the GCP, not coming home for days or weeks at times when you were little. And when she was home, she would act normal and pretend to be this happy mother in front of you. But when our door was shut, she would ... she would let it all out and cry to me. Her heart had died and she wasn't the same with me—or you—after all the tragic events in her life. Most of her family and friends had been killed by the gods, and there was nothing she could really do. No matter how many times she would beat them into stone, more would come and kill twice as many. Her other life was being this journalist, and it was just hard for her to adjust to society with such a burden on her shoulders as a GCP Protector. And on top of her hearing about her own family members dying in different places, we also heard about my own family being killed because of my connection to her."

He paused and shook his head. "I wasn't strong enough to save my wife ... I wasn't strong enough to save my own daughter."

Dad put his face in his hands, trying to calm himself, but he couldn't. I realized how much stress and guilt he carried all these years.

"They took her away from me," he whispered.

"Dad," I said in a soft voice, "there wasn't anything you could've—"

"No!" he said, looking over at me. "Those gods took every-thing—*everything*—from me. I missed out on so many years in your life and now you're all grown up. It left me in such a state of despair that I couldn't even take care of myself. Your mother wanted me to keep you for as long as I could, but she knew it would be too much for me and that's why she asked Lisa to help out ... I failed. Those gods—they took your mother's life. She knew one of them would kill her."

I stared at my father as tears fell from his eyes. I couldn't take seeing him like that. He suffered like I had—maybe more. I leaned over and hugged him. I didn't want to cry anymore though; I wanted him to know I wasn't some weak, helpless girl, but someone strong ... like my mother had been. Even as I hugged Dad, I wondered: *If Mom knew she was going to die, why didn't she wear a combat suit ... or make sure Clark shadowed her everywhere she went? ... And where was Clark when all of this hap-pened?*

I pulled back and said, "I don't understand why Mom didn't wear her combat suit if she knew they were coming for her."

My dad wiped the tears from his face. "Two people couldn't wear the suit," he mumbled. "Two people couldn't wear the suit, two people couldn't wear the suit, two people couldn't wear the suit, two people couldn't wear the suit, two people couldn't wear the suit." He started cry-ing harder now.

"Dad ... what ... what ..." I started choking up. I took deep breaths to keep myself from crying. I squeezed Dad's hand to get his attention. "Dad ... what do you mean? Two people couldn't wear the suit?"

I stared at him, trying to force an answer out of him, but at the same time my eyes were as red as his. We were both hurting inside. But I also felt a mix of anger, sadness, and confusion.

"Your mother ... couldn't wear her suit because she ... couldn't wear it because ... the combat suit only works for one person—to be able to use its power ..." My father took a moment to compose himself. "Your mother was pregnant and couldn't wear the suit. Being pregnant would be considered two people wearing the suit." He hung his head and cried again.

I sat there, totally stunned at what he'd said—and trying to comprehend his words. I replayed what he'd said over and over again in my head. But I knew what it meant: I would've had a brother or sister.

"We wanted to tell you at the right time." He lifted his head and looked me in the eye again. "I missed you every second of the day ... She was young and just lived such a sad life—exactly like what you're going through ... and now they want the only thing I love in this world. I won't let them take you away. I—"

I leaned forward and hugged my dad hard. I wanted him to know that he wasn't alone and wished that I could tell him that I would never leave him. I knew he felt guilty but there really wasn't anything he could've done to prevent what had already happened. He was human, not a GCP member, and there was no way he could have fought back or even protected my mother.

"I love you so much," Dad said. "I wasn't there for you and I couldn't care for you and I'm so sorry."

"Dad, you don't ever have to be sorry. I understand. You're the only thing I care about and I'm glad I'm just here ... I'm fine, really."

He nodded. "Your mother knew I couldn't protect her or you. No matter how much I wanted to help the woman I loved and my child, I couldn't. I allowed the gods to ruin your childhood. What kind of father am I?"

We finally released each other from the long hug.

"You're just like your mother," he said, looking at me. "You cover up your sadness in front of others and show your anger instead. I can see it in your eyes that you're not that innocent child anymore. Those gods ruined your childhood and left you with a deep scar that can't be healed."

Dad got up and wiped his tears, then faced me. "You need to know that when you go back out there, it's game on. Aerozayle will try to break you mentally and emotionally, and when you're at your weakest, she won't hesitate to kill you. I prayed so much to let Gabriel choose someone else but he demanded you. You're all I got. Your presence is what makes me cling to this life."

I stared at my dad, and it was just sad to see how much he suffered without me. And it broke my heart to see my once so tough dad at his lowest. I got up from the bed and we hugged each other again.

"I never want to lose you," I said, then kissed him on his cheek, knowing that Colvin said I had little time left. "Dad, we need to leave." I stepped back and looked into his watery eyes. "We aren't safe here. The gods will invade here at any moment. New York will transport everyone, but I want you with me."

"No." My father backed away and shook his head. "I ain't leaving. I ran away most of my life and served this country. Those damn things won't have me running anymore."

"I won't let them kill you." Trying to plead with him, I raised my hands. "This isn't home, Dad—not anymore. Why are we even discussing the obvious? We have to—"

"I'm not leaving!" His eyes widened. "I won't leave the last memory of your mother. I love you, Angie, but I can't go."

I began to tear up, knowing he had just signed his own death certificate. "Then I won't go anywhere without you, Dad." Unclipping the watch band, I let my arm down, feeling the watch slide off my wrist and onto the floor. "I don't want to be anywhere in the world but with you."

Turning around, I walked back to my room and closed the door behind me. Being back in New York gave me so much pain and grief, which hadn't been what I expected. I felt like I was back at my lowest point. But just as my father needed me, I needed him. Figuring the GCP could get along without me like it had for all those years, I went to bed and tossed and turned through one of the longest nights of my life.

My mind whirled with so many thoughts, keeping me up as I lay there in bed. I considered a lot of things—the past, future, and present. How did my mother handle this life? What would be the outcome and the aftermath of the fight to come? If I was to just leave ... what would happen to my father?

What am I doing? I wondered as I stared up at the ceiling in the near darkness, the only light coming in through the window.

I closed my eyes and pushed aside thoughts of my father. But then I pictured Billy and Lisa. I gripped my covers tightly, angry at myself for letting them die. Imagined images of my relatives dying, bounced around in my head. No matter how much I tried to shove all these thoughts and images away, they stayed in my skull, reminding me of what I'd lost. As my anger finally began to die down, I wrapped myself in the covers and put my responsibility in the back of my head. I stared at the red digital clock that read 3:00 a.m., and I only wished I could stay in that dark place for eternity—that the covers would turn into a cocoon and protect me from the light of reality.

Looking up at the ceiling again, I let my mind ramble:

It looks like it's one of those rare nights. I don't know if I can continue to move forward. Or do I stay here and try to live a normal life?

I can't...

I'm going to kill myself before I get this done. I can't keep running. Pursuing this will blow my engine.

If I don't win this race, I'll be dead inside. If I continue to run this exhausting race, I'll lose myself.

I don't know what to do. The goal is there, and I want to reach it, but it seems so impossible.

Liberation is a long and exhausting road that can kill you.

I just ... I need to breathe ... This race is taking such a toll on me.

I just need to stay in the dark. Maybe then I can find myself and know what to do.

Just die! You can't bring honor to your mother.

You were beaten and forgotten. You can't get this done.

No matter how hard you try, you fail.

Just stop!

It's okay to feel this way.

I'm limited. There's only so much this body can do.

Just let me be happy and take the easy route.

Goodnight.

I closed my eyes, erasing my current reality, and instead drowning myself in my happy place: thoughts of my childhood when everything was okay with my world.

14

Protector Of North Universe- Colvin

Every day, every hour, every second, my memories would flood my head 'til I could no longer think. My past robbed me of my vision.

Standing at the sink, looking in the mirror after awakening, I didn't see an eighteen-year-old guy staring into a mirror, but a woman. Long black hair, dark green eyes, skin covered in marks from substance abuse. I saw my mother; I saw Eve—that day she spoke to me when I was younger.

"You're going to kill them, okay?" she said. "You do that for me." Mom got on her knees and looked me in my eyes. "I'm sacrificing my life to Ominous in exchange to give you power. The god of death's power will flow within you. You'll be more powerful than Gage."

Terror crept up inside of me as I avoided looking into her eyes. "Okay mommy."

"You're so ungrateful! I'm giving up my life so you can kill the man who tried killing you." She reached out and squeezed my forearm. "Look me in the eye when I'm talking to you!"

I looked up, hoping not to get smacked. "I'm sorry ... Thank you mommy."

She loosened her grip. "You're finally going to be of use in this life."

Once again, I thought back on that day—with Gage foreseeing the future of what my mother would do and him killing her and me. But death couldn't take me. Gabriel breathed life back into me and gave me a purpose. My soul was pushed back into my body, and Marie Proctor took me in as her own. In doing so, she told me about Avia, Queen of the Avians, who stayed on Earth with her lover, Gage. She did this in hopes of me feeling loved and having an accepting family, unlike Eve. Knowing where she lived, I visited her. After knocking on the door, I waited until it opened and she answered the door. Seeing her smile down at me, I looked behind her to see her kids running around, laughing. I stepped into her home, and as we locked eyes, she saw the evil within me.

"What are you doing here?" Avia asked, then looked outside. "Who brought you here?"

I extended my arm and opened a portal and Ominous stepped out. He stood by my side and said, "Hello, my Queen. I'm here to kill you at the request of Eve."

Avia looked over at her kids. "Go upstairs and hide!"

As Avia's sons and daughter obeyed her, Ominous stepped toward her, saying, "You won't be returning to Planet Avex when I'm done with you and your children. Your Creator will never know what happened to you. Your soul will be in my possession, where you'll be enslaved for eternity." He then summoned an army of Zaygaian gods. "A female Creator—what a joke."

I headed upstairs as their battle commenced. Going up the stairs, I could hear her kids crying. Opening the door, I saw Cade covering his younger siblings with his arms.

"Why are you doing this?" Cade said as he stood up.

"Revenge ..." I replied as I closed the door behind me.

"You can take me instead," Cade said then shoved his younger siblings into the closet.

I shook my head. "It's too late. Ominous already marked them when he looked at them."

"No!" Cade said. "I'm the future king of Planet Avia. I won't let any of you touch them."

Before I could reply, Ominous entered the room—with Avia's head in his hand. He smiled and threw it at Cade's feet. "Where are the rest of them?" he asked.

I could feel the fear and horror in the room, as both Cade and his siblings knew what was coming next. Ominous opened the closet door and looked down at the kids as tears streamed down their faces. He blew on them, and I could only stand there and watch as the children screamed. Ominous' toxic breath burned their skin until they finally died.

Gage arrived and battled Ominous. Doing my part, I put Cade to sleep and erased his memory of ever seeing me that day. Gabriel arrived and helped Gage defeat Ominous, along with rescuing Cade and me.

Shaking myself back to the present, I filled the sink with cold water, then leaned down to plunge my face into the icy liquid. Standing back up, I gazed into the mirror. "Are you proud of me now, Mother? Am I someone important to you now? Are you proud of me?"

Then I saw the spirit of Ominous appear behind me in the corner of the bathroom.

"I don't know about your mother, but I'm certainly proud of you," he said.

I turned to him. "I don't seek your approval. Our business is done. Get lost."

"Watch your tongue. You kill gods without much effort. Remember who gave you that power."

"I remember it every day. Now get lost."

"Scum." The spirit of Ominous came toward me. "You dog ... Who do you think you're talking to? Our contract isn't over."

I shook my head. "What you and my mother had doesn't involve me."

"It does," he replied. "Don't you forget, you gave me permission to work within you that day. You brought me to his house and allowed me to murder that family in exchange to give you my power and strength. The half earthling still lives. Our deal isn't over."

"You're not touching him."

Ominous smiled. "You turned soft on me. The deal was: I take your mother's life and I make you strong. When that boy finds out the truth, you won't be protecting him. You'll be protecting yourself when he tries to kill you."

"That's none of your concern."

"When the First Resurrection commences ... when I wake, I will kill him—and you won't get in my way ... or I will torture your mother."

I glared up at him as he stood an inch from my face. "Don't—"

"Remember," he said, cutting me off, "I hold her soul. She can go to eternal punishment for your disobedience if I will it. Now, when I return, you will bring me that boy and I will kill him ... or it's your mother."

When a knock sounded at the door, the spirit of Ominous disappeared.

"Hey bro," came Cade's voice. "Everyone is here. We're just waiting for you."

His voice has always helped calm me. "I'll be out in a minute," I said.

I took a step forward, but my body became weak. I fell to the floor and my vision went blurry. Everything slowly darkened and the outside world grew silent.

In the darkness, a light broke through and a man in a hooded white cloak appeared. He looked to be about eight feet tall, with his head almost touching the ceiling, and his cloak moved on its own accord.

He looked down at his garment. "Reveal me," he said. His voice sounded like the voices of a multitude.

In response to his voice, the cloak obeyed his command, and the hood of the cloak slipped off the man's head to show the face of Gabriel. His skin was like burnished bronze.

The floor changed to gold and everything turned bright white—so bright that I closed my eyes. When I opened my eyes again and looked up, I saw buildings made of crystal and gemstones, but they seemed to have been abandoned. The grass was a vibrant green, and the plants and trees swayed right and left in unison.

I got up to further observe my surroundings. "Where am I?" I asked.

"Planet Celestial," Gabriel said. He pointed to the mountains on his right. "The mountains shone upon my arrival, and the trees swayed because of my long-awaited return. Everything in existence moves in excitement at the presence of a righteous citizen, but in loneliness also. What you see before your very eyes, is the home planet of the Angels. This, my child, is Heaven."

Pulling my eyes from the beautiful scenery, I turned back to Gabriel. "Heaven? Why is it so quiet? And why are the mountains and trees lonely?"

"This planet was abandoned by the Celestials. Our Creator went to war against the great evil and we followed. All that remains is the beauty that's everlasting. It waits for the return of its Heavenly Father. I, too, long for his return. But I'm cursed with the truth—the all-knowing truth." Gabriel looked around, then turned to me. "It's time you know the same truth."

"Don't I know already?"

"No, you only know what I allowed you to know. The knowledge you possess currently will only lead you astray from the truth and what's to come. In the beginning, before chaos took root, Angels, Guardians, and Satavians protected the North Universe. We were one of the Elder Races—elite beings created to protect the North Universe—and we even willed the power of our Creator if the circumstances demanded it."

"Why are you telling me this? What's going on?"

"The Angels ... a mighty and proud race, yet a humble presence known amongst this universe. They aid humanity spiritually. My kind was close to the North Creator. The Celestial sector held hundreds of planets belonging to the nine orders: Seraphim, Cherubim, Thrones, Dominions, Virtues, Powers, Principalities, Archangels, and Angels. Each order had their own planet, and they all congregated here in Heaven. Guardians aided the humans and were physically present, as they are now. Then there were the Satavians."

"But ... Gabriel, I thought you were a Guardian?"

I watched him closely as he moved his eyes down to mine.

"Do I resemble one?" he asked. His skin didn't shine like a Guardian and his presence was heavier. His gold eyes continued to blaze. "The Satavian presence alone was enough to obliterate the solar system. They also provided humanity with protection. They were the originals ... timeless beings. The North Creator created a sector for them far away from the rest of the species in the North Universe. There were a multitude of planets for the Satavians. Your sun had multiple purposes—not just to give light and energy to Earth, but to also allow the Satavians to step into your sector of the North Universe and protect you if needed. The sun was filled with Satavians. Then there was Planet Solar within their sector, and then Planet Satavia itself, where Satavians originated from. When the great evil arrived, the Celestial sector was the first to get hit. The Angels evacuated the early humans residing in Heaven to the Guardian sector. There lived the five Kingdoms. Each Kingdom was a planet designed for a purpose. Together—"

"They create a shield protecting the Afterworld," I cut in. "I'm guessing that's where the Angels led the humans."

I walked down the gold road, and as I got closer to the beautiful buildings, I saw that they weren't just abandoned, but some were destroyed.

Gabriel followed behind me. "Step no farther. Beyond that city lies an evil craving for death."

I turn back to Gabriel. "What happened here?"

"War. I witnessed the Heavenly Host go to battle." Tears formed and stopped at the rim of Gabriel's eyes. "I have seen the death of the Archangels as they fought to their last breath alongside the Satavians. The Archangel Michael led me out the realm we battled ... Planet One—the home planet of the Creators. He touched my hand, and within that touch lay his plans to create the GCP. He was given the power of a Creator from the Heavenly Father. He was supposed to watch everything. But he was ambushed and continued to fight the good fight. I escaped and started his plan: The GCP."

I gazed at him and didn't see an Angel who was in pain, but rather someone who held it all in and locked it away.

"I was told the beginning and the end and was told the truth," Gabriel said. "My time here is done. This is the very reason why I brought you here."

"I don't understand ..." I looked around. "There aren't any gods that can take your life. How does this correlate to me being here?"

"I need you to know why the Father gave you a second chance at life ... the reason why I rejected you from entering the Afterworld after Gage shot an arrow through your heart ... why I took you in as my beloved son." Gabriel came closer to me. "I didn't flip you to existence. You were planned from the beginning by Yahweh. You were meant to watch over the North. You're meant to be where you are now."

"I'm next, aren't I? That's why you trained me and showed me the truth and allowed me to die. I was reborn when you breathed life into me. I was given a second chance at life to be—"

"The next Protector of the North Universe." Gabriel smiled at me and snapped his fingers.

I found myself back in the broken home where I'd lived with Eve seven years ago.

"I've been by your side and watched you battle yourself ... to be like Gage, to be recognized," Gabriel said. "I'm proud of who you are without the title, without the accomplishments. I'm proud of what Yahweh created."

I looked up at him, trying to fight the tears from falling. "Don't do this to me! Your work isn't done yet."

"This was never my work or my doing. The Heavenly Father needs me and wants you to lead his people. Don't stray from the path you were meant to walk."

"We can't win ... We need you."

"You need your maker. God's not dead or deaf, nor has he forgotten about his children. Pray without ceasing. Attack with prayer and witness the power of the all-powerful Creator leading you into victory."

Gabriel grabbed both of my hands. "I'm giving you the power of the Creator. I'm passing on what should've been given to Archangel Michael—what the fallen Angels went to war for. You will also inherit the power of my race and become stronger without the need of a suit."

Everything around me began to shine bright. Through the brightness, the eyes of Gabriel caught my attention and continued to shine brighter than anything around us.

"Mold Cade," he said to me. "Have him meditate to bring back Gage. He holds the key. He holds the Kurai and Karui to defeat the great evil ... to save humanity."

Tears began to fall down my face and my vision became blurry. "Y-Yes ..."

"Do you understand? You carry the burden of the North Universe and all its pain." Gabriel squeezed my hands. "Save humanity at all costs and the holy items as well. You'll need them during the end of days when the great evil arrives. Kill if necessary."

A surge of power flowed within me even as the light blinded me. I fell through the floor and back into my body at home.

"Colvin!"

I popped open my eyes to see Cade.

"Are you alright?" Cade held me in his arms, searching my eyes. "You were gone."

"I ... I spoke with Gabriel." I stood up and felt a surge of Zaygaian energy flowing through my body. "What's going on?" I looked up at Cade for an answer.

"You were out for a couple of hours. I tried getting to you ... The Zaygaian orbs turned to planetary size. They're out in the sky as we speak."

I nodded and rose. "They're going to kill everyone at any moment." I rushed out of the bathroom, with Cade right behind. "I need you to meditate five times a day now."

"What? I already meditate three times a day. I'm going to find Dad. Just gotta wait."

"No, time is something we can't afford. Vera is alive and, on the move, as we speak. I can feel her." I lifted my head to look up at the ceiling. "She's at war with Benin even now, and Gabriel is there protecting that country. Addis is going to arrive there. I can feel it. I already know the outcome, but if they win, Ominous will return."

"We're going, right?" Cade walked faster to get in front of me, trying to catch my attention. "He killed my family."

"You want to help, then bring back our father. Now, you said everyone here?"

He nodded, and, having the power of Ominous, I could feel his soul shake in excitement. I headed downstairs to the dining room, now filled with every GCP member in New York. All sixty-two Protectors of New York stood in my presence as I stopped almost at the bottom of the stairs.

Albany walked forward, making her way to the stairway. "You're finally back."

Locking eyes with her, I could see that she knew what was to come. Albany had the ability to foresee major events, a power given to her by Gabriel.

"I know what you're going to do," she said. "If we do this, it'll change everything."

"There isn't any other way." I turned my head toward the other Protectors. "Listen, prepare your designated city for evacuation. Your Guardian will teleport everyone to Planet Peace."

Cade walked down from behind me and stood by my side.

I nodded at him and said, "Cade will watch over Closias. It'll be the last city to leave. Because of headquarters being here, we have to transport all important info to Washington. If I don't return, then Cade will be my successor as New York. Start evacuating now. You'll also hear this news from Moses, but I'm giving you a head start."

"Where are you headed?" one Protector asked.

"To war," I said. Then my GCP armor appeared. "Peace be with you all." Turning to Cade, I gave him a hug. "Wait for my return. I'll be back, I promise."

"I need a time limit," Cade said. "Last time the gods managed to get past our barrier."

I thought about the endless number of bodies that lay beneath the sun then—the lives of so many GCP Protectors who died to prevent the revival of Vera.

"If the sun hits and I don't return," I said, "start evacuating without me. When the orbs shine, they'll take the energy of every living thing on Earth and suck it dry 'til we're all dead."

"They have the Golden Water," Cade said. "I don't—"

His words cut short as everything started to shake, like if an earthquake was happening.

"Outside now!" I shouted.

Then I teleported outside, above the Walker Estate, and faced a red orb the size of the moon. It shined brighter with each passing second.

Cade teleported by my side. "What is it doing?"

"Put a force field over Earth!" I turned to Cade. "Do it quickly." I urged.

"That's insane! I can't do that yet. Even if I wanted to, it won't work. It'll—"

"We're going to die if you don't do it now!"

Cade's eyes shone white and a bright aura emanated from his skin. The red orb turned to a solid sphere, and the dark sky bled crimson as Cade flew closer to the orb. The other GCP Protectors of New York came up behind me.

Brooklyn hovered by my side. "Captain, what's goin' on?" she asked.

"War, and we're losing right now." I turned to her. "Cade is your captain now. Take direct orders from him only."

Reaching up to my neck, I touched my Karui necklace, then I closed my eyes and teleported to the battlefield.

15

The Battle Commences - Colvin

I stood on the soil of Porto-Novo, the capital of Benin, where bodies covered the ground—both Protectors and civilians. I looked up to see that the skies reflected the red of three orbs.

"It's too late," I whispered to myself.

I blinked my eyes red. I was no longer human. I was what my mother wanted me: half-human and half-Zaygaian. With such power, I was immune to the orbs stealing my life force.

Walking over the dead bodies, I saw that the nearby building walls were spattered with blood. Food and clothes lay scattered all over the ground, clearly from innocent civilians selling their goods earlier in the day.

"New Yo'k!" came a shout. "Please 'elp me ... please!"

I turned to see a man lying against a wall. To the naked eye, he appeared to be wearing a traditional long-sleeve dashiki, colored purple with orange designs—but a GCP member would realize it was an outfit made of Guardian cloth, making it impenetrable, even to the power of the gods. I knew this was the GCP Protector for Porto-Novo.

As he called out for me again, I walked over and noticed blood oozing from his scalp and running down onto his face. He looked up at me, his body already starting to resemble a corpse to me.

"Save me … please!" he gasped. "I got … a family. My kids … they need me … Do something—please!"

As I knelt down and held his hand, I gazed into his eyes. "I can't save you … not from this power." I looked up at the red orb as it continued to absorb the life of every living thing it shone its light on. I turned back to him. "Where's the fight taking place? I don't see your headquarters. Did you relocate?"

"Gone," the GCP Protector said. He slowly lifted an arm and pointed to his left. "They a-coming."

I looked in the direction where he pointed and heard chants. Then the ground began to rumble, and the orbs shined brighter.

Releasing my grip, I stood up and looked down at the GCP Protector. "Benin won't fall, I promise. I will save its people."

The Zaygaian power from within me came forth. I extended my hand toward his face and absorbed his remaining life energy before the orbs could take it.

"Adumay," I said.

A bright light shone to my right and I looked that way to see Adumay.

"New York," Adumay said. "You summoned me." He was in battle gear, and his armor was covered in blood.

"Benin is under siege. Where is the rest of Africa?"

"Still in Ethiopia defending their headquarters with Addis. They're battling forces on every front, but so far we're looking good."

I shook my head. "Tell them the real battle is here. We need to mobilize all forces to this front. At this point, I'm a Zaygaian god, and these orbs overhead will bring back the gods you've killed. They're gonna tire us out—the ones controlling the orbs … I can feel it. They're up ahead. We need to take them out if we want to save Earth."

Adumay focused his attention up the hill. "Maybe we should retreat now."

"No, you call the others. I'll stay here to fight. Tell them that Porto-

Novo has fallen and that I'll stay to fight for humanity. Tell them every second that passes, the closer they get to reviving Ominous."

Adumay waited a moment, and I could see he was thinking through my decision.

"What are you waiting for?" I said. "There isn't much time. Get help. I'll be fine."

"Don't do anything I would detest." Adumay rose up into the air and stared down at me. "Call on me when I'm needed."

I smirked. "That's the plan."

Once Adumay disappeared, I flew up and turned my attention to the approaching group of gods, whom I could still hear but not see yet. I gazed down at what had once been a strong fortress that held millions of gods and goddesses as prisoners. Once a sight of achievement, it was now a memorial of dead Protectors. Their headquarters were in shambles, and many Protectors lay dead on the ground next to their Guardians.

Now the sound of beating drums filled the air. Horns followed next, then sung praises. And then I saw the first of them. Two dark-toned goddesses crested the hilltop, holding drums. They walked far apart from each other. They wore no armor, no footwear. Their clothing was made of seeds and stems of plants and beads from their home planet—a short blouse that covered their chest, along with a skirt that stopped around mid-thigh. While bending their knees, they swung their arms to the right and left each time they stomped their feet. They moved to the rhythm of the beat from the drums, and stuck out their tongues and bulged out their eyes. As they continued to move down the hill, my senses were alerted as I sensed a large amount of energy from behind me. I turn back to see a multitude of Protectors and Guardians lined up, ready for war.

Adumay teleported by my side. "Everyone is ready."

The six brothers of Africa came forward to watch the incoming gods. Nigeria, Benin, Kenya, Ghana, Algeria, and Congo stood side by side. Famous for their leadership and combat, the siblings had all become respected leaders of Africa. I looked over to Nigeria, the oldest of the six and also the biggest in stature. Being from the Mapogo tribe, he had markings on his face as a reminder of his ancestors who had lived to serve the GCP.

No matter what happened to the Mapogo lineage, he would always fulfill his duties as part of the GCP.

A moment later, an army of gods came over the hill and marched down the center of the slope. They all wore a black steel-plated armor. None wore a helmet. From their shoulders, hung red capes.

I noted a god with skin complexion similar to the two goddesses, and he also wore the same kind of clothing. He stood around eight feet tall and wore an amulet made of god steel. Dangling from the amulet were eight raw Zaygaian rocks. I knew this was no ordinary god. He had command over the three spheres hovering above. His red eyes gazed up and found us.

Then he clapped his wrists together as if chained, yelling, "Set him free!" He inhaled and exhaled heavily through his nose. "Set my king free!" he shouted. Sweat streamed down his face.

A roar from behind him erupted as the other gods bent their knees and their hands began to quiver.

They're calling to the spirits to aid them. This isn't good, I thought.

More goddesses appeared and began to cry and chant as they looked up at the three spheres. These gods also fell on their knees and began to pray out loud.

"Wait a minute," I muttered. Observing the gods for another moment, I turned back to Nigeria, saying, "Those aren't regular gods. In the Zaygaian culture they're called 'worshippers.' They're the key to Ominous success. Zaygaians have never lost a war." I pointed at the hill. "And they're the reason for it ... Now it all makes sense! They stayed under our radar and awakened Vera without the Golden Water. This time it's a whole army of them and they plan on reviving Ominous and every Zaygaian god. We need to kill that god standing there. He controls the three orbs. Doesn't matter how many of them we kill; those spheres are going to drain our life away."

A loud trumpet sounded, and the three Zaygaian spheres glowed simultaneously. Then a large planet came forth from out of the sky, bigger than the three spheres combined. The planet covered the skies, sitting above Earth. It was black and sparkled with red lights.

"That's Planet Zayga," I said. "They were calling to their planet to—"

"Then why are we waiting here like sheep ready to get slaughtered?" Nigeria shouted. He opened his hand and his spear appeared. He plunged it into the ground as he stared at the god who stood at the top of the hill. "You are not welcome here!" He turned to his brothers. "We kill all of them!"

Our army of Protectors and Guardians all shouted in agreement.

"No survivors, no weakness, no mercy, no forgiveness!" Nigeria bellowed to those behind us. Then he turned back to the gods up ahead. "Only vengeance and war!"

Nigeria ran forward, and I followed. The god commanding the army extended his hands in our direction. As we ran up the hill, Protectors and Guardians alike beside me fell to the ground, dying immediately as the god absorbed the life force of anyone coming his way. I summoned a force field to prevent any other GCP members from having their energy stolen.

Seeing this only angered the commanding god. He charged forward. Nigeria launched his spear at the god. So powerful was the force of the spear as it tore through the air, that the ground split open beneath it as it passed over. The spear went straight through the heart of the god and out his back, landing among the army behind him and breaking open the ground, causing all the gods and goddesses to disperse.

I ran toward the gods while they were still recovering from the impact. Not bothering to summon my bow, I opened my hands and shot arrows into the back or chest of any god I laid my eyes on, turning them to ash.

"Kill all of them!" I shouted. "No one is innocent!"

Seeing the worshippers continue to pray, I summoned my dark spirit beings. They were female beings born from the North Universe—with no face, name, or birthplace. They all looked the same but wielded different weapons.

After summoning thousands of them from all directions, I looked around, then commanded, "Kill every god and goddess. They are all a threat to Earth, so leave none alive!"

As the dark spirit beings flew off to obey, I noticed that some of the gods and goddesses had fallen to their knees to pray. So I began swinging away with my sword, slicing their necks open until my arms started shaking.

Different-colored energy blasts from gods came from all directions. More gods began flying down to Earth. Others were being resurrected back to life by the Zaygaian spheres above. As they crash-landed, I ran forward to absorb the life force of any injured gods who were regaining health, even as my body took multiple hits from the energy blasts. My heart beat hard as I ran forward into the fray with the other Protectors and Guardians.

Then I stopped when I heard loud screams from behind, but I could barely see because of all the endless blasts. I looked back and saw the gods slaughtering Guardians and Protectors alike.

Then a thick mist came rolling over the battlefield, and a moment later I saw a massive figure emerge from it: the commanding god whom Nigeria had killed.

The god thumped his chest and then opened his arms, summoning more gods to stand by his side.

"I'm Katakula," the god said, "loyal servant to the All-Knowing ... eternal servant to Death and the Death Seeker. I don't die!" His eyes shone red. "Colvin, son of the great Gage Walker—the man who's never been touched by his foes ... they say you were mentored by Marie Proctor, the strongest GCP member to ever live. You even adopted their greatest attributes making you one of the rare members to never lose a battle ... Well, from what I see, the praise doesn't justify the reality."

Summoning my scythe, I pointed it toward Katakula. "Stop talking and come and find out."

Katakula walked forward as his skin shone bright. "Your confidence will be your downfall. I will resurrect Ominous."

"You're still talking," I said.

Katakula turned to his comrades. "Kill that boy!"

A swarm of gods charged my way.

"I don't lose." I said.

Sensing a god coming at me from behind, I lowered myself. As his hand went over my head, I grabbed his wrist and threw him forward, causing him to collide with the incoming gods. Seeing the bodies crash into each other, I extended my arms and opened my hands, shooting a barrage of black arrows that struck the gods and turned them into ash.

I looked over to Katakula and yelled, "Come on!"

"As you wish!"

Katakula launched himself at me and threw the first punch. When I caught his fist in my hand, the ground beneath us shook and then cracked open from the force of the blow. Keeping my eyes on Katakula as we both fell to a knee, I swung my scythe at him, but he ducked it easily. So I opened my hand, aiming at his head. As I released my arrows, the Zaygaian rocks on his amulet shone and absorbed each arrow I shot.

Katakula smirked as he shook his head. "No more powers."

I headbutted him. With him stunned momentarily, I looked up and absorbed some of the life force from the spheres above. Gaining new strength, I grabbed Katakula by the back of his head, then drove my right knee into his temple. As he jerked back from the blow, I followed with a right hook, then threw an elbow to his jaw. Pressing my advantage, I grabbed his throat with both hands and shoved him to the ground on his back, making sure I landed squarely on top of him. Before he could make a move, I let go of his throat, then shot my arrows into his neck, severing his head from his body. Then I grabbed his amulet and placed it around my own neck.

Sensing a god coming my way, I reached into a pocket hidden near my belt and withdrew a blade that I hurled, connecting with his throat. Seeing a goddess battling Benin a few yards away from me, I got up and ran to the god I'd just wounded. As he knelt there, flailing, I yanked the blade out of his neck, then ran forward and drove the knife into the back of the goddess, sending her to her knees. Another god lunged forward toward me with his sword in one hand. He came at me fast and at an angle that pinned me between him and the wounded goddess, still on her knees. So I turned, braced myself with a hand on the goddess's shoulder, and then front-flipped over, just eluding the god's attempt to slice me with his sword. When I landed, I saw the goddess glaring up at me, then she lifted her hands and began channeling energy. I saw that the god was already pivoting for his next move, so I quickly snapped the goddess's neck, then opened my hand, summoning a sword and plunging it through the god's heart as he came at me.

Closing my eyes, I knelt and touched the ground. Thanks to the amulet, I had a view of the entire battlefield from the perspective of the three orbs overhead. As I noted each dead body of a Protector, I restored it back to life. Having the power of Zayga, I was everywhere and knew the plans of the gods. I felt millions of bodies around the world being emptied of their life energy by the second. The three Zaygaian spheres were taking in energy from the Earth and sending it to Planet Zayga. But I noticed something different about the lives of those on Planet Zayga. I didn't sense gods but rather something stronger and ancient. The spheres, I realized, were reviving a different army. One being from this unidentified race would be strong enough to wipe out Earth with little effort.

Opening my eyes, I stood up and pointed my scythe forward. I looked back at the Protectors and Guardians fighting with the remaining gods. "We move forward!" I shouted, then ran ahead while several Guardians flew over.

A Protector from Africa came up on my left. "What are we looking for?"

I glanced over at him. "Kill all gods worshipping. As long as they're alive, they'll—Watch out!"

I dove to the ground as an orange energy blast shot out from the thick mist and took the head of the African Protector clean off. Gods from above and our right and left began shooting endless different-colored energy blasts. Some blasts killed slowly, and others instantly. The only thing I was able to see through the mist were the colored energy blasts.

Nigeria and his five brothers formed a circle, protecting themselves. I looked over at them and shouted, "We need to push forward!"

I stood up and instantly got struck by multiple blasts from both sides. Falling back down to the ground, I could feel the pressure of the energy blasts superheating my suit. I got up and ran ahead again, this time not stopping when I got hit with a blast. Each blast shifted my body, and I felt like a pinball, with no control over where I was going. I felt a blow to my chest, and the blast burned the sun symbol onto my chest plate. Feeling the heat through the armor, I looked around as more gods came my way from every direction. I opened my hands and began shooting arrows as I ran forward over the dead bodies of gods.

I came to a halt when Katakula teleported in front of me. "Meet the old gods!" Katakula said, then got on his knees and opened his hands, looking up at Planet Zayga. "Ancestors, come and aid us!"

A light from the planet projected down onto the battlefield.

"Retreat now!" I yelled. Turning around, I waved toward the Protectors and Guardians. "Turn back now!"

A red flash blinded me and a loud thunder shook the earth. All became quiet for a moment. The skies started to rain dead gods. Endless bodies fell to the ground. Then Addis appeared and descended slowly from the sky to the ground as all the surviving gods on the battlefield stood still in awe.

"I'm Addis, supreme commander of this continent of Africa," Addis said. She pulled her red and black locks back, revealing her face. "And you're all dead."

At the snap of her fingers, lightning came down from the sky, striking down the surviving gods and turning them to dust—except for Katakula, who did indeed seem immune to all attacks.

Addis looked up at the light from Planet Zayga. "Prepare for the real battle," she ordered.

I summoned an extra scythe. "This isn't a battle. What's about to come—it's going to kill all of us. Alice was right." I looked at Addis. "Where is Gabriel? We need air support and we need to get everyone off this planet."

"I'm here, boy," Gabriel said as he came up from behind.

Alongside Gabriel were Clark and Adumay and other high Guardians.

"You've done your part," Gabriel said. "Go home and help evacuate this planet."

Then I saw what appeared to be an army of Titans standing at hundreds of meters. They were in different heights, some two hundred feet and others much taller that it was impossible to see past their knees. I took a step back in shock. The Titans all wore crowns. These beings, I realized, were the energy I'd felt from Planet Zayga. *They aren't Titans!* No ... they were the old gods—the original gods. After the South Creator made them, they realized the potential of their power, and they rivaled their own Creator. Banished from the rest of the universes, they lived in darkness. The South Creator made Genesis the leader of the South and gave his power to him, the first super god who was deemed worthy.

Now each of the three spheres shone a bright beam of light onto the battlefield, teleporting more gods who held hand drums and immediately began beating their instruments. From one of the beams of light came a giant three-headed wolf that stood at the height of one of the old god's knees. Its black fur was on fire but it didn't affect the wolf. It wore a collar that had Zaygaian rocks embedded in the collar. This made it impossible to kill the wolf, and it was untouchable because of the fire. Next, hellhounds came forth from the light, all of them the size as a regular wolf of Earth. Having read my history on the Zaygaian culture, I knew the hellhounds moved at the speed of light. The three-headed wolf also controlled them all and saw through their eyes if ordered by Ominous.

The old gods, three-headed wolf, and hellhounds all stood in place side by side. Planet Zayga and the three spheres simultaneously shone together and projected a single beam of light in front of this new army. Within the light above the ground appeared a ruby statue of a man, and it slowly landed on the ground. A moment later the ruby transformed into Ominous, who fell to his knees.

"No way," I whispered, then watched as Katakula placed a black crown on the head of Ominous. I looked over at Gabriel. "How did this happen?"

He said nothing, but I could see regret on his face.

Then, from behind Ominous, came Vera, Galoriah, Aerozayle, and Lucius.

Ominous opened his eyes and they shone red. The battlefield had gone quiet, and in the silence he said, "I've returned."

An uproar from the gods went up behind Ominous. As the gods cheered and cried, Planet Zayga continued to revive gods back to life.

Standing there, I looked Ominous over. He wore black pants, and his long black hair was tied back. Vera placed a black fur coat over his shoulders, then planted a kiss on his cheek.

"The old gods rivaled the South Creator and almost took the South Universe," Ominous said. "Now they're here, stronger than ever. This is their universe now." He looked up at the old gods. "Kill these humans, find my father, and this universe is yours to keep."

Gabriel looked back at us. "Kill without hesitation."

At those words I felt my heart beat rapidly, and the only thing I wanted to do was kill.

Ominous opened his hand. "Kill them!" he shouted.

I flew forward even as every Protector and Guardian gave a war cry and charged ahead. Ominous launched a fist forward, sending out a wave that hurled everything and everyone back, except Gabriel, who stood still as dust and debris filled the air. I tried to get my bearings, barely able to see anything, and then out of the dust-filled air came a hellhound. I saw a little more than a red flash as the dog ran past me and sunk its teeth into the neck of another Protector. More hellhounds emerged from the cloudy air.

A moment later, Addis flew forward from behind me, with the surviving Protectors following. She flew above me, then yelled and threw a fist forward. Fire tornadoes descended to the ground and plowed through the army of Zaygaian gods. Lightning formed around the fire tornadoes and struck out at any god in its path. Then the tornadoes sucked in any god, turning them into ash with the flames. This was the power of Addis; this had helped her rise through the ranks to become the supreme leader of Africa.

As the air cleared, I ran forward, even as dead gods continued to fall from the sky. Looking up, I saw that an all-out battle had commenced high overhead. The old gods decreased their size to that of an average human and strode forward in unison. Ominous walked ahead of them and pointed down at the ground, unfazed by the chaos around him. At his command, the orbs flew down out of the sky like meteors.

Gabriel responded by shooting miniature-sized suns from his hands to destroy the orbs. The little suns grew in size as they rose into the air, but the orbs consumed them on contact. Then the old gods disappeared and rematerialized in front of Gabriel, with the closest one landing a direct strike to his stomach. The shock wave of the blow sent everyone to the ground. I felt like the entire world must have shaken from that blow. Every god, Protector, Guardian, and hellhound rose from the ground and watched as the old gods continued their attack on Gabriel.

I felt fear for the first time. One old god grabbed hold of Gabriel's head and roared, then drove its knee into his face. The impact of the blow shook Planet Zayga and the orbs above. Gabriel's eyes rolled upward. Ominous walked in from behind—and sliced Gabriel's head off with one swipe of his sword.

My mouth fell open as I watched Gabriel's body fall to the ground. The ancient god who had killed Gabriel now opened his hand to the sky, and a bright light emanated from his hand, rising into the air. Every Protector and Guardian hovering overhead met death, falling from the sky.

"No way," I whispered, staring up as dead bodies rained down. "We need to leave," I told myself.

Ominous extended his hand toward Gabriel's body and his eyes shone. "Watch what true power looks like."

He flew into the air and every orb shone at once.

I began to run, shouting, "Everyone get out of here!"

I charged past the gods who were opening their arms toward Ominous and cheering.

"Run!" I yelled as I sprinted across the battlefield, passing by shocked Protectors who couldn't see, to process what had just happened—and what was about to transpire.

Being connected to the orbs, Ominous was going to use the power of the orbs and wipe out every living thing on Earth.

"Phase two!" I whispered.

My entire form turned charcoal black and imitated the image of the universe, showing planets and stars as they moved. My armor disappeared in the process, consumed by this overflowing power that had my body hot and my blood flowing fast for the first time since my death.

Summoning a large amount of energy, I clapped my hands together as everything became red before my eyes. I yelled, then closed my eyes and teleported from Earth into space.

Opening my eyes, I floated inside a force field, viewing the Earth. Everything felt unreal as I thought about being in England not so long ago and all that had happened until this moment. Within minutes of his revival, Ominous had ended the battle. Now, gazing down at the red atmosphere that covered the globe, I sensed billions of lives had instantly ended. Ominous had just partially killed every living thing still on Earth.

I wiped the tears from my face as the carnage overwhelmed me.

But then ...

Wait!

I detected a hint of energy still active in cities where GCP headquarters were located. The orbs apparently weren't strong enough to penetrate the force fields of those cities—which meant Cade should still be alive.

I stayed there, not sure what to do. *I need help ... help me.*

16

∽

Till Death Do Us Part - Cade

You're the future, heir to the throne, lucky, blessed, son of Gage, great. I appreciate you; your father works within you.

You're all of these, Cade, to the outside world. But what are you really?

I don't know ...

I just want to be happy.

I'm scared of not being happy.

I'm on the road pursuing happiness and strength, but it's a hard one.

Maybe I can stop and end it all; maybe then I can see my family

No, I can't ...

Just find your pleasure and take the easy route.

I can't keep doing this ... Father, where are you in my time of need?

This trip I'm taking is a lonely one.

I know the sacrifice that comes with this.

It's why I always want some sort of company. It's temporary but I'll take the immediate pleasure because it's something.

I've been so lonely and I've finally found someone ... Alice.

We're connected and she's everything to me.

She wants someone strong, reliable, and fearless. I want to be that for her and for you, Dad.

But the only way to be this person ... to be like Colvin ... I have to release myself from her.

I feel like I'm at home when I'm with her, and to lose her is to lose a piece of my soul.

This fight is taking a toll.

This love is taking a toll.

Something tells me to be careful with you.

But my eyes are attracted to what it sees.

I don't know, but if you leave, I won't hold anything against you.

I know what this lifestyle comes with.

I think this is why the Creator built me this way.

I know this route would cost me love and friendship.

Maybe she boosted my attributes so I could be loved by many ... and attract those so I could never feel ugly because it does get lonely.

Maybe I'm misunderstood.

Love is my weakness and it's something I can't afford.

But I have it and it's ruining me.

I can't count how many times it has set me back.

I don't know if I could actually continue with love.

It comes with a lot.

Love comes with magic.

It gets you up.

It makes you happy.

It makes you do things you normally wouldn't do.

But it's hard to contain.

If you leave, it's okay.

Been mentally bleeding to get things done.

Been depending on myself; I think it's how my back got so strong.

I carried my own weight.

It's okay if you leave.

I don't expect anyone to stay by my side at this stage.

I continue to walk this road until I reach my goal or until I mentally fall.

I won't lie to you.

I could say that I will make time for you.
That I will stop fighting.
But I'll come up empty-handed.
It's the cost of true strength and happiness.
I'm built to walk this path.
If I walk this path, I could maybe help those I love, and at the end of the road, I could find happiness and love.
I won't be mad if you leave like the rest.
But if you stay ... I don't know ... I would be grateful.

Opening my eyes from meditating, I got up and thought about what this world could come to at any second. I wondered if I should spend my time prepping for what was to come and continue to meditate to get stronger, or if I should spend what could be my last day with the love of my life. Constantly trying to get stronger, I felt tired of trying. Alice came to mind, and my heart longed to sleep with her for an eternity. I hated myself for being soft-hearted and not rushing into the fight, but I wasn't coldhearted like Colvin. I knew I would regret it—I would hate myself for not spending the short amount of time I had left to be with her. I loved her and I didn't want to be separated from her.

I teleported to Alice's bedroom, where she was sleeping. Walking over next to the bed, I stared down at her and my heart ached as the thought of losing her came to mind.

I lightly touched her shoulder and whispered, "Alice."

Opening her eyes, she quickly sat up. "Cade, what are you doing here?" She looked out the window. "It's late."

I sat on the edge of the bed. "I couldn't sleep and I missed you."

She looked away and covered one side of her face with one hand. "Well ... what do you want?"

"To be with you. I'm sorry for everything ... for yelling at you. I don't want to lose you. I'll go through hell and back to be with you ... to protect you."

"I'm always going to be here for you no matter the obstacle. You have my heart." She scooted to the opposite side of the bed, making space for me. "Come here. I missed you too."

Removing my sandals, I got into her bed, and she laid her head on my chest. Putting my arm around her shoulder, I sat up against the headboard and stared into the near darkness that consumed the room.

She looked up at me for a moment. "What are you thinking about?"

"You said you had a vision of the end: you were dead and everyone on this planet. I think what you foresaw is coming to pass. If that's true, it means I lose you. You don't know how hard I train to protect you."

"Baby, it's okay."

I shook my head. "You're special to me. I can't allow anyone to get to you ... and tonight or tomorrow, I'll be tested. Me being captured has put everyone at risk."

"If I'm going to die, then let me do it fighting. I just can't see you die protecting me. You're important—"

"You're more important. Feel like I've been cursed to fall for you yet be an Avian—half-Avian at that."

"What do you mean by that?"

"Avians are created to be perfect, without flaw or temptation. We don't age nor are we mortals like humans. Years and age is nothing but a number when you're immortal, time is your friend and not your enemy. I get to fall in love like a human but the Avian part of me allows me to live forever and remember everything in detail from birth. Humans say you heal with time after any loss but that part doesn't apply to me and I just want to keep you and love you."

"You have me." Alice slid her fingers in between mine and planted a kiss on the corner of my lips. "Sleep with me. If this could be our last night, then be with me."

I pulled her in close, squeezing her body against mine, and placed a cheek on her forehead. I did this for a while, savoring the moment. "What I'm about to commit myself to will change everything. I'm going to call upon the great Avex army to aid the GCP. That many Avexes takes a master who's completely in tune with themselves and their Creator. I'm going to get in contact with the West Creator and see if she'll respond. In the meantime, you're going to be transported to Planet Peace. You'll be safe there."

Alice shot up, facing me. "I'm not leaving you. Not—"

"I love you." I looked into her eyes. "As much as I hate leaving you, I have to. My brother is out there. I'm going to meditate now, and a Guardian will come to get you."

"Wait! Just wait a minute." Alice held on to my hand.

The door opened to reveal Alice's personal Guardian standing there. He was from the Blue Kingdom, which meant he had been created for war, like Adumay—except that he'd been created in perfection and would only listen to Gabriel ... and of course kill anyone who was a threat to Alice.

The Guardian flipped on the light switch, and his brown skin shone. "Alice Lombardo," he said, "we need to move. Get what you need."

Alice looked over at him and frowned, but she knew what to do. I watched as she got up and put a few clothes in her bag, then took a couple pictures of her family and friends from her wall and dresser. "What about my mom? Can she come with me?"

"My obligation is to defend and protect the individual holding the soul of Genesis within them—no one else. We need to get moving." The Guardian paused, then said, "In a few minutes people in this country will start dying."

"Listen," Alice said, staring at the floor. I could tell she was thinking things through. "I can't go," she said, "not yet."

The Guardian came forward. "I don't have much time for—"

"Just wait please!" Alice backed away from her Guardian. "Colvin's out there fighting—fighting for everyone's future. He's due to come back; that's his duty as New York. I won't leave until he gets here safe." She looked at me. "I won't leave him out there, nor would I ever leave you or Angela." She then looked at her Guardian again. "I can be helpful. Just let me stay."

Her Guardian studied her and turned away. "Fine, but the moment things go left, we're leaving."

Alice zipped up her bag and placed it on the bed. "I'm staying here with you."

"Whatever," I said. "Just don't go anywhere without me."

I shut off the lights and locked the door, then proceeded to sit and meditate on the floor. Once I'd folded my legs and hands, something didn't seem right. I sensed death surrounding the Earth. Changing the position of my hands, I clapped them together and then began praying to the West Creator for her guidance and strength. Keeping my eyes closed, the darkness bled into white and then I found myself in a land filled with white grass. The sun shone white and projected different-colored rays. Looking closely, I saw that the sun was pulsing like a heartbeat, and it was the only thing you could hear—with no wind or birds or voices, even from afar. It wasn't as bright as the sun I was familiar with, as I was able to look into it and see the core beating.

"Hello, my King," came a female voice.

I turned to see a girl who was young like me, wearing a white gown with her hands folded in front of her. Her platinum-colored hair reached her lower back. "You've been gone for some time." Her pale blue eyes stared down at my clothes. "You've called for guidance and strength, my love?"

I looked down to see I was wearing a white shirt and white pants, but they were dirty. "Uh." I quickly got on both knees. "West Creator, I didn't—"

"No. Please stand. I'm not the West Creator, but she sent me to you."

I got up, looking around the vast land. "Is this Avia?"

"You're in the purest of the realms, owned by the West Creator. She heard your needs and I'm here."

I looked up at the sun again. "The sun ... I've never seen something like that."

"Without the sun, inhabitants die off like every race in the four universes. Each sun tells us the time. But time is useless when you're bound to immortality." She smiled. "But my mother told me to not critique our Creator's creation. But in the West, if you remember, we call it Ava, not the sun, my King."

I squinted at her, trying to recognize her face. "You ... Have we met before?"

"We haven't, but we are connected. My name is Tivonia, your loyal servant 'til death, the other half of Cade, the defender of the West, the Queen of the West, and your other half—wait, no, I said that already." She blushed and covered her face. "Can I start over, my King?"

"Tivonia? My mother told me about you." I looked down at my filthy clothes. "I'm in the purest of the realms, but my clothes are dirty." I looked at Tivonia. "It's because I have Earthly desires. It makes me unholy ... not pure ... because ..." Gazing at Tivonia, I didn't want to say *love*.

"You hold on to Earthly desires, and it's the reason why you're calling out for help. You're in love with Alice and with things that don't serve you ... I can feel it."

"You can be the Queen, but I'm not the king of the West. My place is on Earth, protecting Alice."

"You're needed here ... I need you. Together we—"

"There is no *we*, my Queen. My heart is with Alice. I'm leaving you with the duty to protect the West Universe."

She shook her head. "There are bigger problems than the gods your father wanted you to handle."

"The gods are the ones that took him away! I'm sticking to my decision. I need an army. Earth is in trouble."

"To call upon the great army of the Avexes, you need to be filled with our pure essence. You hold Earth ties. It won't work."

I slit my eyes at Tivonia. "It won't work ... or is the West Creator refusing to help if I don't side with her?"

Tivonia stood quiet for a moment. "I know how much the Earthlings mean to you. If you need help, then I'll aid you." Her gown transformed into Avian steel armor. Then an owl appeared on her shoulder. She placed her hands on the hilt of the sword that hung from her waist. "The current state of Earth will come to an end, but I can face the army with you."

Sensing her energy, I could tell she was confident in fighting against and killing whatever Colvin was fighting in Africa.

"No," I said. "I don't want to put your life at risk. This is my fight, but if I can't use the Avexes at full power because I hold on to Earthly love, then I renounce my title as king of the West Universe and my birthright."

Being connected to her, I could feel her heart ache as she said, "You've made a mistake ... but I'll always love you."

She turned away, and I opened my eyes to see Alice's bedroom again. As I sat on the floor, I saw that the sun was now high in the sky. I'd forgotten the time difference in traveling into another dimension. What seemed like minutes in the West Universe were actually hours in the North Universe. I looked around and saw I was alone. I got up, looking out the window and seeing there were still planet-sized red Zayga rocks hovering over Earth.

I left Alice's room, only sensing myself and Alice's mother in the house. I entered the living room and saw Miss Lombardo in the kitchen, cleaning.

When she saw me, she stopped wiping the counters. "Cade?" she asked, confusion written all over her face. "When did you get here?"

"I stayed the night with Alice ... Today could be the end of my life and Earth itself, and I wanted to spend last night with your daughter."

Miss Lombardo shook her head. "Why isn't the city evacuated yet? Where's New York? I heard the news and just trying to keep busy. I know other places around the world started transporting lives to another planet."

"He's at war in Africa, but it looks like his time is up, so I'm going to start evacuating."

She nodded, and I teleported myself to the central hub of the GCP US headquarters. I found chaos there, as members hurried in all directions, grabbing things before they would head for Planet Peace.

I walked to the front of the building, where the communicators sat below Heaven's Eye, watching over America. Moses stood down in front, where a small camera picked up his image and projected his face onto screens in all four buildings.

"Okay," Moses said, "we've received orders to start evacuating. Please allow your fellow Protectors to do their job in transporting the people in their designated cities to safety. Do not interfere in trying to save your own loved ones. Once you're on Planet Peace, please remain there until you receive further instructions."

Striding up to where Moses stood, I looked up at Heaven's Eye and saw a graphic that showed the world's population drastically decreasing in number by the second. "Unbelievable …" I whispered.

Then I turned to my right and noticed Washington standing there with his arms folded over his chest as he also stared at the dwindling numbers, surrounded by Guardians.

I watched as Washington looked down at the communicators typing on the keyboard. "Show me the list of every city and town in this country and its population," he said. "I want to know the status of where they're at for the evacuation. I need Guardians in all the cities of America and evacuating all life—not just humans, but all living animals. And send out support to the Protectors fighting gods at this moment."

Then, Washington turned to the Elder Guardians who stood ten feet tall. Their eyes had no pupils, only shining blue. "Go to Zulu's body and get it to safety," Washington said. "It's bad enough that Africa allowed things to get this far. Ominous was revived, so he'll be looking for his brother."

"Ominous?" I said.

Washington turned and froze upon seeing me.

I went on, "They allowed him to—"

Washington interrupted, "We don't know how. He just did." He walked over to me while cracking his knuckles. "Colvin told me you'd be taking over New York. What's the status of evacuation on your end?"

"I already talked to my Protectors, and they're transporting the people in their cities at this very moment."

"Some are falling behind. When this idea came to mind, it was expected for the human race to leave here in an instant. Things aren't going according to protocol, so I need you to send everyone on Earth to Planet Peace."

I nodded. "But I need to head to Benin. Ominous is out there. Colvin is going to need—"

"You need to understand your purpose and Colvin's. Colvin is well aware of what's at stake. He was bred for war, to win by any means necessary. It's the reason Gabriel forbids him to die. He's the last of his kind, and losing isn't in his blood. Trust your brother that he'll win no matter if the odds are against him. You were brought here to save humanity. This is your chance. Send everyone off this planet. Once Colvin senses this, he won't hold back and neither will anyone else on that battlefield." Washington placed his hands on my shoulders. "Can you do what your father did ten years ago and save the Earth at its most critical time?"

I let my emotions reach out into Colvin's heart from afar, and I could sense his need for my cooperation. So, I nodded to Washington and said, "I can. I'll head to an empty room and begin, but I'll need a boost. Teleporting a couple thousand people, that's fine. Millions will have my heart beating fast, but billions ... that'll kill me."

"We got that covered." Washington backed away and turned to one of the Elder Guardians. "Assist New York and make sure those who have died are brought back to life and sent away as well."

As I turned to leave with the Elder Guardian, I stopped when I saw someone walking up the stairs—Jerusalem, the supreme leader of the GCP on Earth. After him, came every other supreme leader from other universes. Jerusalem wore a tunic that stopped at the laces of his white boots. The all-white tunic made him look like a monk. Over his tunic was a short white cloak that covered his arms and chest, stopped halfway down his back. Dangling from his neck was a Karui necklace like mine. Like me, he also had a replica of the most powerful item. We were the same—except he was completely human.

Jerusalem stood next to the Elder Guardian who had been appointed to help me. "Together the three of us will send humanity to Planet Peace," Jerusalem said to me. "Let's move."

I nodded, then followed the Elder Guardian and Jerusalem toward a room where I would meditate. But I sensed fear in the air as we walked. Entering the all-white room, with walls covered in foam, we sat on the floor in a triangle formation, legs folded and holding each other's hands, with me in the middle.

The Elder Guardian looked around at each of us. "I'll start first. I will accumulate my power from within," the Guardian said, then turned his head to Jerusalem. "Then, with a portion of my power, I will transcend myself into your body. You will have full access to my accumulated power, as well as the Karui you hold, and I'll be guiding you into the mind of Cade."

The Elder Guardian then faced me. "We'll be in your head. Jerusalem will provide you the extra power of the Karui that will be in sync with the Avian power you lack to teleport the human race and other living things from Earth. I will accelerate your healing so you don't die and allow them to continue to revive the dead. It's important you focus on the task of shifting the living from Earth to Planet Peace. If you fail to focus, you could transport the lives of those on this planet to an unknown destination or even to another dimension. I will focus on healing you as you use your Avian power. Jerusalem will assist you in the transportation of the living."

Now the Elder Guardian looked at both of us. "Gentlemen, what we're about to perform is something that requires a lot of focus and power." He closed his eyes. "Let's begin."

Closing my eyes, I increased my power. Everything turned white in my view, and I felt the Elder Guardian and Jerusalem's hands go cold as I physically became distant from reality. Power from a Guardian entered through me, and Jerusalem's voice sounded like an intercom that spoke to me inside my head. I had an overview of the US GCP headquarters and as my sight zoomed out, I saw the region of New York, then the East Coast, and finally the entire planet—still surrounded by multiple glowing orbs feeding off the lives of every living thing.

"New York, this is Jerusalem. How are you feeling?" I could hear his voice within me, and I could feel his presence all around me.

I felt different, filled with an abundance of power and spiritually connected to every living being on Earth. *"I can sense everyone,"* I replied in my mind, and then I realized what I was seeing. *"Earth will be gone in a matter of seconds! We don't have much time."*

A black being whose body sparkled like the universe caught my attention. It hovered above Earth, and I could feel hopelessness showered over it.

"Colvin!" I cried out in my mind.

"We have to focus on getting humanity and every animal to safety," Jerusalem said, lowering his voice. *"Colvin will live."*

My spirit, soul, and vision connected to Colvin. He was holding back, scared, and sorrow was clouding his judgment and his ability to make a move. He clearly wasn't in the right mind-set. Death would take him if he returned to Earth. I continued to stare at Colvin and my senses told me he would lose if he was to return. Not wanting to believe it, I gazed down at Benin, where only bodies could be seen scattered on the ground. Sensing danger in space, I again looked away from Earth to see an enormous orb approaching at full speed. It would kill us all.

"New York, we need to focus on the objective even if it costs us our lives," Jerusalem said, his tone impatient. *"Time isn't on our side."*

With a boost from the Elder Guardian, I unleashed my power across the Earth, reviving the dead. Then, I sent white rays of light onto all people still on the planet, protecting them from the orbs. In doing this, I was also connected with billions of individuals in a matter of seconds. I found myself flying at the speed of light across the globe, spreading my power. Seeing the oceans, deserts, jungles, forests, cities, mountains, and islands, I took account of every living thing. The orbs surrounding Earth, all shone brighter in unison, wanting my power. As I poured out more energy, I could also feel the orbs absorbing my power, quickly weakening me. Picturing all of the Arks—our evacuation spaceships—across the world, I teleported everyone I could onto those ships. Then I began to lose my grip on the power I'd sent throughout the Earth, and the orbs immediately started stealing the life energy I used to revive the dead. Sensing the death toll again increasing, I closed my eyes and pictured Planet Peace, then teleported some of humanity there.

Opening my eyes, I felt myself back in my body, crashing to the ground. I could see heavy sweat on Jerusalem's face and the Elder Guardian's as well, both of whom had fallen to their knees. The orbs were strong enough to take away their life essence, even in the spiritual realm.

How did the gods manage to find material this powerful and use it to their advantage? I wondered.

Slowly getting up, I felt my body regenerating its strength. "I managed to get everyone to safety except the people of this city," I said, locking my eyes on Jerusalem as he also got to his feet. "I couldn't—"

"You couldn't do what was expected of you," Jerusalem said. "You couldn't let go of that girl you love. You couldn't do your job. You wasted valuable time on your brother." He pointed a finger at me. "You paid attention to one life and forgot about the rest. Now we have thousands in this city and billions still around the world still needing saving that will die because of your poor timing."

The Elder Guardian walked toward me. "You brought out the power of the Karui—and of my power and your own. Utilizing those three elements alone, you witnessed things that even I myself couldn't see. What did our power reveal to you?"

I clenched my fists, thinking of the knowledge I unlocked by meditating. "Colvin will die if he fights. No one in the four universes is currently strong enough to take down Ominous. He's going to reign over the North and kill every man. He'll have his Zaygaian gods descend to Earth and rape every woman who is of age to give birth. He'll have the women of Earth bear halflings and they'll fight at his command. What Colvin and the rest of Africa battled today weren't Zaygaian gods." I stared at the Elder Guardian. "They were fighting halflings from different races around the four universes while the Zaygaian gods studied our tactics from a place of safety." I turned to Jerusalem. "The survival of the North Universe solely depends on Colvin. He may be one life, but his life alone is more valuable than anyone in this universe."

I turned and walked toward the door. "You can save the people of this city and I will get Colvin and head to Planet Peace."

17

The Last Stand - Colvin

Standing alone on the battlefield, I saw death everywhere. No matter where I turned or how far I looked ahead, only the dead and dying could be seen. The hellhounds paced the battlefield, sniffing for bodies where life hung. They didn't feast on meat or blood but on the life force of the injured. Soldiers plunged their swords and spears into any Guardians who managed to survive.

Seeing Gabriel's body, I slowly walked over to see what had become of him. As I drew closer to him, everything felt unreal. Looking down, I didn't see an Angel but my father. I knew that Gabriel, at full strength, would've had no trouble defeating Ominous, as well as the old gods. My father had given a majority of his power to me. He'd entrusted me with his will. Standing over Gabriel's body, I couldn't believe I was seeing him this way. I turned away, only to see Benin lying nearby, barely breathing, trying to get up. I ran over and fell to my knees, then cradled him in my arms. Gazing down at him, I saw his life was disappearing. He'd survived the attack of the old gods, but now the orbs were taking away the remains of his energy. *How is he still fighting?*

"I got you, brother," I said.

I placed my hands over his face and tried pushing the Zaygaian power

I inherited into him. Seconds passed and nothing happened—nothing came out. My body started to weaken and then it hit me: I no longer had access to this ability. I threw away the amulet I stole from Katakula.

"I'm really dying," Benin whispered. He opened his eyes, with tears falling down his face. "Where am I going?"

I let him rest in my lap as I dug my fingers into my hair. I couldn't cry, couldn't scream, couldn't do anything. I could only close my eyes and do what was logical. I knew what to do—to press forward—but I lost all hope at that moment. I thought of all the things I needed to do, but it felt like it would be impossible to defeat Ominous.

"Someone help me!" yelled a voice from behind me. "He's dying!"

I turned to see a female Protector holding a lifeless body. "You need to get up and fight," I said, staring down at the corpse she held in her arms. "Listen to me! He's gone. I need you—"

"Oh my God oh my God oh my God!" the Protector shouted as she pointed up at the sky behind me and then started to cry.

Whirling around, I saw one of the planetary orbs begin flying down into Earth's atmosphere. Glancing down at Benin, I hurried and gave him a hug, remembering when we'd first met ten years ago as kids. The image of the Mapogo brothers accepting me and treating me like family after Marie's death came to mind. I planted a kiss on his forehead as the orb broke through the upper atmosphere and the air temperature increased dramatically, with the soil all around starting to slowly melt.

Standing up, I whispered, "My God ..." Looking back at the battle-field, I began to run—fleeing from what was about to come, hardly able to grasp the magnitude of the impending impact and how the sheer size of the planet would decimate Earth. I flew up into the sky, not looking back at what was about to come. The only thing I could see ahead of me on the ground were countless bodies—the dead and the injured. The gods and their hellhounds disappeared, knowing what was to come.

"Adumay!" I shouted, searching the ground and trying to come up with a plan with only seconds left.

I mustered all the strength I had. Breathing in and out of my mouth, my vision began to get sharper and every cell in my body became more fully alive. My blood rushed hot through my veins, and my heart awoke as I called upon the full power of the Kurai. The dark power of my necklace shone as the universe poured its energy into me. I came to a stop in the air, then landed, facing the orb. Extending my hands toward the orb, I braced myself.

"Phase three!" I shouted, feeling a surge of pain as overwhelming power from within me unleashed itself from my body.

This dark energy then lifted me up into the air as it formed itself into a humanoid avatar around me. I found myself held high above the ground within a being made of pure universal power. Lifting my hands, the avatar imitated my movement. I walked forward, shaking the Earth. Focusing on the incoming planet, I extended my hands toward it. Hearing the cries of the surviving Protectors behind me, I looked back and saw the hopelessness in their faces as some stood still and others limped away while losing their life force because of the orbs overhead. Facing the incoming planet again, I could feel its intense heat. I kept my hands pointed toward it, then yelled out as I released every bit of power within me. From my avatar's hands, came forth a massive ray of black energy that shook the ground, the noise of which sounded like successive explosions.

I wanted to stop myself, to tell myself to slow down. *Colvin,* I thought, *you let out this magnitude of power, it's going to backfire. You won't be able to fight efficiently.*

But I couldn't think about myself—only the survival of the human race. Continuing to yell with my hands extended, I closed my eyes when the planetary orb shone bright red, and then the pressure of its presence pushed my avatar back. As this happened, my energy blast grew weaker and the size of my avatar began to decrease. My armor began to burn up, revealing the skin on my arms and my chest.

Flying up at full speed toward the orb, my surroundings grew bright red. I stopped and hovered in the air as the orb broke through into Earth's lower atmosphere without any damage showing on it at all.

"No way." I muttered.

As my gloves burned away, I extended my right hand toward the sphere, bracing it with my left hand. I could hear a feminine voice screaming from my avatar. Channeling the remaining energy I had, I unleashed a large black arrow. My avatar disappeared once the arrow was released, and I dropped to the ground. My right hand went completely numb, and the only thing I could feel was pain all over. I watched the arrow disperse into light as the orb absorbed it. Staring at the orb, I saw only death, and everything in my body told me to flee. My entire body turned numb as rays of red energy shot out from the orb. Some of the rays struck my body directly and sucked the last of the energy and life within me. Everything turned black.

Who am I?
Who am I if I'm always touched by you?
Always yelled at
Always beaten
Always used
Who am I?
What's a mother who didn't see you but the man she use to love but now hates
What's a father who didn't see you
But sees a seed that'll kill him
But sees a seed of pure evil
Who am I?
Used by both accepted by none
A tool mentally, verbally and sexually abused
A tool killed by his father
A tool resurrected and still used
Who am I?
Don't know who I am mother
Love me mother, maybe I'll be human
Accept me mother, you're all I have
I hope I make you proud mother
I forgive you mother just love me
Who am I?
I'm Death, a tool to kill
I accept it.

I didn't know how long I was out for or what had happened after being hit with the power of the orb. I did know that I shouldn't still be alive after facing that power. My sight was blurry and the sky continued to bleed red, but Earth's sun shone among the orbs and the Planet Zayga. The ground started to shake beneath me. Realizing where I was, I attempted to get up. My body resisted my efforts. I felt an arm lift me from behind, and then I felt a swell of energy within as I stood up. Looking back, my eyes locked onto Cade's.

He studied me. "You died ... I gave some of my life to you. I don't know what's going on here but I'm staying." Cade looked ahead at Ominous, now approaching with his army. "We have to take him out together."

I looked down at what little remained of my armor, then I shook my head and stared at Cade. "Listen, I need you to leave. It's not safe here." My legs began to shake. "I got this."

Clearly shocked by my words, Cade said, "But—"

I raised my hand, stopping him from continuing further. "Win or lose, this is my fight."

I paused and took a deep breath. Even with the life force Cade had given me, my body still felt tired. I figured that the orb must have left a piece of itself within me, continuing to feed off whatever energy I had. My body had been damaged beyond healing. I overdid it, but I couldn't hold back now. This was war.

I raised a hand toward the orbs but nothing happened. I wasn't able to receive their energy. *Ominous ... he took away my Zaygaian powers. This is it.*

"He's coming to kill me," I whispered.

"We're stronger together," Cade said, then leaned in close. "Our dad would've wanted us to fight together."

I looked into his eyes and saw someone who was clueless. I wanted to tell him the truth. How I had set him up but ... I loved him and didn't want to hurt him—not right now.

"I love you, okay?" I said, saying those words ignited tears that I didn't know existed within me. I wiped them away as they trickled down my face. "A lot of things are not as they seem." I looked down, thinking back on that day and what I had done. Then I gazed up at Cade. "You were never meant to fall in love with Alice. I ... I put a spell on you—to make you fall in love with her in order to protect her at all costs. If the strongest being in the four universes was to protect the single most important person, then the North Universe could be saved even if the gods took all of the holy items. We would always have the upper hand."

Cade stared at me for a long moment then said, "What? ... what are you talking about? You never put a spell on me."

I said nothing, but shook my head and frowned.

He squinted his eyes at me, reading me. "Really? ... when?"

"The day your family was murdered. I set the spell and was given the green light to do so by Gabriel." I reached out a hand toward him. "Let me touch your forehead and I'll release you from the spell. I realize that I'm only protecting Alice and making you vulnerable to death."

Cade backed away. "With or without the spell, my love for Alice is real. If that was holding you back, then know I still love you ... despite your mistakes."

I wanted to say more but this wasn't the time. Putting a hand on the back of Cade's neck, I looked into his eyes. "I'll always love you. If I don't save Earth, then I want you to finish what I couldn't. Promise me that."

His confidence washed over his face. "I promise." He looked away. "I know what's expected of me but I can't block out the love I have for Alice. My love runs deep for her but I will save this universe and be in love with her at the same time. That, I promise."

I removed the Kurai from around my neck and placed it in Cade's hand. "Then be with her and make sure the gods don't capture her." I looked over my shoulder and saw that Ominous drew closer. "This war is lost and Gabriel is dead," I said to Cade, looking at him again. "Be the light our father intended you to be. Study what happened here and learn from it. Learn to defeat them. Now get!"

"I love you too, brother." Cade's light shone bright and then he disappeared.

Bracing myself, I turned and focused on Ominous. "You all are enemies to humanity. Every last breath in my body will be used to save the—"

"Save who? Look around," Ominous said, glancing to his right and then his left. "Swallow that pride. Blood will continue to shed as long as I'm here." He glanced over at Vera. "Get the prince of Avia and retrieve my father's soul inside that human ... Forward, all of you!"

The approaching army charged toward me. I tried to run forward, but my right knee buckled, causing me to fall. As I jumped back up using my one good leg, I was met with a spear flying through the air and striking me in the chest. At the same time, I felt another spear pierce my back. I cried out as I twisted quickly, knocking aside the spear that had hit me in the chest and seeing a god to my rear, holding a spear that had my blood on its tip. I elbowed the jaw of the god, then grabbed his head and snapped his neck. Sensing three more spears coming my way, I held on to the dead god and used his body as a shield to take the impact of the spears. Hearing approaching footsteps from behind, I dropped the dead god and yanked one of the spears from his body. As I turned around, I saw Vera running at me while extending her hand. I hurled the spear at her, but she easily blasted the spear away. Pulling another one of the spears from the dead god's body, I threw it at Vera's head. She ducked, and the spear split open the head of a god right behind her. Three small orbs then flew up to my body and hovered there. I felt them deplete nearly all my remaining strength, dropping me to my knees.

I knew I needed to get away, sensing gods coming toward me from every direction. Closing my eyes, I activated the powers given to me by Gabriel. I opened my eyes just in time to see a host of swords and spears pierce me. As I stifled a cry, Vera came forward and stood over me, a spear in each of her hands. She stuck one spear in my chest and the other in my stomach. I groaned quietly as the shock of the pain washed over me but kept my eyes set on her, not showing any emotion as other gods pushed through those around me. They pierced my body over and over again with their swords and spears. Steadying myself, I tapped into my inner self and awakened my true power—the power of a creator.

I then waited calmly as several gods grabbed me and lifted me to my knees, forcing me to face Ominous and the old gods as they stood before me. I also noticed Katakula nearby.

"This planet is too small for my kind," Ominous said. "I feel this wasteland seconds from crumbling at my feet. My gods will not fight this war."

Ominous kept his eyes on me as he talked to the old gods: "Name what you desire."

"The Kingdoms of the Guardians and the Afterworld ... Heaven and all of the Satavian territory," said one of the old gods, wearing a silver cape and a crown that showed the universe.

Ominous waved a hand and scoffed. "You might as well claim the entire North Universe."

"Yes," said the old god as he walked forward, shaking the ground with each step. He looked down at Ominous, grinning. "We will take the entire North Universe."

Ominous shook his head. "We find the kingdom of the Guardians and conquer it, then you keep the North Universe."

The old god stared at Ominous. "You fight the humans. Give me the coordinates of the Guardian kingdoms and victory will be ours."

Ominous crouched down, keeping his eyes on me. "I am Death and Zayga. With a single thought, I can absorb every single being, dead or alive, in this universe. Right now, there are hundreds of my planets in this universe that I've been secretly planting while my brothers fought." He pointed up to the sun. "The real war was out there not here. The stories of this great universe will fall on deaf ears."

Taking my chance, I allowed him access to secrets and knowledge within me.

After absorbing all of this information from me, Ominous stood up and turned to Katakula. "I just transmitted you the coordinates of where the humans are hiding and of the Afterworld. Retrieve the holy items, then find me on Planet Genesis." He turned to the old gods. "You also now have the location of the Afterworld. There you'll find the kingdom of the Guardians, and finding Heaven and the Satavian sector should be easy to find."

I watched as Ominous took his leave, flying up into the air. He stopped overhead, hovering as he looked down at his army. "Enslave the humans. Kill all the children and men, and then breed with the women. Once you're through with the women, dispose of them to the hounds." He glanced my way. "As for the boy ... kill him."

Vera nodded, then drew her sword and plunged it into my heart. Ignoring the pain, I fell to the ground even as an uproar of cheers filled the air. Everything went blurry, and I lost control of any movement.

I could barely see the gods as they began to leave, and then everything went quiet and dark for me.

18

I'm Ready - Angela

While sleeping, I fell prey to my nightmares. Everything became so real as my surroundings turned pitch black. A light from above showed my father running toward me in fear as Aerozayle trailed behind him. Dad's sweat and tears told me he didn't want to die—not before me, not when so many gods wanted me dead. Aerozayle aimed her hand at Dad's back. He was a few feet away from me when Aerozayle's scorching flames struck him. As he fell forward into my arms, I froze in shock as the flames shaped themselves into a living entity and then consumed every inch of his body while he screamed in pain. His body soon disintegrated, and then the flame entity faced me and latched onto my body. The flames blazed up into my eyes and began burning every inch of my skin. The cells in my body went into a frenzy, feeling like they wanted to burst as my blood boiled. I felt sure that I was dying. I blinked repeatedly, and for a moment I believed that this was my actual reality, but then the flames turned into a blinding light.

This great light turned everything orange, and I opened my eyes, waking up, and seeing that it was nearly light out. I sensed someone in the room with me. Without thinking, I visualized Black Beauty and leaped up as the armor appeared on me. Standing on my bed while aiming a pistol at the light that stood before me, I said, "You're dead."

Then I saw Clark there, on one knee with his head down. He raised an arm in my direction. Seeing him put me at ease. I hurried to the door and turned on the switch, then caught my breath when I noticed he was covered in blood.

I ran to Clark and looped his left arm around my neck, then helped him up so he could sit at the end of my bed.

"What happened?" I asked. "What's going on right now?"

Tears fell from Clark's eyes as he ran his hands through his hair. I could see the blood mixing into his hair. His hands shook, and his knees bounced. He looked up at me. "We need to move," he said. "I found Amentous, but it ended up being a fake."

"Right, Colvin told me." I backed away as Clark stood up, composing himself. "Galoriah and the rest will be looking for me. We can attack them then."

Clark shook his head. "This isn't the time, Florida. We need to evacuate the people of Everglades City."

We both looked toward the window as a bright light came from outside.

Clark walked over to the window. "That's Cade." Clark looked back at me. "He's well aware of what's going on. He's trying to teleport everyone on this planet to Planet Peace."

"Then I need to stay and continue fighting." I looked deep into Clark's eyes. "I need to do this. The real Amentous is out there even if he was put to stone by Gage. There's a chance he can be revived."

"Do you hear yourself?" Clark pointed out the window. "Everyone is going to die! This war is going to kill every single person on this planet and possibly in the Afterworld. The gods that are here, they won't let you touch Amentous. You somehow find the real Amentous and you kill him, you will ignite a war on both sides. Planet Peace will come to kill you, and we need them. Planet Zayga will come for you, and if they succeed, Planet Genesis will come for you. Right now we need to evac—"

Clark stopped talking, and his eyes shone blue before an immense energy erupted from his body, pressurizing the room. Everything began to cave in. The ceiling grew cracks and the bed started to crush itself to the floor.

Then Clark faced the window, clenching a fist as he shouted to the outside, "I'll kill you all, I promise! Come and get her!" He looked back at me. "Stand behind me!"

Clark faced the window again as a loud deep growl came from outside, sounding like a large wolf. Another light appeared beside Clark. Out of the light came Adumay.

"Leave here and save Florida," Adumay said to Clark. "I'll take care of the city of Closias."

Clark nodded and faced the window, then gripped my hand. The next second I found myself back at the safe house, where we were surrounded by GCP Protectors and Guardians.

"How did we get here?" I asked.

Looking around the place, it seemed clean and in order, like it had never been abandoned.

"I'm Miami," said a Protector as he came forward. He looked to be Hispanic and in his mid-thirties, with his hair in a ponytail. "I made sure every city in the state of Florida was cleared. All that's left is this city. What's your command?"

"We leave," I said, then faced Clark. "Get us and every person in Everglades City to safety. But I need to go back to Closias to get my father. He needs me."

"Adumay has it under control," Miami said. "He won't allow a single god to touch your father. You have to have faith in us."

I looked into his eyes and I wanted to trust him, but I had no trust in my heart to give. "Fine," I said. "We save Everglades City, then get my father if he isn't on Planet Peace already."

Clark nodded. "We're leaving now." He extended his arms and everything in the safe house began to shake as his eyes shone blue.

In the blink of an eye I found myself with thousands of other Protectors and Guardians outside in a grass field. Above us, hovered thousands of giant green aircraft that looked like shipping containers, but much bigger than anything I'd ever seen. The aircraft were big enough to hold skyscrapers and large statues atop their upper hull. Some of the aircraft landed, and I saw the various flags of the nations they'd apparently come from. Protectors and their Guardians protected their respective ships.

I looked around and saw a white marble wall. Atop the wall stood both Guardians and gods, shoulder to shoulder, all wearing the same golden armor and purple capes that looked like silk. I didn't see any weapons on them, and the Guardians' eyes were all different colors like Mandroid had told me.

"Why are gods and Guardians together?" I asked.

"This is Planet Peace," Clark answered. "Gods and Guardians live in unison, without quarrels, differences, and they share the same ideals."

"What ideals do they share?"

"That fighting between their universes isn't the answer. They oppose the ways of Gabriel and the gods. They choose no sides, and any outsider that steps onto this planet is not to battle any opposing forces. Planet Peace is the only place where fighting isn't allowed in all of the four universes." Clark walked forward. "They follow the rules of their king." He stopped and looked back. "Their king is Amentous, and even now they don't fight."

"Those things up there ..." I pointed up at the aircraft as more of them slowly descended to the ground. "These airships or aircraft ... they're holding people inside them?"

Clark nodded. "We call them Arks. Biggest ships known to exist. Made of Satavian metal. The only material that doesn't originate from any of the Guardian kingdoms."

Before I could ask more questions, a set of gates in the marble wall began to open. GCP leaders walked up to the gates with their Guardians. I followed behind Clark as he walked past Protectors that seemed scared to present themselves to whatever was behind those walls. Aligning myself with leaders and captains of the GCP while facing the wall, the gates opened to a female Guardian standing by her lonesome, with a city in the background. Her cool gray eyes observed all the inhabitants of Earth standing before her. Her olive skin emitted a light glow. Her silk garment was the same color as her eyes. It touched the grass that shone green. Her dress was a low cut V-neck, and the arms of her dress extended past her hands. A thin gold band sat atop her head. The headband held a diamond-shaped gem at the center of her forehead, with the gem changing colors. Something told me she was different, that she held some impor-tance and was not just some messenger.

"It's been a while since I last saw all of your faces, my brothers and sis-ters." She walked forward. "It almost seems like yesterday when I watched my mother form and shape you all into existence."

Clark stepped forward. "Armia, we need your assistance. Earth is on—"

She raised her hand to stop Clark from speaking. "As you know, Planet Peace doesn't affiliate itself in any conflict under any circumstances without Amentous's approval. Our laws are governed by his rule and Genesis." Armia glanced at all the GCP members from around Earth. "You come here without consulting me. To send eleven billion lives to this planet. Your urgent need for help shows your lack of respect."

"We just need a place to have the people of Earth stay as we devise a plan to take out Ominous and his army," Clark said.

"Gabriel has created a planet for cases like these."

"I know," Clark said. "But at this moment it is surrounded by—"

"Armia's word is law."

I saw a large Guardian fly down from the top of the wall, landing at Armia's side. He had shining wings and carried a long sword on his back. His long blond hair wisped in the air from the blowing wind. He looked directly at Clark and said, "Your plea falls on deaf ears. Take your lot somewhere or have them perish for your arrogance."

"Easy, Zodiah," Armia said as she looked over at the Guardian. "This is Clark, the Guardian who protected my mother and myself." She looked back at Clark. "His loyalty cannot be questioned despite where he stands now. I will not have a single human reside on my land. To do so is to dis-obey my brother's command."

Clark walked closer to Armia and pointed back to me. "Then have me train the daughter of Marie Proctor here—Angela Proctor in the flesh."

Armia moved around Clark to get a full view of me. Her eyes grew wide. "She's grown so fast!" She switched her attention back to Clark. "She stays here, then. She won't fight."

"You and I know that's not possible," Clark said. "Dark times are ahead and she needs to prepare for them. We'll train outside the gates to prevent harm to those living inside the city."

"Fine, but no harm comes to the girl." She looked at me and smiled. "Come here, child."

I walked up to Armia as the gods and Guardians from Planet Peace flew out to instruct the GCP to head to another planet.

I stood in front of Armia and observed her facial features. She was beautiful. "Yes?" I said.

"I am Armia." She held her hands together and didn't seem so strict anymore. "I knew your mother when she held you in her arms. She made me your godmother—to protect you and to guide you. You're welcome here anytime. Whatever you need, just call upon me."

"Thank you ... but I'm fine." I didn't know why my mother made Armia my godmother or how she came to meet Armia, but I wanted to know more. "If you can get the people of Earth safely to their destination, that would be nice."

"Of course." She smiled and looked up, and her eyes shone.

I looked back to see the field was now empty. Turning back to Armia, I said, "Where did everyone go?"

"They were transported to New Earth—I believe that's what the GCP calls it," Armia said. "I'll take my leave, so good-bye for now, Angela." Armia turned and headed back into the city with Zodiah.

Clark turned to me and then sat on the ground in a meditating position, crossing his legs.

I stared down at him. "We don't have time for this. I thought we were training."

Clark closed his eyes and placed his fists against each other. I watched as his eyes shone through his eyelids. "I'm the Guardian of meditation," he said. "If you want to get stronger, this will be the quickest way. Quickly imitate my meditation position."

"Meditating? No, I need to get stronger now. I need to protect my father."

"You want to help your father?" Clark spoke in a calm voice while his eyes were closed. "Then you have to follow instructions and trust me."

I stared down at him and realized this was the only way to get back at the gods. If this was the Guardian my mother trusted, then I couldn't go wrong. "Alright," I said, then sat on the floor across Clark and crossed my legs, placing my fists against each other like he did.

I closed my eyes and waited for what felt like hours but was only minutes. My body began to ache as I stayed in the same position for so long. My breathing grew slower and then my body became numb. I couldn't hear anything. Everything in the outside world was nonexistent at this point. It was as if my body was dead but my soul was trapped inside. My five senses slowly died down. The darkness from closing my eyes became pitch black, and I was deaf to even my own breathing. I couldn't feel my knuckles touching each other, my nose had no sense of smell, and it was impossible for me to move. When I felt as if I was drowning into a dark dream, I suddenly heard a loud crack, like someone tried to break a piece of glass. I got up and opened my eyes to everything being black. I knew I wasn't outside the gates on Planet Peace anymore. A large screen floated in the air, showing memories from my life. I saw myself laughing at my fifth birthday party ... my mom picked me up from the supermarket. I saw bad memories: the funeral, being left alone, the embarrassment as a child with Billy. Things I'd forgotten: memories of how close Colvin, Alice, and I had been. Then everything turned bright white. The screen disappeared, and Clark appeared in front of me. He wore ivory-colored armor from neck to toe.

"This is where I trained all of my previous Protectors," he said.

"Where are we?" I asked as I looked around and saw nothing but white that stretched for miles. "I saw memories that I ..." I stared down at the ground as more memories of the past came to me.

"You essentially died. It's the reason why everything in your body stopped working. It's why you saw those memories. A living being can't be here—only spirits and Guardians."

"And about this place?"

"This is one of the Afterworld's realms. But onto more important matters: I created this place; that is what makes me different from other Guardians. What makes this place so special is that the time is based on the Afterworld's time. But at least we'll be together."

"Wait—pause. How long am I here for?"

"Well, in the Afterworld a day on Earth is a hundred thousand years here, so you—"

"Shut up shut up shut up! Clark, I'm not spending a thousand years here!"

Clark gave a nervous laugh. "Technically we'll be spending a couple centuries here—"

"What? Are you—"

"But it's only a few minutes on Earth, maybe a few seconds on Earth if you're good. My job is to make sure you're ready for the worst to come. You'll be facing gods who have been fighting for centuries. They're fighting for the revival of Genesis and their existence. They're fighting with a real purpose, which makes them more dangerous." Clark began stretching. "Is there a better way to learn a lot in a small amount of time?"

I stared at Clark. "Don't you think it would have been important to tell me the time I'd be spending here before you told me to meditate?"

"Nope, and don't get so dramatic. You won't get hungry or tired here, and you won't miss your family or friends. So any more questions before we begin?"

"Yeah ... fighting Galoriah, it was like his skin was impenetrable. I have super strength but it's impossible to hurt him, so how does that work? And how am I supposed to train without Black Beauty on?"

"You have to believe ... The more faith you have in your punch, the more power you'll have. And there's no need for your combat suit. Here you'll be the same as if you had the suit on. Your memory is also enhanced. Everything you learn will be remembered. Anything else?"

"Nope, let's get started."

Clark began teaching me new fighting moves. He taught me a defense technique for when an opponent would throw a right hook. I would give a low right kick to that person's leg. It was somewhat of a defense-fighting style without dodging or blocking. I spent a hundred years learning to perfect every countermove that existed. Then he taught me to fight with movement. He told me the best fighters knew how to move quickly and precisely without thinking, that it was instinct. In Clark's world anything he said or imagined became tangible. So part of my training was becoming aware and learning how to use the different types of weaponry the gods wielded, and knowing what armor they wore for certain occasions. With these perks I learned to use submission maneuvers, quick takedowns, and pressure points.

Then with a snap of his fingers Clark turned his place of meditation to a deserted rocky planet with a red sun shining down on us.

"What is this place?" I asked.

"This was a planet used for war. This was where the second great war took place between the GCP and the gods. This was where your grandmother was killed and it's what changed your mother." Clark turned and looked up at the red sun. "That is what gives energy to millions of planets that belong to the gods. Genesis created it in case he ever died. It symbolizes his heart and his divine power—an everlasting energy source that makes the gods natural-born leaders."

I stared up at the red sun. "Genesis created that?"

"He can do more that we don't even know. I never had the honor to fight him. But he's the only ancient god to have power to last this long. His power lies in that sun. He made himself weaker when he created that sun to protect the super gods and the gods. He wasn't just looked upon as a king but as a Creator. He was the only one who was deemed worthy to talk to the South Creator."

I continued to look around and saw Guardian weapons and flags from different countries on Earth. The ground was unbalanced, with craters from fighting between Protectors and gods.

"This isn't the actual planet," Clark said. "It's an exact replica. I want to teach you how to use stealth in certain situations if we were to ever go to war."

"War ..." I couldn't imagine myself fighting in an all-out war with Colvin by my side. How many gods and GCP members would lay down their lives for items that could mean the end of either of our universes?

So we practiced stealth maneuvers, and Clark taught me war tactics and moves I could use if we were ever ambushed by a large group of gods. All this led to the second most important thing, which was knowing what to use. Clark would use various types of fighting moves, and it was my job to know whether to counter or dodge and to know which move was best to use at that moment. I spent decades perfecting that course of training.

In my last stage of training, we went back to the original realm, where everything was white. I spent two hundred years perfecting a fighting style known as "Fast pace," only used by ancient gods—like Amentous—or powerful Guardians, like Clark, who had perfected it himself. It did not mean fighting fast, but rather letting the body fight and react to any attack without stopping or thinking about what to do next, as if everything is automatic, predicting an opponent's next three moves at every step. After I perfected this style, I then had to do it blindfolded. Then Clark taught me to block and deflect any energy blast coming my way or at any bystanders, and in doing this I had to remain quiet and totally focused.

After the final training session, Clark grew in height and then sat on the ground.

Feeling tired, I sat down beside him. "Why grow in size?"

"The usual height for an Elyzian is eight feet when we're not in the presence of humans," he replied.

I nodded. "Tell me more about your race. Washington said something about Habaranians and Elyzians. Mandroid showed me Guardians with different eye colors. Wondered why I never came across those kinds of Guardians."

"We're Guardians, as you're human. But there are different kinds of Guardians. It's what you humans call subspecies. Each planet is considered a kingdom, and Guardians have a distinct eye color that coincides with the color of their kingdom. Six of the seven kingdoms surround the Afterworld and create two force fields. One is an outer force field to protect the seven planets and the second force field protects the Afterworld. The seventh planet is ahead of the six planets and monitors Earth."

Clark looked sad for a bit then glared ahead and his blue eyes shone.

A figure of himself stood in front of us. "Blue-eyed Guardians like myself are known to be great in combat, wise in decision making, and perfect in almost everything. My planet is called Elyza. I'm one of the oldest Elyzians. To the outsiders, they call it Blue Kingdom because our planet shines blue from space. Guardians with orange eyes are called 'Hadimites."

Clark summoned another Guardian, this time the Guardian had jewelry all over its arm and head. This Guardian had shiny skin like an Elyzian but had three halos; each one wider than the other.

"What you see before you is an image of a Hadimite. Hadimites come from Planet Hadi, otherwise known as the Orange Kingdom. They create the laws and are known to be wise and they grow up to be advisors. They oversee all operations in the seven kingdoms and in the Afterworld. The three halos you see above their head is their crown and grants them three lives, it's not an indication that they're dead. They're the wealthiest Guardians in the seven kingdoms. They wear excessive jewelry and precious stones to show dominance."

I looked over at Clark. "They're the only Guardians that have three lives?"

"Yes, the three halos also represent the sacred meaning of three. Elohim, our creator, placed three halos on the Hadimites to show complete and perfection. It shows his three elite creations: Angels, Guardians, and Satavians. There's Power, Dominion, and wisdom in each halo. Power beyond anyone comprehension lies within their halos and it's used as a coat of rings for protection when in battle. Elyzians are physical beings but Hadimites can be physical or spiritual and live in the Afterworld if they please."

Next to the Hadimites was a Guardian that looked like a human except his eyes were neon green. His left eye was dark green and his right eye was light green.

"These Guardians are called Evites from Planet Eva. They're the workers and builders of the seven Kingdoms. This kingdom is the defense planet of the seven kingdoms, and most importantly it produces the force field that protects the Afterworld. Amongst the other Guardians they're called the Misfits because of the treachery Eva, their ancestor committed. But we the Elyzians call them the essential Guardians."

"What was the treachery?"

"Too much history. You'll soon find out the culture of the Guardians sooner than you think."

A gray-eyed Guardian appeared next to the Evite. It was tall and had eight wings. I stood in its presence. Each wing showed a visual of fire, lightning, pulse waves, rocks, black holes, space, and one of them just shined bright. "Woah, what is that it looks amazing."

"What you're looking at is a Catorian, born from planet Catori. Catorians are the Guardians for the people in the Afterworld. They have eight different sets of abilities which you see showcased on their wings."

I turned back to say "Guardians in the Afterworld similar to the Guardians on Earth!"

"Right, but they aren't limited to deceased GCP members. They only protect the souls in the Afterworld. The male Catori you see in front of you have dark gray eyes. The female Catorian has silver-like color eyes. They also enforce the rules and laws the Hadimites place for the Guardians and humans in the Afterworld. Like the police on Earth, the Catorians maintain order and they have the largest planet. The prison is located on their planet for wicked Guardians and bad people in the Afterworld."

"What else do they do?" I walked closer observing the Catorian.

"Well, they're spirits and can't be physically touched. Everyone on the planet is considered siblings so they don't mate with each other or with any Guardian. They can be very uptight and serious. It's how they were created. Catori or the Gray Kingdom is a planet most never enter; it's said it's meant for outsiders to never leave."

Three other Guardians appeared next to the Catorian. I walked over to see a pink eyed Guardian. She was beautiful and her skin sparkled. Her brown skin was flawless and looked smooth.

Clark got up and stood by me. "She's an Althean from Althea. Pink-eyed Guardians are our caretakers and healers. It holds the most advanced hospitals in the four universes. She has two arms now but when an

Althean goes into deep healing for someone she can summon two extra pairs of arms. Having six arms she'll use each pair to heal the body, soul, and spirit. They are kind and meek. They can be spirit for a limited time and when they're in their spirit state their entire eyes turn pink. Their healing doesn't just stop physical harm but also mental and all sorts of damage."

We continued walking to the second to last Guardian who had dark purple eyes. They looked like the Elyzians.

"Now, purple-eyed Guardians are our peacemakers and messengers. Their purpose is to travel the four universes and send messages and create peace treaties. They originate from Airini. Airinians are middle class and some don't mind living low. They can turn into spirit beings to deliver messages. There are other Airinians who become warriors or advisors and can adapt to any role to maintain peace. It's rare to find one living in a luxury lifestyle like the Hadimites. They're fast learners and oftentimes viewed as soft or passive. The Purple Kingdom holds our history and our greatest secrets."

I stood toe to toe with the last Guardian with white hair and white eyes. "They must be special."

Clark smiled at the replica of the Guardian with white eyes. "Habaranians are the last Guardians to be created out of the seven kingdoms. Planet Haba is their home planet but they live on all planets. They are privileged and loved by everyone. They are entertainers and warriors. Their job is to Guard the entire North Universe. It's why Washington talked to the Elyzians and Habaranians. They supply aid in the East and the West but they're not spiritual. Could be lazy at times and live a regular life."

"Okay, interesting ... but why go by your eye color? What if someone is born a certain way and doesn't want to be what he or she was born with?"

"We are a superior race born to perfection. There are no mistakes in fertility. Going by eye color easily tells us what each one is destined to be. That way you can focus on your destined craft. This makes you flawless."

"They said you could've been an Elder. Why did you want to work in the GCP?"

"Sitting around a large table making rules and talking about war and security isn't what I like to do. I'm a warrior. I was offered the chance to be an Elder because I'm one of the oldest remaining Guardians. I'm a first-generation Guardian."

"What does that mean?"

"It means I have no parents. I was created by the North Creator. Almost every other first-generation is dead. Actually, I should tell you about our history."

"Well, we are stuck here for centuries." I looked around at the whiteness that stretched on for an eternity.

Clark smiled, then said, "The first Guardian to be created was a female Guardian. It's the reason why they are valued higher and treated with the highest respect. Now I know they told you the Afterworld is a planet. But it's technically not. It's more of a fortress where humans go after death. As I already said, the Afterworld is surrounded by seven Guardian planets. Each planet contains about a trillion Guardians. The Afterworld is the most sought-out planet in the whole universe because of what it holds inside. Our history then started with the first Guardian, whom we've always called 'Mother' but to outsiders was known as Maresa. She didn't live long. She created our seven planets alone and then took control of them. She later created seven female Guardians. The first, Hadi then in order Elyza, Catori, Althea, Airini, Eva, and Haba. They held their own kingdom and in them like a vineyard they produced good fruit. Descendants that multiplied to trillions. The Angels had been on the brink of a universal war. God created a race to protect the holy items against the super gods or any outside force that posed a threat. It's why we're called Guardians. Mother would always negotiate with the super gods' leader and founder, Genesis. What we didn't know was that they had a secret relationship. It was only later that we found out, when she gave birth to Genesis's child, Amentous."

"What? Amentous is half-Guardian?"

"He is indeed half-Guardian. You could've seen it in the real Amentous's eyes. We Guardians have every colored eye in the spectrum, but you can identify us by the neon colors. Neon green, blue, purple ... you name it, if it's neon based, it's a Guardian. Amentous has neon gold. It's why he's the greatest threat. There's no GCP base he can't enter. He can even enter the Afterworld without being detected as an outsider. To us he's royal blood because Maresa is his mother."

"What happened to Maresa—Mother?"

"Once Gabriel was left to watch the North Universe and he found out about this pregnancy, he charged her with treason and took her life. He divided her power and created Elder Guardians amongst us so that a sole individual wouldn't go corrupt and retain any secrets."

"You know a lot about your history. Why didn't they tell us this at orientation? And no one ever revolted?"

Clark looked down. "Ever heard of unnecessary information? Armia didn't want to see Guardians fighting each other because of any disputes. It's why Planet Peace was created. The Evites created that planet with Armia. The other Kingdoms saw the Evites as traitors and lost everything."

I could see the hurt in Clark's eyes as he took a long pause before talking again.

"Our sole purpose is to serve humanity," he went on. "To grow up and to possibly die guarding the Protectors of the GCP."

"Not to sound negative but that doesn't sound like much of a life to live. I mean, I haven't been living as long as you, but for the past ten years all I did was serve—just following orders from my adoptive parents."

"Yes, and that's the reason I urge you to be different from your predecessors." Clark looked into my eyes. "Become the bridge of peace so that children from our home planets can actually live a life worth living. I don't want you to be just the peacemaker between two universes, but rather be a hero for gods, humans, and Guardians alike. There's more to you than you know. Your mother dedicated her life to the GCP and nothing came before it—except for one person, and that was you. She told me if there's anyone who can make a change, it would be—" Clark cut his words short and got up, looking ahead. "Cade failed to transport his city home. The force field will break, so we need to head back."

"What? But ... my dad!" I jumped up. "I'm ready. Let's go!"

Everything turned bright white, forcing me to close my eyes. When I opened them again, I saw the outside gates of Planet Peace.

I thought of Black Beauty and felt the armor cover me. "What exactly is going on?" I asked.

Clark's eyes shined again. "An invasion ... This is bad."

At that Clark turned to me and teleported us away. We arrived at the front entrance of a building that looked like an open-air stadium or arena.

I looked around and everything looked exactly like Earth, but I knew it couldn't be. "We need to head back home, not New Earth," I said.

Clark said nothing, but hurried toward the entrance. "We need permission to go to Earth now. Miami has already transported all of your state's civilians. You have no reason to go back unless asked by New York." He looked up at the sky. "Ominous and his army will make their way here—sooner than we expect."

We walked inside and through the halls, hearing Jerusalem's voice by way of the speakers along the way. Farther along in the halls I saw GCP members sitting on the floor, with many covering their faces with their hands. Some were crying and others looked zoned out.

Clark opened a door that led into what appeared to be an arena, and we headed up the stairs. As we walked, I saw banners of various continents hanging on the sectioned wall of the arena. Under each banner sat GCP members who represented the countries and states/provinces located there. I looked over at the banner for North America. I didn't see Colvin or Cade.

In the center of the arena sat one table and a chair, occupied by Jerusalem.

He picked up a microphone and began to speak again: "Ninety-five percent of Africa died on that field. They fought their best and lost against the greatest army in the four universes. The United Kingdom almost met defeat but the gods took mercy and left." Jerusalem looked around at everyone. "Earth is on the brink of destruction and the remaining humans left there are in the city of Closias. There lies the enemy, so who will go to save those who remain?"

An Indian man stood up, wearing a burgundy kurta. He picked up the microphone from that section's table, then waited a few seconds until the mic went red, indicating it was live. "Let's look at the reality of this," the man said. "Gabriel is dead, and survivors from the battle saw it with their own eyes. All of the greatest Protectors around the world took part in that battle and died. We are all that's left. Asia will not take part in this plan to help the city of Closias."

Jerusalem leaned forward and looked around the arena. "What say the rest of you? Who will extend a hand for New York and his brother?"

"Florida!" came a voice from behind me.

I turned to see a boy running up to me. I figured he had to be one of the communicators at the GCP US headquarters. He stopped and caught his breath. "The gods have broken through the barrier and are looking for you. Adumay tried to protect your father but he couldn't. Aerozayle is going after your father."

Those words were like an anchor to my heart. I knew that anything could've happened to my dad. He was all I had left, and I didn't want to lose him. My dad had already lost too much to be facing any other emotionally or physically harmful situations.

Clark turned to me, appearing concerned. "He's probably still alive." He looked at the boy. "Do you know her father's exact location?"

"Yes. Adumay teleported him to the city's high school, and that's also where Cade is. They plan to teleport everyone in the city at once in one location."

I looked back around the arena. Everyone was quiet as Jerusalem waited for someone to volunteer to help those in Closias. But no one stood or raised their hand.

I walked toward the stairway that led down to the arena floor, but Clark grabbed my arm. He shook his head. "This war ..." he said. "What was out there, not a lot of people could survive it."

Pulling my arm away, I shot a stern look at Clark. "I'm guessing they did this to me when Lisa and I were running for our lives—when Lisa was frightened and fought to save me. My friends and family are still on Earth. I won't stay here only to hear that they died." I headed down the steep stairs to the center of the arena floor where all eyes were on me. "Florida will aid the people trapped on Earth." I projected my voice loud enough for Jerusalem and everyone nearby to hear me.

"I'm afraid that isn't your call." Jerusalem spoke into the mic.

He just stared at me as I stood there before him and the leaders of the GCP present.

"What?" I said, "You asked for Protectors who'll help, so here I am."

I glanced around and saw that everyone was staring at me now. Then I returned my attention to Jerusalem.

"Washington gave me orders to not allow the Protectors and Guardians of North America to assist. He will return and we can discuss this, but for right now, you will wait. That's final."

"With all due respect, sir," I said, "if staying here and taking orders despite it being wrong, then I don't want to be a part of any of this." I turned and headed toward the exit.

Jerusalem cleared his throat. I stopped and looked back just as he stood up from his chair. "Rebellion," he said. "That's something I won't tolerate. You will listen or you'll find yourself before me and your superiors for your actions."

Just standing there, knowing my father might still be alive, didn't sit well with me. It just wasn't in my character to leave someone I love out to die. "I'm done with this," I said to myself.

I continued walking forward across the arena floor, and two Guardians approached me. One of them stood around eight feet tall, and his hands were folded in front of him. His eyes shone blue, and I noted that he was well built, with a short haircut.

"You're not permitted to leave this—" he said, cutting his words short as he looked up.

I saw that every other Guardian in the arena also was looking up.

"They're here ... the gods," said the Guardian in front of me.

I walked past all of them as a commotion arose among the Protectors, Guardians, and leaders.

Clark followed behind me, awaiting my orders. "Angela," he said, "if we do this, there's no going back. The gods are outside, and if we leave, it could mean death. You're a leader. They will notice."

"Screw the GCP," I said. "I fight for the people I love." I looked up and saw red planets hovering above us.

Clark got in front of me. "Listen, I failed with your mother and—"

"You won't fail now. I'm not my mother. I'm Angela Lopez, and my father and my friends need me. Transport me to Closias High School now."

Frowning, Clark looked up at the planets above us, then reached out to lay his hand on my shoulder—and we were gone.

19

My Last Battle - Angela

Clark and I arrived in the middle of the gym, and I could feel the floor begin to shake. Giving me a quick glance and saying he needed to check the situation outside, Clark ran toward one of the doors.

"Aerozayle!" I yelled, looking around. My eyes searched throughout the crowded bleachers of students, who looked to have mixed reactions at seeing us—with some no doubt wondering how the hell I'd appeared out of thin air, while others seemed like they couldn't take their eyes off of Black Beauty. "Aerozayle!" I shouted again.

Aerozayle walked out from under the left side of the bleachers, picking at her nails. "When I sensed that your father was home by his lonesome, I was tempted to repay him a visit." She turned toward the students. "Listen, you diseased species, kill the woman standing before you now."

The students looked at each other, confused, but then their pupils enlarged. They all stood in unison and came pouring down to the gym floor, circling around me.

"Surrounding me with humans?" I said, "You think I won't kill them to get to you?" I kept my eyes focused on Aerozayle while the sound of hurrying footsteps continued to fill the air as more of her newly made slaves piled onto the gym floor around me.

Aerozayle said nothing, but watched as her minions finished getting into position, ready for her next order.

I looked around at the students, carefully planning my next five moves.

Aerozayle grinned as she turned her green eyes on me. "Go," she ordered.

At her command the students charged. I punched the air, causing enough wind shear to knock everyone in front of me off their feet. They got up from the floor like they were robots. They didn't seem to feel a thing, and there was no expression on their faces. But then a wave of white light passed through the gym, causing them all to fall down, unconscious.

Then I saw Clark appear at the exit doors behind Aerozayle. His eyes shone bright blue as he said, "This planet is going to blow. Get your father and head back to New Earth!" he shouted, then disappeared along with all the students.

I kept my focus on Aerozayle, but said nothing.

Aerozayle shrugged. "Doesn't matter. You're—"

"Shut up!"

I leaped at Aerozayle, kicking her in the chest. As Aerozayle's body bounced off the wall behind her, I teleported right in front of her and began throwing jabs at her face. Each punch sent her back against the wall again. Finally, she managed to dodge one of my blows, and she threw her first punch. But I jumped back and avoided her punch, then delivered a hard uppercut to her stomach, lifting her off the floor and sending her up into the air. Teleporting above Aerozayle, I elbowed her in the back of the head, sending her back to the floor.

As her body collided with the floor, I followed up with a hard kick to her temple. Reacting to the kick, she got up and retreated to create distance between us, but I charged forward, grabbed her leg, and body-slammed her over my head, destroying that part of the floor. She managed to kick me in the face, sending me onto my back. Ignoring the pain, I jumped up and flew forward, grabbing her hair, not wanting to give her any time or space to throw her fire.

She held onto my hands and bent her legs, then burned my knuckles, forcing me to release my grip. She twisted and hurled me into the bleachers. She flew toward me. I slammed my fist against the bleachers in rage and leaped forward at her. I was closing in on her fast when I attempted a roundhouse kick. She dipped down and spun around, causing me to miss. Slowing down time while in midair, I reached for the pistol in my shoulder holster, even as Aerozayle grinned at me. Time resumed, and before I could get a shot off, she grabbed me by the throat and threw me across the gym, all the way into the locker room. I smashed into a wall and then a set of lockers. I got up on shaky legs, my body screaming in pain as I brushed debris off me. My body screamed for mercy as I stood there.

"You're hurt, aren't you?" Aerozayle said as she walked into the locker room.

Before I could do anything, she threw black fire from her hands. I jumped behind some lockers that still stood, but my knees buckled and I fell hard to the floor.

"Stop hiding, daughter of Marie. You're the one who's supposed to change everything. But you're going to die just like your mother and her ancestors. Let me tell you the truth before I send you to the Afterworld. Your mother wasn't what you thought she was. She was a whore. She slept with a god. In fact, it was the same god who killed your grandmother and your relatives."

I clenched my jaw, trying to find the strength to get up and kill her.

"You'll soon meet your delusional, soft-hearted father too." She laughed. "He couldn't save his own family and soon he won't save his country."

"Shut up! Shut up!"

I got up and stood across from Aerozayle.

She smiled at me. "Good," she said. "That's how I like it. Die with some dignity." She nodded toward the doorway, then walked backward, creating space between the two of us.

My knees finally felt mostly healed, and so I started to run toward her just as she stepped into the gym. Aerozayle took to the air, throwing five black fireballs at me. I could feel the scorching heat coming my way. I dodged the first fireball, then ducked beneath the second one. Slowing down time, I hopped over another. Time resumed and I spun around another fireball, then slid beneath the last one. Hovering overhead, Aerozayle looked down as I tried to stand. She flew at me, grabbing my pistol from my shoulder holster and aiming it at my head.

My breath caught, waiting for the shot. But when she pulled the trigger, nothing happened.

"What?" Aerozayle shouted.

When she looked down at the weapon, I threw an uppercut to her chin, snapping her head back. I grabbed her hair before she fell to the floor, kneed her in the face, propelling her back into the wall. Before Aerozayle could do anything else, I dashed to her and punched her sternum. The loud crack told me I'd broken it. I karate-chopped her neck, then grabbed her by the throat and yanked her forward, dislocating some of the small bones there. Aerozayle fell to the floor and attempted to speak but failed. I watched as she tried to suck in oxygen.

I knelt down in front of her. "Breathe," I said. Then I placed my right hand on her neck and squeezed the pressure points beneath her jawline. She tried to break free of my grasp but was clearly in too much pain.

"It hurts, doesn't it?" I said, "Imagine how Billy or Lisa felt, or all those innocent people in my state." I squeezed harder, using my super strength to hold her in place as she tried to move back. I pushed her down to the floor, holding her still. "My father—where is he?"

As Aerozayle opened her mouth, some blood trickled out and she smiled. "No," she said.

I thought of the safe house and who was there. *"Mandroid,"* I mindspoke. *"I need her to squeal. Make that happen."*

"Do I have your permission to appear in plain sight?" came his reply.

I looked into Aerozayle's eyes. *"You do."*

Mandroid appeared by my side and looked down at Aerozayle. "Not in the best shape, I see." He looked over to me and handed me a case. "These daggers pack quite a punch. I suggest you create some distance once you've driven the blades into your opponent."

Using one hand to keep Aerozayle in place, I grabbed the case with my other hand and nodded at Mandroid. "Find my father, then you're good to go."

Seeing Mandroid take his leave, I opened the case and found two daggers within. The steel blades were blue, and the handles were black. I took one of the daggers and jammed it into Aerozayle's shoulder, then shoved the other one into her back. I got up and walked off, smiling.

I could hear Aerozayle scrambling to get up. "You ... think I'm going to ... die from an attack like that!"

I kept walking, smiling again when I heard her scream as lightning from the daggers now electrifying her body. I could see the gym walls in front of me reflecting the blue lightning burning Aerozayle as she screamed in pain.

Turning back, I saw what looked like a burnt statue propped against the far wall. I pulled out my pistol from the leg holster, and the GCP rules came to mind. "Who cares?" I said to myself. Pulling the trigger, I sent a bullet to Aerozayle's head, causing her to crumble to dust.

I walked out of the gym into a connecting hallway and found a bunch of students still inside the building, rushing around and shouting something about hoping the place wouldn't collapse on them after all the explosions. I knew the so-called explosions had come from my battle with Aerozayle, and I started to tell everyone to calm down, but then a group of security guards shoved past me, calling for backup because a "crazy man" was terrorizing the students.

What's going on? I wondered ... and then I saw him: Lucius.

When the security guards got to Lucius, he hurled them back through the air. Once everyone saw what he could do, the students yelled and turned to run in my direction, screaming for help.

Lucius saw me and shouted, "You're dead!"

I saw that he wore no shirt, just a long raincoat, leather pants, and boots—all black. I noticed that the veins in his forehead were visible, and his face was turning brighter red.

The three guards began screaming, holding their heads as if someone was pushing a drill to their temple. Their screams of agony turn to laughter. Their hair turned blond, and their physiques leaned down to Lucius's size. All of them had become replicas of Lucius. Then some of the students also turned into his clones.

Other students began crying out, not knowing what was going on. Then I saw Alice in the crowd. As several students around her began to shake and transform into copies of Lucius, I yelled to her, "Alice, get away!" I ran toward her, shoving students out of the way.

"No!" came Cade's voice. "Florida, stand back!"

I turned and saw Cade running in my direction. He pointed overhead. Looking that way, I saw the real Lucius flying toward me, coming so fast that the lockers blew apart as he sped past them. Above Lucius, running on the ceiling, were two of his clones. My eyes went to Alice as a group of clones held her against a nearby wall, with one of them choking her. They didn't attack her like they did the rest of the students; they clearly wanted to kill her slowly.

"Leave her alone!" I shouted.

The clones running on the ceiling shot massive energy blasts at me from their hands. I continued to run forward and dived in between the blasts, feeling their immense heat. I tucked and rolled, then my ears as the blasts impacted. Nearly half the school collapsed into rubble. Everything behind me was gone. The ground began to move, and I turned back to see the hallway leaning to the right. Classroom doors flew open and desks fell out into the hall. The fluorescent light tubes went out and exploded. I could hear the screams of trapped students underground and the scent of smoke filled the air.

One clone above me jumped down at me, fist-first. I teleported to his right and gave him a kick to the ribs. Twisting around, I elbowed the throat of the clone behind me. As he stumbled back, I teleported to him, grabbing his throat before pointing my gun in between his eyes and pulling the trigger. As the body hit the ground, it changed form into a dead student. I felt sad but knew I didn't have time to grieve.

The other clone on the ceiling flew down at me, yelling. I teleported in front of him and gave him a right cross to the face, then ducked his hook and kneed him in the gut before landing another punch, this time to his jaw. I grabbed him by his jacket, then shot him in the heart with my pistol. The clone fell dead into the debris and transformed back into the lifeless body of a student.

Now Lucius stormed toward me. I teleported just above and in front of him, slamming my knee into the bridge of his nose. He flew back from the impact, tearing up the hallway as his body crashed and skidded. The remainder of the school building shook and then the floor opened.

"Angela!"

Alice's pained shout had me spinning around. I saw her eyes turning red and her face turning blue as two clones held her in place while another continued to choke her.

Then I noticed movement to the left of Alice, and a second later both Colvin and Cade rose up from out of the debris, covered in dust and looking like they'd been hurt.

"Alice!" Cade yelled. His eyes widened and shone white as he flew past me.

The three clones stopped their attack on Alice and charged at Cade. The first clone swung and Cade ducked, launching an arrow at that clone's head. The arrow went right through the first clone's head and then changed direction to pierce the second clone in an eye, dropping both of the clones. The last clone teleported to the side, dodging the weaving arrow, and it shot an energy blast at Cade. But Cade deflected it with his bow, causing more of the school to collapse. Ignoring the loud crashing, the clone followed up with a punch that Cade blocked. Cade gave the clone a kick to the knee, then followed with an uppercut. As the clone stumbled and tried to keep its balance, Cade jumped back and sent an arrow into its Adam's apple, dropping it to the floor.

Cade teleported to where Alice had collapsed against a pile of rubble. He knelt before her and said, "Are you hurt?"

"M-My ... th-throat." Tears fell from Alice's cheeks. I could see how blue her face was even from across the hallway.

"Shhh, it's okay." Cade's hands shone white, then he carefully placed his fingers around her neck. "Everything is going to be alright. I'm healing you."

Alice's skin color returned to normal before Cade wiped her tears away with his thumbs. "Can you walk?" he asked.

She wrapped her arms around Cade's neck and buried her face in his shoulder. Cade lifted her off the ground and faced me.

"Your father is outside," he said. "Go out there if you want to save him. Any injuries he had from Aerozayle are gone; I made sure of it."

Relief swept over my body. "Thank you."

A bright blue light came from the middle of the hallway, and I saw Adumay appear there. Covered in blood, he looked at Cade and shouted, "Leave with Alice now!" Then Adumay flew to me. "Florida, tell everyone to evacuate to the football stadium now—you lead them. I got it from here." He grabbed hold of my arms. "Do you understand?"

"But Alice—"

"Cade will protect her. Right now there's about three thousand clueless kids outside, along with some staff. You can save them. Lead them to the football stadium. It's safer there, and then I can start transporting everyone off of Earth, but right now they're still in harm's way."

Cade nodded at us, then flew off with Alice.

Lucius stumbled out from beneath a collapsed wall. "Every human in this city will die!" he said, then took a knee, clearly not in the best shape.

I looked at Adumay and asked, "You're going to take him on with students still trapped inside the building?"

"I got it," He said. "Clark should be here any second. They're sending the remaining survivors out of the school, so the rest is up to you, now go."

Lucius wiped rubble off his jacket and began to laugh. "You don't know what you got yourself into, little girl," he said to me. "Leave now like he said. I'll come after you."

I eyed him, then flew up and out of the school, leaving Lucius to Adumay. When I reached the parking lot, I could see the terror in the students' eyes. Girls cried while trying to comfort each other, and boys were shouting about what they saw. Other students were on their phones, recording the school. As the red planets above began to shine, some fell to the ground.

One girl began to panic, looking around. "Oh my God, where's my sister?" She fell to her knees and cried.

"Yo, what's going on?" said one boy, pointing as one of the remaining walls of the school began to tilt to the side.

Another boy pulled out his cell phone and started recording the scene. "Everything is going to hell!"

I heard energy blasts from inside the school, and students were still screaming.

I flew up high enough to have a good view of everyone. "Listen up!" I shouted. "If you want to live, follow me to the football stadium!"

One girl pointed in my direction. "Look, that man is coming our way!"

The entire crowd of teenagers started yelling and spreading out.

I looked down and spotted a clone of Lucius coming their way. I flew down and threw a kick to his neck, sending him flipping over a car. The clone scrambled to his feet and then kicked the damaged car in my direction. I ran forward and leaped over the car, then threw two Guardian knives at the clone's chest, but he swayed out of the way. I drew in close and the clone swung at me. I ducked, grabbed his arm, broke his elbow, then reached up and snapped his neck before throwing him at the same car. As he flew through the air toward the car, I used my pistol to shoot the vehicle multiple times, causing it to explode into flames, consuming the clone.

All the students around me froze in awe.

I looked at them. "If you want to live, go to the football stadium! You'll be safe there."

Wasting no time, everyone swarmed inside the stadium. I looked around, scanning the area for more clones. *How long does it take for Adumay to teleport the people of this city to New Earth ... and where's my father?*

Once everyone was inside, I closed all the gates to the stadium. It was crowded, and everyone talked over each other. I flew above the crowd and hovered over all three thousand students and staff. "All of you need to shut up!" I shouted. "Right now, there's more of those things outside wanting to kill more humans. I can't protect all of you, so again ... shut up!"

"No!" one teacher yelled. He walked toward me, with several students following behind him. "You need to tell us what's happening. Who was that?"

"That person you saw was a god," I replied. "He wants me dead, and all of humanity."

"Gods? They aren't real." The teacher turned to the students. "Come on, people! They're myths used to entertain us. They can't be real ... It's not possible."

"Look around!" I flew down and got close to his face. "Do you think a human can turn another human into an exact replica of himself or move a car with ease? You better start praying, because I'm not saving all of you."

"Angie!" came my father's voice.

I looked and saw him pushing his way toward me, with Mandroid by his side. "Dad!"

As I ran toward my dad, I saw him and every student around him looked up into the sky behind me. Everyone fell silent. Several students dropped their cell phones, even as their mouths hung open while staring up into the sky.

"Jesus!" one kid cried as he pointed to the sky.

I started to turn around as a female student dropped everything in her hands and shouted, "Watch out!"

Before I could fully turn around, a massive wave of gravity knocked me and everyone backward. I closed my eyes out of instinct but soon felt my body crashing into other people. We were no longer in control of our bodies but just rode the gravity wave up into the sky. The wave of gravity cleared everything in its path: the scoreboard, bleachers, and pieces of large turf. Then we all suddenly froze in midair. I looked around, trying to figure out my next move. Countless students and teachers were crying out in pain or screaming in terror, and others ... well, some just hung in the air, dead. I looked ahead to see a familiar man with his arms extended to his sides: Galoriah.

"Help me please," shouted the teacher who had been arguing with me. His face was covered in blood. "I believe now! P-Please ... Please help me get down!"

I knew I was responsible for their lives, but everyone was at Galoriah's mercy. I looked down to see the football stadium destroyed, even as the survivors around me wailed in pain.

"Your mistake was fighting back!" hollered Galoriah.

I watched as poles, pipes, and bleacher rails fell toward the ground, then stopped and pointed upward at us—like swords. We all knew what was going to happen next.

"Let me give you a chance at life, liberty, and the pursuit of happiness," Galoriah said, then laughed. "That's what you pathetic humans believe in, right?" He looked directly at me. "Tell me where Alice Lombardo is hiding or everyone falls to their deaths!" he said, then flew down to the damaged field.

I could feel my body slowly healing as I locked my gaze on Galoriah. "You're going to pray you never laid eyes on me."

"Miss!" called one girl who was covered in dirt and blood.

I turned and looked at her.

"Please," the girl said. "I don't know you, but please just tell him where this Alice is. She can't be more important than all of our lives." She started to cry along with many others.

I saw Galoriah point his finger downward, and at that, we rocketed down toward poles, pipes, and rails, all still aiming upward—now awaiting our arrival.

Everyone around me screamed, but the only thing that ran through my head was finding my father. Some of the bleacher rails launched upward into the sky, impaling some of the students and staff. I flew to my right and tackled a girl, saving her from an oncoming rail. Then I teleported below a male student and kicked another rail out of the way.

"Grab the nearest person to you and I'll send you all somewhere safe!" I shouted.

Everyone grabbed hold of each other's hands, but before I could move a single muscle, Galoriah took control of my body. He sent me flying downward, separating me from everyone. Unable to move, I could only look on as multiple pipes and poles launched upward at the crowd above me. My eyes went to one end of a bleacher rail waiting on the ground for me. I only had a few seconds. Everyone above continued to scream. I took a deep breath, ready to meet my end, when Mandroid appeared beneath me, ready to take the hit.

"Don't worry, ma'am! I am here to help!"

"No! Go save the others—now!"

Mandroid teleported away, and I closed my eyes, bracing for impact. But then I heard a familiar voice: "Angie!"

Opening my eyes, I saw my father off to my left.

Then I heard Galoriah laugh. "That's your father?"

I suddenly stopped in midair. Then I saw my father begin to fall toward a long pipe below.

"No!" I screamed.

Dad's body hit the pipe, and it impaled him.

I cried out, but then I started falling again, toward the same pipe. I didn't care—I'd lost my dad. Tears streamed down my face. I closed my eyes and envisioned my school clothes and welcomed death.

20

Whatever It Takes- Cade

I teleported Alice to her home, where we found her mom. "Oh my God! Alice, are you okay?" Her mother rushed over as I held Alice in my arms.

"Get in a room with her and don't come out for any reason," I said, then glanced all around the living room. "They're coming—a lot of them. I'll come back. I need to get Colvin."

I thought of my brother and where he might be. With him not having his GCP item, I couldn't locate him, and I didn't want to teleport the remaining people of this city without him.

I froze when I sensed energy blasts coming toward us from all directions. I handed Alice to her mom. "No way!" I shouted, extending my arms and unleashing a powerful force field that covered the three of us.

Everything around me exploded into flames. Hearing Alice and her mother screaming, I kept my eyes open, sensing life all around me. My sixth sense told me there was an unfamiliar force field covering this city. Looking straight ahead, I sensed a familiar life force through the debris: Vera.

"Your time is up." Vera said. Her eyes shone red as she locked her focus on Alice. "The resurrection of Genesis and the end of this universe starts with you."

My heart was pounding. I knew this was it. Colvin wasn't here, and no one was going to save me. I glared at Vera. "As if I would ever let you touch her." I wanted to summon an Avex, but I was restricted from it after renouncing my birthright and giving up my title as King.

Vera flew forward, and I clenched my fist. "Phase One," I said, shining a light over everything using my body. Even with her eyes closed, the brightness still overwhelmed Vera. I opened my hand to my bow. I pulled the string and launched an arrow at her head. She dodged it as if she had seen it coming, but I knew she couldn't with the bright light. Sensing orbs above me, I looked up, and something told me that Vera could somehow see, thanks to the orbs.

I ran forward, dropping my bow, and threw the first punch, only to see her dodge it. I turned and threw a left hook, but she ducked. Throwing a right hook next, I saw Vera move her head back. When she lifted her arms, I jumped back and threw a quick jab. This time she grabbed my fist with one hand and punched my head with the other, sending me crashing to the floor. She pointed her hands toward me, sending out three small orbs. The orbs hit my chest like bullets and immediately began sucking a tremendous amount of life out of me.

Miss Lombardo ran at Vera but was kicked back to where Alice was.

Vera looked down at me. "You should've been dead the moment the orbs got in contact with your armor."

I looked up and grabbed hold of the three orbs in one hand and teleported them to another dimension. My strength came back. "I'm immortal," I said. "A billion lives reside within me."

Then I sensed a life force beside me.

"No more tricks," came a strong male voice as he struck my back, sending me across the room.

Getting to my feet I saw a tall, dark-toned god whose eyes were red like Vera's. He wore a skirt made of stems and beads. He hovered over Alice's mother while looking at me. "I'm Katakula, and death has come to you." He turned to Vera and said, "She's too old to breed."

Seeing him look behind me, I turned around in time to see Vera swing her blade. It struck me, and I saw red, then black, falling to the floor again. I covered my right eye as blood began to trickle down my face. Hearing Alice scream, I tried to get on my feet, but a planetary orb hovered over us and shone down, causing me to be weak and stay on the floor. My senses told me that the life force of Miss Lombardo had disappeared.

Vera wiped blood from the blade on her face. Closing her eyes, she received more energy from the orb, and then she shot open her eyes, stuck out her tongue, and spread her legs as her hands trembled. Looking down at me, she smiled. "Tell me if you see your father." Then she sat on top of me and pulled my hand away from my face before plunging her blade into my right eye.

Clenching my fists, I screamed, feeling pain pulsing through my head. Vera flipped me over, giving me a view of Miss Lombardo's body lying on the floor as blood ran from her throat.

"Take the innocence away from this girl," Vera said to Katakula, then lowered herself down to my ear. "Now watch."

With one eye working, I could see tears falling down Alice's face as she looked over at her mother in shock.

"Just kill me please!" Alice shouted. Backing away from Katakula, she began to cry. "Kill me!"

"Leave her alone ... please," I said, not much above a whisper. The pain radiating from my eye kept me from fully focusing, even as blood flowed down into my mouth.

Katakula walked over and threw his hand over Alice's mouth as he got on top of her. "She's good to breed with, but she's already carrying," he said to Vera. He placed his hands on her stomach and they began to shine red. "But that isn't a problem."

"No! Stop it!" Alice yelled. Blood began to pour out of her mouth.

"No!" I said outraged.

But then I sensed three life forces inside her stomach disappear in an instant. My one good eye opened wide. "No!" I screamed, feeling more power forming within me.

Then my skin peeled off and a bright light came forth. "Get off of me!" I yelled.

Screaming at the top of my lungs, I released a large amount of power, destroying everything around me and not caring who it affected. I got up and remembered that I was blind in one eye. I placed my hand over my right eye to stop the bleeding. Sensing that Alice was still alive, I teleported to her side and saw that she laid unconscious. I put my hand on her stomach and restored life into the triplets she was carrying. Within a few seconds, I sensed the two life forces again, but Alice remained unconscious.

I looked up and saw Vera in the sky, controlling the orbs and merging them into one.

She aimed her fists down toward me. "You don't understand," she said. "The entire South Universe is on the brink of extinction. Without Genesis every child, every goddess, every living thing will die. I will take back the soul your universe stole and save my kind."

The single giant orb rose higher into the sky and now blocked the sun, turning everything completely dark. I couldn't even see my own hands in front of me. The next second, a red giant orb appeared out of the darkness.

"Even if it kills me!" Vera shouted.

A red beam of light bigger than anything I've seen shot out of the orb. I glanced over at Alice, then I looked up and summoned a force field to cover the two of us. I watched as everything outside my force field turned to ash. I could see the ground split open and lava erupt from the fissure, all while feeling the pressure of the energy beam trying to break through my force field. I screamed while keeping my hands extended. Then, suddenly, the red ray stopped and Vera crashed to the ground. I looked up again to see Addis.

She hovered above us, keeping her eye on Vera. "That's for Africa." She looked untouched, and then her eyes changed color from scarlet red to electric blue.

Addis darted down and shot lightning at Vera, which had no effect.

Vera stood up. "All of you are going to die here—just memories of the billions of lives I've taken. You'll end up like Colvin."

Addis and I flew toward Vera, and I threw sparks of light that erupted into stars, which exploded and sent her crashing down into the lava. Enraged, Vera got up, wiping lava off her body like water. I saw Alice's Guardian appear behind Vera, then lunge forward to grab her sword with her right hand. Nigeria appeared on Vera's other side and threw a spear to Alice's Guardian, who caught it with his left hand. I summoned a force field and enclosed us all together with Vera, preventing the orb from giving her more energy.

Even though she was surrounded, Vera smiled.

A moment later, Kenya appeared and flew through the force field and tackled Vera, sending her to a knee. I summoned my bow and launched an arrow to the same knee Vera knelt on, causing her to scream in pain. Ghana showed up and grabbed Vera's left arm, then Algeria appeared and grabbed her right. Alice's Guardian plunged the sword through Vera's back. She shrieked and tried to fly away, so I made the force field smaller, trapping her inside with us. But Vera grabbed the spear from the Guardian and stabbed Algeria in the shoulder, then tossed Ghana aside.

Now Congo teleported directly in front of Vera. "For my brother!" he yelled, then drove a hooked sword into Vera's chest, lifting her off the ground.

Turning myself into an astral being, I flew through Vera's body, placing small stars inside of her body, then I teleported everyone to the GCP US Headquarters. I returned to my regular body and stood in front of Heaven's Eye. It showed lights shining inside Vera. The lights levitated her into the sky, resisting her control to use the orb. Once she was high enough in the sky, the lights within her exploded into a supernova, turning the sky white and Vera into dust.

Death no longer loomed over the North Universe. I could sense the orbs surrounding Earth and New Earth begin to simultaneously disappear. I looked around at the people still at headquarters—but no Colvin. Some huddled together, hoping Earth wouldn't explode, while others were watching me, waiting for my next move.

I looked at Heaven's Eye and approached it. "Locate Colvin Walker," I said.

Addis grabbed hold of my face. "Listen to me," she said as she focused her eyes on mine. "Get us out of here. Colvin is gone and you know—"

She cut her words short when Heaven's Eye gave off a sound that we all knew had changed its viewscreen to my brother. "Colvin Walker located in Porto Novo, Benin," the computer said.

I gently pushed away Addis's hands and turned to the large screen, which now showed Colvin. Staring at the screen, I saw an unrecognizable person lying on the ground, facing the sky, a host of spears and swords sticking out of his body—some of them looking like they went all the way through him into the ground. His Kurai armor was in tatters. Blood covered him and tears streaked his face.

"That's ... That's not him," I whispered. My throat choked up as I tried to tell myself it wasn't Colvin, but everything within me told me I was wrong.

Nigeria turned me away from the screen, and I could see tears forming from his eyes. "I lost a brother today too," he said to me, "but we need to go." He looked back at the others. "We've won because of you. Now let's leave."

The building began to shake from beneath us as the ground split open, causing everything to cave in. I heard screams all around me as the ceiling began collapsing overhead. Closing my eyes as tears fell down, I sat on the floor and got into my meditation position. With my legs folded, I floated in the air and I soon had a mental view of the entire world. Placing a force field over myself and over every surviving human and every GCP member, I tried to invoke the power within me to teleport everyone to safety, but Colvin came to mind and I just couldn't leave him.

"What are you waiting for?" Addis's voice rang out. "This planet is going to explode!"

With my eyes still closed, I probed out to sense every survivor, and then I teleported everyone to New Earth.

I opened my eyes to see thousands of civilians lying on a grassy field, all unconscious. And then my eyes came across Alice. My heart raced at seeing her, and I could see that she was still alive, but also unconscious. I'd have to wait to go to her.

I continued to look around. We were in the city of New Closias, an exact duplicate of the original. I walked up to where Addis was throwing her arms around the Mapogo brothers, all of them hugging each other.

Addis turned to see me and ran my way, wrapping her arms around me. "Thank you," she whispered into my ear. "He fought well and died a hero."

I nodded and then pulled back when she let go of me.

To my right Clark rose into the air, covered in dirt. "Angela!" he shouted.

I could see his worried expression as he flew back and forth over the masses. He came back and landed in front of me.

"What did you do?" Clark asked. "Angela isn't here."

Even as he said it, I felt a wave of guilt shower over me, knowing I had left Colvin behind. I pursed my lips and stared at Clark, then said, "That's impossible. I teleported every surviving human and GCP member from Earth to here." I turned toward Addis. "Unless ..."

"No, she was alive," Clark said. He paused before saying, "She isn't completely human." He looked off into the distance. "She's the daughter of Amentous."

"I knew it," Addis said. "She's like me: half-god, half-human. Marie told me this years ago, but I thought she was bluffing."

Clark frowned. "Angela isn't like anybody else. She was created to be a hundred percent human and able to turn her DNA into a full super goddess, not half." He looked up into the sky. "And right now she isn't human." He clenched his fists. "She needs help and I'm going to save her."

Nigeria walked up to Clark. "Earth is unstable. It'll explode and likely kill you. If you go back without permission, you could be sentenced to—"

"I'll take my chances," Clark said. He looked up at the sun and teleported away.

Seeing everyone in safety and knowing Alice was okay, I walked away and then teleported to the house that would be our home in New Closias.

Everything was dark. Looking around at the empty house that had been prepared for Colvin and myself, I fell to the floor and began crying. Memories of my older brother through the years, and the sacrifices he'd made for me, flooded my mind. I got up and ran to the nearest wall and began bashing my head against it, hating myself for leaving him. I knew if the tables had been turned, he wouldn't have left me even if I was a corpse. Feeling the blood trickle down my forehead, I turned and leaned against the wall, then slid down, crying in silence. Then all the lights in the house came on.

Gabriel stood before me and gazed down at me as I cried. "Talk to me," he said. "I'm right here." He sat next to me. "What's on your heart?"

I stared at him. "I thought you died." As the light dimmed, I could see Gabriel was wearing his silver armor. "We needed you—we still need you."

"Everything that happened was part of a plan that was followed accordingly. The question is, are you going to follow what's meant for you?" He paused, then went on, "I was created to be a messenger to the Most High. He's called for the strong-willed, the holy, the clean, the obedient, the pure—not the lukewarm, not the weak-minded, not the easily persuaded. He called me to remind you of the path you were meant to walk."

I shook my head, knowing what he was going to say. "It's easier said than done. No Avian is like me. It's easy for an Angel or an Avian born of purity and holiness, but I'm half-human. I have desires to be loved and to be in love. I love someone, so why do I have to lose something precious to me? I tried letting go of Alice. I listened to you, to do what's right. When I did ... I left crying, and it hurts. I went back to her because that's where things made sense ... with her."

"You need to focus and pray to the Most High to fulfill your purpose. People are counting on you. You've been called to do the Lord's work. He calls for his sheep, and in the midst of things it may seem like you will lose everything, but meditate and pray. There you'll find true love and a satisfying life."

"I don't want a life without Alice. Why can't I have both?"

Gabriel turned toward me. "That's not how things were meant to be. You and Alice shouldn't have happened. There's a special connection between you two, but it shouldn't have gone that way. You were never meant to be in love ... to have sexual relations with her ... to be spiritually bound to her. That was all set upon you by Colvin and your own flesh. I'm here to release you from this bondage. Let me deliver you."

As I gazed into his eyes, our surroundings changed. I looked around and it felt like home. "This isn't Avia ... but just as pure." I said.

In front of me lay a sparkling lake. From afar I saw buildings made entirely of rubies and diamonds. The grass around me shined and swayed left and right.

Then Gabriel lifted me off the ground, "Do you want to be delivered?"

"I don't want a life without her. I'll find another way. To take away, to erase, to vacate the love I have for her is murder. I don't want this deliverance. Tell the Creator I'll find another way."

Gabriel lifted his hands as our surroundings shone brightly. "This is his divine plan. You have to walk the path Jehovah has set for you. Lean not on your own understanding."

I shook my head at the thought of losing the connection I had with Alice. "To lose everything to attain peace ... it's a calling not meant for me. He made the mistake by choosing me. The West Creator made the mistake of calling me. I'm sorry. I'm going to end this my way."

"Things will only get worse," Gabriel said.

Then he turned around, and everything flashed and I was back in the darkness of my home.

21

Our Final Moment - Angela

My surroundings were dark for a minute, then a burst of light illuminated the place. I looked around, and everything was bright white. There seemed to be no end to whatever this place was, and I stood still for several minutes, remembering what had occurred on Earth.

Thinking of my dad, I sat on the ground and started to cry. I lost the one thing I'd wanted to protect—the one thing I cared for. I drew up my legs and wrapped my arms around them, then I pressed my forehead into my knees as I continued to cry aloud. I thought about how I had failed to protect Dad. Why did it seem misfortune always followed me? Why was I cursed? Crying louder, I didn't care about the world, my surroundings, or anyone. I sobbed even harder as memories of my father came to mind. I clutched at my own arms and pressed my fingernails deep into my skin, wanting that pain, wanting to die ... to end all of this.

"My Angie, stop crying," came a female voice that I didn't recognize.

I didn't care who it was. I kept my head down and closed my eyes, wishing for complete darkness.

Her voice came closer: "Baby, look at me."

I lifted my head but kept my eyes closed, as I wanted to take in every second I had in darkness. Slowly opening my eyes, I saw a young woman standing in front of me. She looked calm and at peace. She seemed familiar but I couldn't figure out who she might be. She wore a pure white cloak. Her smooth, pale skin shined, and her hair was dark purple, hanging down to her lower back. She had a beauty mark above her thick, rosy lips. She looked beautiful. Her piercing blue eyes looked right at me, but I averted my gaze.

"You're in a different part of the Afterworld," she said. "The higher-ups sent me here to direct your path. It seems that you're lost." She leaned her head to the side, trying to catch my eye. "My name is Elizabeth. I'm the mother of Marie, the previous GCP Protector of Florida."

I got up and faced her. Remembering what I'd learned about her from Mandroid, I started crying again. I covered my mouth, wanting to stop my emotions from pouring out. I hated to be so vulnerable or to allow someone to see me at my weakest. I turned away from my grandmother, placing my hands on my hips and looking up while trying to stop the tears.

"Why me?" I said, "Why does everyone want me dead?"

Elizabeth walked over to face me. "You're special."

I looked directly at her. "Just stop, please. I don't need you feeling sorry for me or using words to make me feel better." Wiping the tears from my face, I closed my eyes, feeling mentally and physically exhausted. I opened my eyes and said, "Everything in my body is telling me to just stop and die."

"Angie, listen—"

"Please! Just let me be. I'm done fighting. I'm done trying to be happy. I'm done getting hurt. I never wanted this. I just want to be happy. Why do I always get the short end of the stick?"

Elizabeth was quiet for a moment and then I could see her eyes start to get watery. "I'm sorry you're all alone in this, but you have the power to end it. You were holding back."

"What?" I said, "I gave it everything I had. Mom died, then I was sent to Lisa, then these gods ..." I wanted to cry some more and just tell her everything. "I feel like I'm in this cycle of pain and regret and there's no getting out. I'm fighting for my life and I feel so alone. I got to live in New York and I can't ever be that happy seven-year-old girl again—because everything back home only reminds me of what I lost."

I began to break down again. "I lost Mom. Now, dad is gone. I feel so alone. I just can't be the person I want to be because I'm always in constant trouble or involved in something I don't want to be in." I wiped away the tears. "I want to be happy, to be loved, and I can't have that."

"Of course you can. You have people who love you."

"They feel sorry for me!"

My grandmother shook her head. "Where is this coming from? I've been watching over you, and I've seen people love you as you get older."

"Who—Lisa? That's what you call love? The woman was supposed to comfort me! And she was really my aunt all along!"

Elizabeth reached out and put a hand on my shoulder. "Listen to me. Everything that has happened in your life has happened for a reason—as ordained by the North Creator."

I scoffed and pulled my shoulder away from her touch. "Tell the North Creator he can play with someone else's life, not mine. I won't endure anything for nobody, and I won't fight someone else's war. Mom made the choice to fight and get herself killed rather than be with me. You can tell her I'm done fighting her fight."

"The Afterworld is at risk of desolation. Earth is at risk of being taken over. You're not fighting her fight. You're fighting the fight every GCP member has put their lives on the line for. If you don't fight, everything will be lost; everyone you care about will cease to exist. We'll be cast into oblivion for eternity, where only pain exists. Even the Guardians are fighting; it's not just you."

"You can't just tell me to fight when there's other things in my life that are messed up! You don't get me. I'm not some type of robot! I almost died fighting for Mom's past mistakes, and she was barely there for me! If she truly cared for me, she would've left like Alice's mom and took care of me. She doesn't love me."

"Shhh ..." My grandmother came closer to me. "Relax." She wiped the remaining tears from my face. "Do you know what it means to be human?"

"Yes."

"Humans experience love and know that mistakes and bad events will happen—and sometimes they're inevitable. You're too hard on yourself.

You don't know what love is because your whole life you've been focusing on what you lost. Your father was in the army a lot and your mother was in the GCP. Then you were with your adoptive parents, and they showed you no love. I understand, but you don't know anything about love … and that's what worries you. You're so worried about the evil things and what could happen that you close yourself off from everyone, but that's all you know. I see why you do this, but look at the good things in your life and give it a chance." She took my hand. "I want you to live a life worth living. You don't have to live a life bent on anger, hate, and revenge. You're going to kill yourself."

I backed away, gazing at my grandmother. "But I'm in the GCP."

"Being in the GCP does not mean your life has to be miserable."

"But Mom—"

"Your mother … my daughter … her story is over. I tried talking to her but she never listened. Listen to me: don't go after Amentous because of what he did to me. You understand?"

"Yes."

"Amentous never killed your mother. There's no need to go after him. He only went after me and he did what he did to save his people and that's natural. You have to forgive and forget. You don't have to fight for me. My fight with Amentous ended years ago on the battlefield."

"I just need some answers."

"You're the daughter of Amentous and Marie. Your mother fell in love with someone who she never knew was a super god. She only found out after my death and realized it was her lover who had taken my life. He didn't even know my relation to your mother. He fought to protect you—and fought Gage Walker for killing me … and he died doing it." She inched forward. "Our Heavenly Father brought me here to tell you that you have a purpose, and to stay strong, and that he's with you. You just have to seek him. He'll work within you. It gets better. Nothing that happens to you goes unnoticed by God. Know there's purpose in your pain. He'll never forsake you. Someone else will go through what you experienced and won't have the strength to carry on like you and God won't be there physically but he'll send you, his daughter."

I let those words sink in, and all the negative thoughts and energy disappeared. "So protect the Afterworld?"

She nodded. "Yes, everyone you ever cared about is here and war is coming. I need you to bring peace on both sides. You have the power of the super gods. You just have to use it."

"But I'm dead, aren't I?"

"Not quite. He made Gabriel give up his life to give it to you. You can't die. Not now." My grandmother touched my heart, and it felt like everything within me turned bright white. "Remember, you have to win or—"

Everything turned black and went quiet.

A loud scream broke the silence. It got louder and louder until I finally opened my eyes, looking up at the sky. I could see the actual molecules in the air—the dust particles that the human eye couldn't see. All five of my senses seemed enhanced.

I awoke to the sun shining down on me, and a steel pipe impaling my stomach. I wrenched myself free and then saw my father also impaled on the pipe, dead.

"You're back!" Galoriah said, then lifted his war-hammer and walked toward me. "Where's the Golden Water? There was—Wait, your eyes are ..."

I went into super speed to slow down time, and I threw a punch to his chest, sending him across the field. Flying at top speed, I bolted toward him, and the ground split open below me. Before I could follow up, Galoriah lifted his hand and I gravitated upward. Then he pointed his finger down and my body smacked hard into the ground.

I got up and ran at him again. Before he could aim his hand in my direction, I teleported behind him. I swung at his head, but he ducked without looking back. Twisting around, he grabbed my arm and flipped me over his shoulder. I opened my hand and unleashed a gold ray of energy to his face, sending him onto his back. I leaped forward and landed on top of him, placing one hand on his neck to hold him down, and then I started beating his face with my other clenched hand. He screamed, unleashing a pulse wave that pushed me off of him. As I flew back in the air, I shot multiple blasts at him, hoping one of them would take him out.

Galoriah teleported out of harms' way, appearing right in front of me. He lifted his war-hammer above his head and brought it down. I blocked the war-hammer by catching its handle with one hand while keeping my eyes locked on Galoriah. I could hear Galoriah grunting as he used both hands to push the hammer toward my head. Even with the Black Beauty suit, I knew I couldn't be that strong or perform the things I just had. I had to be a super god.

I shoved aside the hammer and threw an uppercut to his stomach, lifting him off the ground. The football field's turf beneath him split open from the impact. He groaned as he held his stomach, and I watched as drool escaped from his mouth.

I leaped at him, grabbing him by the neck. I felt my power increase, and so I threw him up and out of the stadium. Galoriah caught himself and stopped above me, then threw his war-hammer at me. I easily caught it and this time broke it in half over my knee. As I flew up toward him, I could feel his telekinetic energy in my bones, trying to control me—but it had no effect.

"No!" Galoriah yelled. He landed and slammed his fist against a nearby car, then flew at me and threw a punch.

I caught and held on to his fist, then kicked his shin, which twisted and wrenched apart his knee. I grabbed his head and drove my knee into his face, crushing his nose. Before he had time to process the pain, I struck his throat a fist, sending him down onto the football field. He bounced along until he crashed through a wall and landed on the street. I teleported in front of him as he tried to get up.

"No one is going to save you," I said, then raised my hand. A gold energy orb emerged from my palm.

Galoriah scrambled to get up and then looked around for anything to use as a weapon. I shot the energy blast from my hand, destroying the whole street. Cars, telephone poles, bushes, and street signs all turned to dust as I unleashed this new power. When the dust settled, in the middle of all the destruction I saw Galoriah standing there, now turned into stone.

Feeling safe now, I fell to my knees and realized that my body was completely drained. I didn't feel the power of the gods flowing through me anymore. My vision returned to regular, and I could now only hear a ringing sound in my ears as the ground beneath me began to cave in.

"Ma'am, what will you do now?" came Mandroid's voice in my head.

I observed everything falling apart around me. *"How long do I have?"*

"Ten seconds until Earth's destruction."

It was impossible to transport myself to another planet. The distance was too great for me, so I teleported to the front of the safe house. I ran inside, and the closer I got to the main bedroom, the more my heart pounded—and I realized how much I valued my life. I barged through the door and grabbed a frame picture of my mother and me. Using my super strength, I broke through the floor to find Mandroid standing there amidst the crumbling underground base, with a silver container in one hand—ready to pour The Golden Water over a gold statue of a kneeling man who wielded a spear in one hand and a shield in the other.

"Wait, what are you doing?" I aimed my pistol at Mandroid's head. "Don't you dare! I'll kill you!"

"Forgive me, ma'am, but these were orders from your mother." Mandroid poured the Golden Water over the gold statue.

An energy wave shot out from the statue, and the power overflowing from this being sent chills throughout my body. The gold statue transformed into a living god—but no ordinary one. It was a super god, shining bright. The energy I felt from him seemed similar to mine but much greater. The light shining from the super god decreased, and I saw that it was Amentous.

I redirected my pistol at him. "Don't move!"

Amentous looked exactly like the clone, but his presence felt different than any other god I'd been around. It felt more like the holiness I'd sensed with the Guardians and the absolute power of the gods I'd faced.

Amentous looked around the underground base. "How many years have gone by?"

Mandroid immediately responded, "Seven years, sir."

Amentous's eyes met mine, seeming to try to find an answer to some question that bothered him. "I'm lost ... Where's the daughter of Marie?"

Hearing her name come out his mouth brought back memories. He knew what he had done and I figured he was taunting me by saying her name. My eyes turned gold, reflecting my change back into a super god. I pulled the trigger repeatedly, aiming in the direction of Amentous, only to see the bullets disappear as they came out of the barrel. I dropped my gun and ran at him, throwing a hard blow to his forehead, causing everything around us to shake or fall.

"Damn it!" I yelled as I jumped back and held onto my broken knuckles. "Don't taunt me!"

This time I went for a kick to his neck and managed to break something in my leg, causing me to fall to the floor.

Amentous reached down and grabbed both of my wrists, gazing into my eyes.

"Get off me!" I shouted.

I pulled back and freed myself, then threw a strong hook that broke my good hand. I fell back down to the floor and held my hands together as pain pulsed through them. I rose and went for another kick to his neck, but again only caused damage to myself.

Amentous stood still, his face placid. Even as a super god, I was no match for him.

He extended his arm toward me, and I felt my body heal instantly—the broken bones and my wound from being impaled on the pipe. "Angela?" he said, then looked around and raised a hand.

Everything stopped moving, including Mandroid, and the destruction halted.

"That's better," Amentous said.

"How did you get here?" I said, then pulled my pistol from its shoulder holster and aimed it at Mandroid.

"You're dying," Amentous said, "and this planet will blow once I release my hold."

Amentous walked over and stood beside me. "I'm sorry you had to endure the labors of what your mother and I left behind. A queen like you should have never had to go through that and I deeply apologize."

I backed away from him.

"I'm your father," he said. "It's okay."

His gold armor disappeared and I saw it reappear on my body. "What?" I whispered.

"This armor was made by the North Creator—made to protect you from anything. I don't know where to take you, but you'll survive the destruction of Earth. Bring your companion there along, because he'll guide you and protect you, just as he did with your mother." He looked at Mandroid, then at me before he slowly started to turn to dust, and I could feel all his power surge through me.

Tears fell down my face as he poured his life into me. The ground began to shake. He was losing control of Earth as he gave his life away. A moment later he disappeared.

Mandroid grabbed my hand, and I found myself back on New Earth—facing an orb while I hovered in midair. Looking down, I saw two armies facing each other. The surviving GCP members stood opposite an army of black-armored gods. The gods began to charge forward and then the GCP did as well, but I flew down and landed between the two armies. Extending my hands toward both sides, I created a force field, blocking them from moving forward.

Looking at the gods, I could see they were amazed at my new armor. I turned and faced them. "As the daughter of Amentous, I order you to go home." Releasing both force fields, I switched my focus to the GCP. "It's done. You don't have to fight anymore."

One of the gods walked forward. "We don't have to listen to you."

I opened my hand and my father's spear appeared in it—a weapon that could kill anyone or anything. All of the gods stepped back, many of them gasping.

Staring at the god who had come forth, I aimed my spear at his chest. "You're an army with no leader, your orbs have no effect on me, and I alone have the power and weapons to change the tide of this war. With a single shout, I can call upon Planet Peace to assist in eradicating all of you.

You stand in the presence of a super god now, so I won't tell you again. Leave or I'll eliminate you where you stand."

The god looked back at his comrades and then turned toward me. I could see fear on his face as he said, "We go back to Ominous."

He looked up and all of the gods disappeared, along with the planets.

I released the power of the super god within me and lost control of my body, fainting on the spot.

22

The Battle For Heaven Begins - Colvin

I awoke to nothing but darkness and stars gleaming from a distance. There was no telling how long I'd been out or the condition of humanity. I looked down to see that I lay on a piece of rock that floated in the middle of space. My armor was ruined, which reminded me that I had lost the battle—*But not this war ... I'm coming for you Ominous.*

This rock was the only tangible item of Earth remaining. It was a reminder that death was real but also a reminder of my presence. Death couldn't touch me wherever I might be. I stood up and sensed home, along with New Earth, the Afterworld, and every planet in the North Universe. I sensed no orbs, which meant Cade did it. He saved humanity.

But then I sensed trillions of gods being revived, and it sent chills up my spine. I looked down into the darkness. Billions of miles away was the South Universe. *He actually did it. He revived every god in his universe using the Golden Water, for the purpose of waging war.*

Light emerged from behind, and an abundance of power filled the space around me. I turned to the Seven Elder Guardians kneeling before me on the rock. They wore Guardian-plated platinum armor, and within the plated armor white clothing hung below the waist, reaching their ankles. The clothing had imprints of eyes all over it. Each imprint showed a different color among the Guardians, symbolizing what kingdom they represented.

One Guardian lifted his head, revealing green eyes that shone brighter than any of the Guardians in the GCP. His tan skin had a shine to it as well, along with his curly brown hair. "My lord," he said to me. "Great danger lies ahead."

"Stand," I said, then lifted my hands to see my ruined skin.

Heal and return, I thought. Instantly my body returned back to its normal state and my armor looked as if it had never been worn.

"Prepare your kingdoms," I said to the Elders. "War is headed to the Afterworld. Split your ranks and protect New Earth."

"Greater danger lies outside the walls the North Creator built," said the Evite. He looked to his right and then his left. "The walls built were not to separate species from each other, but to prevent the great evil from entering."

"What is this great evil Gabriel told me about?" I said, then watched as all seven Elder Guardians stood on their feet. "What lies outside these walls?"

"The great evil is an entity that created a few of the holy items," the Evite said.

The Elder Guardian ruling the Blue Kingdom walked forward. "No, it wants the beings living in the four universes. It consumes energy and we're its food."

"I was given the task to protect the beings in the North," I said, looking at each of the seven Elders in turn. "The old gods' plan is to kill everything here. They're not doing it in a few days, not in a few months or years. They're not like the gods. They move with haste and will kill without hesitation. Right now they're making their move on the Afterworld—trillions of gods." I pointed to my left, where Earth used to be. "They'll be arriving to take New Earth and create their own history and wipe out ours. I understand about this great evil being deadly, but we can't ignore what's about to happen."

I stopped to take a moment to remember all the lives that were lost—the pain and suffering that occurred throughout the world because of the war in Benin. Then I said, "The North Universe will end up like Earth. This is real, and if we ignore it and focus on this great evil, what we fought to protect, will be taken from us before we know it. Ominous may not be as great as this great evil, but he has the capability to take out every universe and thus, he's my main focus right now." I walked up to the seven Elders and looked at them and then at the stars. "Protect our home from the old gods and the gods. Let's prepare for war."

The Catorian smiled at me. "What will you do first, my lord?"

I sensed the Afterworld and its image came to mind. "First, I will direct the ones that died to the Afterworld and then," I said as I glanced over at him, "send aid."

I teleported to the Afterworld.

23

I'm Alive, Not Dead - Angela

My sense of hearing was the first to work. I could hear the panicking of many people, numerous phones ringing at once, doors being opened and closed, and a few voices yelling out instructions.

"You're up," came Clark's voice.

I opened my eyes and saw him sit down on the edge of my bed.

"How are you feeling?" he asked.

I looked down and saw that I was in normal clothing. Then I glanced around the empty room I was in and figured I was in some kind of hospital. I remembered everything that had happened on the battlefield—and when I was in the Afterworld, when I killed Galoriah, and then stopping a war.

Looking down at the white sheets, I felt so tired emotionally. "I'm ... I don't know if I'm okay—normal, I guess." Touching my knees and then staring at my hands, I looked over at Clark. "Forgive me if I was ever rude to you."

"I forgive you," Clark said. "I'm proud of you for doing what was needed of you."

"Why me? What makes me so different from everyone else?"

"Our God gives all of us a talent, gift, or purpose. Yours happened to be this." He smiled. "We needed you and you delivered."

"I want out." I shook my head, still trying to make sense of it all. "I'm done with this. When the world really needs me, I'll be there. Now,

243

though, I think I'll get in tune with myself spiritually and learn to control my anger. I'm thinking about meditating and praying ... Maybe I could find peace in that."

Clark nodded. "It's for the best. I think you're changing into a better person. The universe needs you; don't you ever forget that." He placed his hands on top of mine. "I talked to the leaders of the GCP, and they re-opened your mother's bank account in the GCP. For all the missions she completed, she made a lot of money. They can transfer everything to your account, so don't worry about living expenses. And if you ever want to talk to me, I'll be in the Gray Kingdom."

"What?" I looked over at him. "You told me the Gray Kingdom was for prisoners."

He frowned. "We both disobeyed orders, and you broke some of the rules. I should've led you better as your Guardian. I had them add your sentence to my own and asked them to pardon you." He crossed his wrists together and gave me a reassuring look. "You're fine. Live the life you want, but there's no denying what's coming. Train every day, okay? And be sure to go see your dad. They brought his body here, down the hall."

Two Elyzians appeared and took hold of Clark's arms, lifting him up to a standing position. One of them said, "We must go now. Your fate has been decided." Then they placed white handcuffs on his wrists.

"Listen to me," Clark said, looking at me. "The prince is coming. I've heard of him. If there's one thing he's good at, it's taking planets. At this point, I'm terrified for Earth if I'm not here. Keep to yourself and learn to control and awaken your super god abilities. I need you to be faster, stronger, and sharper. A sharp mind beats a sharp sword. Go over what I taught you. Repetition is key—and don't let your anger guide your judgment. From this point forward it only gets tougher, with a lot more people dying. You can make a difference if you're willing to work hard."

Clark gave a small smile. "You are the Creator's artwork, created to do good works. May your life be a gift of beauty back to him. I love you."

Before I could say anything, Clark disappeared with the two Elyzians. Clark's last expression stuck with me. I couldn't tell what he was thinking, but more than anything at that moment, I wish I knew. It would've told me how he thought of me.

I got up and left the room, entering a busy hallway. I saw kids on the phone, crying, and the elderly were being assisted by doctors. I found teen students crying at almost every corner in the hallway.

I was making my way down the hall to find my father's room when someone behind me said, "Miss, thank you."

I turned around to see a girl around my age holding a girl's hand. "My sister and I just wanted to say thank you for what you did in the stadium. We don't know how you did what you did but we wouldn't be here without you ... so thank you."

"You don't have to say thank you," I said, then continued to walk down the hall.

I found my father's room and entered, closing the door behind me. It was mostly dark inside, but I could see his body lying there. And even with all the crying and yelling in the hallway, it was soundless in my father's room. I slowly walked over to his side, and my heart turned weak.

Looking at his innocent face, I finally shed a tear for him. "I thought about being here with you but I only got you killed and I'm so sorry."

As I continued to talk to my father, I started to feel more hurt inside. I wiped tears from my face as I said, "They love me ..." I didn't know if I was telling my father or myself again. "They appreciate me ..." I started shaking my head, trying to get those words in my skull to stay. "Daddy, I don't think I'm alone anymore." I stared down at the bandages that covered his face and then kissed his forehead. "Bye."

I opened the door only to find myself staring right into Alice's face. "Alice!"

With my face still covered in tears, Alice didn't wait for permission to hug me. "I don't have the best words," she said, "but know you're not the bad guy here."

I shrugged. "I caused the fight at the high school."

"And you saved half the freakin' school today! Not to mention when everyone was about to fall to their deaths or when those clones tried to kill everyone outside ... I heard everything and so did everyone in the GCP."

"It was my job."

"No, it was Cade's job. New York isn't your state. You did him a favor, and for that I'm grateful—and so is every member." She smiled as tears formed in her eyes. "I know how it feels to lose the last person you hold close. All this feels like a nightmare—losing my mother and Colvin. I don't know where I will go from here."

I felt at a loss for words, and I could only stare at Alice as she fought to hold back her tears. "Alice, I'm sorry." I gave her a hug, then whispered in her ear, "You keep moving. You're stronger than I'll ever be. Move forward. If you stand still, things will only get harder. Move for the betterment of yourself and your child."

She nodded and smiled, then said, "Children, actually. Triplets."

I smiled back at her and hugged her again. The thought of Colvin and our last time together played in my head as I held her. I always cared for him and losing him and a lot of others in recent days had numbed me to the feeling of loss. Maybe I'd cry about his death days from now, but at that moment I would be a shoulder to cry on.

We held each other for a few more seconds, then I took a step back. "Move in with me," I said. "We're sisters after all." This time I smiled a big smile. "I would really enjoy your company."

"Yeah." Alice fixed her hair. "You can live with me, okay? I'm actually not ready to leave home."

I laughed. Using her personal Guardian, Alice teleported me to the new headquarters. We arrived in the Communications Center, then walked to the elevator and waited.

"What are we doing here?" I asked.

"Need something from Cade," Alice said. She walked inside the elevator when the doors opened, and I followed. She clicked on the Lobby button. "Won't take long."

We waited as the elevator went up, and the doors opened to a large crowd of people cheering when they saw me. I looked back at Alice, who grabbed my hand and walked me to Heaven's Eye, where the screen showed live footage of other members around the world cheering.

I looked around during the ongoing uproar of cheers. The headquarters was filled with Guardians, Protectors, and other members applauding for me. I even saw signs with pictures of my face, and other signs with encouraging words.

Cade came forth from amongst the crowd and gave me a hug. "Thank you for saving the people in my city. I'm forever grateful." He released me from his tight grip. "You have family here; always remember that."

"What's all this for?" I asked, still unable to believe the praise was for me.

"You took out Galoriah and Aerozayle," Cade said. "And everyone knows you defeated Amentous." He looked around at the crowd. "Despite losing their hero Colvin ..." He looked back at me. "They gained a new one."

I took a moment to gaze at everyone. Through the pain, loss, and suffering I'd gone through, I felt glad I had made it this far and that I hadn't given up.

I smiled as everyone cheered for me, and then I looked over to Alice and Cade—my new family.

Epilogue

Katakula bowed before Ominous. "My lord, Cade killed Vera. The mission to take over New Earth was a failure."

The all-powerful Ominous stared off into space. "Her death will be accounted for. Every human shall pay the price. We're going to wipe out an entire planet with twenty trillion gods and an army of super gods. There will be no escape for what comes to the humans now that Clark and Gabriel are out of the picture." He looked down at Katakula. "Have you located Zulu?"

Katakula looked up, smiling. "Yes, my lord."

"Good. Resurrect him. That will be all." Ominous snapped his fingers. "Oh, I almost forgot. Please tell my poor nephew La-Naious the news of my brother's death."

Katakula nodded.

Ominous looked back out into space with deep malice in his eyes. "Angela killed her own father. An army of gods will wait for Planet Peace to begin the first assault toward the resurrection of Genesis."

Acknowledgement

I just say thank you to my parents and siblings who were there and prayed for me, became my readers, and advised me every step of the way. To my friends Khris, Tyrone, Yasmine, Chrystelle, Sean, and Chrystelle for being there and supporting. Chrystelle and Salena thanks for being beta readers. Marie-kerline, Erns, Marieange, Cedric, and Marjorie thank you all. John David Kudrick thank you for your amazing edits. To God, thank you for guiding me along the way. I'm creative from the Creator of all things. I love you God always and forever.

Thank you to everyone I didn't personally mention. You know who you are if you're reading this. You had a lot to do with this process and I want to say thank you for being there to listen, read, and to suggest. The experience I went through formed an Alice and Cade relationship and it turned me into Angela for some time and in the end, I developed to be Colvin and ultimately Addis.

This process started in 2012 and being lost, depressed, feeling sad, in "love", being firm in the Lord, and truly going from being lost to found again was just wow. Through it all, I continued to write because this story had to be told and something told me to keep pressing on because there's a purpose for me. To anyone reading this keep pushing forward and give God a chance because you're a Protector and your destiny is tied to someone else who needs you. Thank you everyone for being a part of my life even if it was temporary.